THE GOODBYE
SUMMER

the GOODBYE SUMMER

SARAH VAN NAME

sourcebooks
fire

Published by Sourcebooks Fire, an imprint of Sourcebooks, Inc.
P.O. Box 4410, Naperville, Illinois 60567-4410
(630) 961-3900
sourcebooks.com

Library of Congress Cataloging-in-Publication Data

Names: Van Name, Sarah, author.
Title: The goodbye summer / Sarah Van Name.
Description: Naperville, Illinois : Sourcebooks Fire, [2019] | Summary: Eager
    for the end of summer when she and her boyfriend, Jake, plan to run away
    together, Caroline finds herself drawn into Georgia's life and begins to
    question to whom she should say goodbye.
Identifiers: LCCN 2018043063 | (trade pbk. : alk. paper)
Subjects: | CYAC: Dating (Social customs)--Fiction. | Friendship--Fiction. |
    Summer--Fiction. | Aquariums--Fiction.
Classification: LCC PZ7.1.V353 Goo 2019 | DDC [Fic]--dc23
LC record available at https://lccn.loc.gov/2018043063

Printed and bound in Canada.
MBP 10 9 8 7 6 5 4 3 2 1

For Elyse,

like I promised.

JUNE

1

Here at the aquarium gift shop, we sell posters, puzzles, and stuffed animals of everything under the sea. We've got dolphins, sea turtles, penguins, fish, sharks, whales, whale sharks, and more!

That's the pitch—what the tour guides say before they lead their groups into the store. It's technically true, although the stuffing falls out of the dolphins through their mouths, the puzzles are sometimes missing pieces, and the posters are just stock photos with the watermarks removed. We also sell seashells, though we are nowhere near the seashore. As a landlocked girl, I have never been to the ocean.

We don't sell the animals themselves. Some people ask.

We also don't have the live versions of most of these animals at the aquarium. But the gift shop is here to make people feel like they've visited a truly impressive place. It has glass walls and lighting that makes everyone's skin look gold.

I began working here yesterday, the first Monday after my junior year ended. It would've been nice to have a bit of a break, but I wanted to start making money, and my parents wouldn't let me have a job while I was in school; academics, they said, were too important, though I have never been a straight-A student. They'd even told me I didn't need to work this summer.

"It's fine to be at home all day, sleep in," my dad said.

"I can teach you how to sew," my mom said.

"You don't get many chances in life to relax," they said. Both of them had worked full-time jobs during every break from the age of sixteen, and I think they mourned the loss of their teenage summers. They must have felt they were giving me an immeasurable gift in the option of leisure, a gift they'd never had.

But I told my parents I wanted to do something with these three months. They said it was good that I had a work ethic, but Mom looked sad.

I got the job through Toby, Jake's cousin, who has worked at the aquarium since he graduated high school two years ago. Jenny, the manager, chewed gum all during my interview a few weeks ago. Her office in the back of the store had a window looking out on the parking lot and a giant, faded poster of a shark on the wall. She looked young, in her twenties or thirties, but for the entire half hour of our conversation she bore an expression of ageless exhaustion.

"...so I really think being a part of that science fair team gave me some stellar organizational skills," I finished. She stared out the window. In the parking lot, a minivan was failing to complete a three-point turn.

"Can you work a cash register?" she said without looking at me.

"I can learn, definitely—"

"Could you yell at a kid if they were trying to steal something?"

"Um...yes."

"Do you have a passion for ocean life?"

"I—"

"Nah, I'm just messin' with you." She opened a desk drawer. "Toby recommended you. So you're probably okay."

"Toby's great, right?" I said. "I hear he leads great tours."

"He's okay," Jenny said. "When did you want to start?"

It's early afternoon my second day on the job, and there's a burst of sound and a flood of hassled parents and children surge into the lobby, finished with their tour and heading my way. A second later, the doors from the outside open too. They admit a steady stream of kids, all chattering and holding matching plastic backpacks. Two guys wearing blue shirts herd them toward the front desk. The door falls shut behind the last child and then opens again, too quickly, as if it's about to be yanked off its hinges.

And that's when I see her.

I notice her first because she is a girl my age, and the aquarium mostly employs guys. She is wearing a Junior Aquarium Camp T-shirt that says COUNSELOR in big letters on the back. The N and the S are obscured by a wet band of dark, frizzy hair. In Junior Aquarium Camp the counselors take the kids to the pool and tell them to pretend to be fish. If they learn about a certain type of fish on Monday, they practice being like it in the pool on Tuesday. I know this because I went when I was little.

The girl is shouting at the kids in front of her and shooing them toward the front desk where the other counselors wait with stickers. One child dawdles behind, and she picks him up and balances him on a wide hip. As she carries him to the desk, her eyes flick around the small atrium and toward the gift shop. They meet mine and roll upward as she smiles, like she's saying: *Can you believe this shit?*

As our eyes connect, I have a peculiar sense of déjà vu, as if I know this girl already and have seen this eye roll and this smile many times before—in front of parents, teachers, other and lesser friends. It feels like a familiar and thrilling inside joke, like we are halfway to friendship already, though we have never met.

Then one of the guys yells, "Georgia!" and she looks away, sets down the kid, and starts passing out stickers. They walk through the door into the aquarium itself, and she is gone. I look at the lobby where she was, now empty and silent, floor littered with waxy sticker backings.

After that, it's a quiet day. Most days, Jenny tells me, are quiet, with occasional bursts of post- or pre-tour activity. It's true that the aquarium gets the most traffic in the summertime, but even then, she says the gift shop doesn't make much revenue. Last week I spent most of my time straightening displays and texting Jake, and it looks like this week will be the same.

Jenny wanders out of her office at 5:15, fifteen minutes before I'm supposed to close up shop.

"Might as well leave early," she says.

"Maybe things will pick up this week," I say. "With the campers."

"Maybe." She shrugs. "Now go ahead and start closing up. I'm supposed to supervise you for the first seven days and I've got shit to do."

I complete the closing tasks at the store under Jenny's watchful eye with her correcting me every other minute. But in the end, there's not that much to do. We walk outside together.

"See you tomorrow," I say.

"Mm," she responds, already halfway across the parking lot. I sit on the curb and pull out my phone. I'm alone for a couple minutes until a woman wearing a business suit comes outside, talking to someone on her phone. She glances at me and her eyes linger. Normally, Jenny told me, Junior Aquarium

Camp parents pick up their kids at 5:30. Today, though, there is a special welcome-to-camp party in the activity room. This woman must need a break from all the fun.

I feel incredibly awkward.

With the waiting and the heat and the looks from the parents, I'm in a shitty mood when Jake's truck pulls into the roundabout at 6:15. He would have been late even if I'd gotten out of work on time, and as it is, I'm stiff and sore from sitting on the curb so long. The sun is still high, and the air hangs around me, wet and syrupy. When I get up, lines of sweat have gathered in the crooks of my knees.

I throw my bag behind me into the back seat and get ready to sit in annoyed silence until he apologizes, but then Jake reaches over and grabs my face with both hands and kisses me so long and sweet that I cannot be angry. He pulls away a little. We are so close that I can see only one of his eyes at a time, and I don't know which to focus on, both dark and deep. I look back and forth and get dizzy.

"Missed you," he murmurs.

"Missed you too," I whisper back.

When we get home, we lie on the porch of his house. We stay there, talking and laughing and occasionally making out as it grows dark. The kudzu rises like a wall down in the valley. He smokes a single cigarette, the smoke clouding the air inside the screen porch and then disappearing. Inside, his roommates are making dinner, and all I can hear are cicadas and the sound of hot dogs sizzling in the pan. The air is blue and purple. Mosquitos drift through the holes in the netting and wander lazily in the air above us. One alights beside my belly button. I slap it dead, leaving a spot of someone else's blood on my skin.

I'm drunk. One of Jake's roommates recently turned twenty-one, and Jake got him to buy us a bottle of wine to kick off the summer. I look at Jake next to me and I think it's the wine that's making me dizzy, but I can't be sure. He rolls on his side to face me, props his head under one arm.

"So, I've been thinking," he says, raising one eyebrow and wiping his mouth, "about the end of the summer."

"About leaving?" I say.

"Yeah. I figure with your money from the aquarium and my money from the grocery store, we can probably get just about anywhere. But I think somewhere nice and cool. Northeast, maybe, or the upper Midwest. After this summer, you know you're gonna want some snow."

I look out at the backyard. The air shimmers, blurry with heat.

"I don't know," I say. "I like being hot."

"You *always* complain about being hot."

"But I complain more about being cold."

"That's true," Jake says, laughing. "But, baby, you've never lived anywhere cold. You don't even know what snow is like."

"It snows almost every winter!"

"Once. Maybe twice. And that's not real snow."

"Well, you don't know what real snow is like then either."

"I do not," he says. "Listen, though. I honestly think you would hate it if we went somewhere hot. I think you're already sick of it, and you don't know it yet. But we can go visit Florida if you want. On vacation. One of those beach resorts." He reaches out for me, and I scoot closer to him, his strong arm wrapping around my waist. "We've got no limits, Care-bear. No limits in the world."

I tip my head back to kiss him and imagine us alone in Arizona, Texas, Vermont. He is right. No limits in the world for us.

We lie like that, looking at each other, until finally his eyes droop and his breathing changes. I study him in sleep. His skin is even and brown from his forehead down his chest, shimmering with sweat and grease, his breath calm. I wish again for September, when we'll be able to fall asleep and wake up together, beholden to no one. If I didn't have to go home in two hours, I would curl my body around his and stay like that, entangled until the morning.

His roommates turn on the porch light and moths swarm toward it like they finally have a destination. Jake opens his eyes slowly and turns to me. I drape my arm across his chest and settle my head on his shoulder. He sighs.

"This is the life," he says.

He unravels the skin of a clementine with his thumb and

presses a piece between my lips. It bursts upon my teeth. Juice runs down my chin.

At 10:45, I pick up my bag from the kitchen counter, slip on my flip-flops, and change from my sundress back into the sweaty aquarium uniform: khaki shorts and the polo with the dolphin on the pocket. My parents don't know I keep a set of clothes at Jake's. I guess if they saw me, they might think I brought the dress to work today, but I don't want to worry that they'll worry.

Jake turns the radio to the country station as he drives the dimly lit five miles to my house. First his neighborhood, with its small, tired houses, then mine, green grasses and red doors, stopping before we get to the bigger, nicer houses. The long way home. Thirteen minutes from his door to mine.

To my parents' door, I mean. I'm trying to think of it as my parents' house. I think that might make leaving easier.

He's quiet. He's not usually quiet when he drives me back.

"Are you okay?" I venture.

He doesn't answer. The passing streetlamps create a shifting palette of orange and black on his skin, light and shadow. The song on the radio fades away and is replaced by a commercial for a mattress store.

Out of nowhere, a thought pops into my head: Where will we sleep when we move? A hotel? A house? An apartment? I guess we can sleep in the back of the truck for a while. The more

I think about it, the better it sounds. Especially if we're in the southwest, where it's warm and dry and it never rains. They don't have mosquitos there, do they? Only snakes and scorpions, and those stay on the ground. We could sleep under the stars, out by the side of some long, slim desert road.

These thoughts have been coming more and more recently— the flecks of logistics that orbit our love like asteroids.

"I'm fine," he says. He breathes out a long sigh. "But it sucks. Having to take you to your parents' every night. It's shitty they won't let us stay together."

He's right.

"I'm sorry I'm so young," I say. I feel helpless in the face of this immutable, inescapable fault—the fact of my age and all the many burdens it implies.

"Can't you ask them if you can stay over?"

"They would say no."

"But you can't know that, if you won't ask them."

"I don't want to ask them. They like having me at home. Besides…"

"Besides what?" he says, and he turns off the radio and it's silent.

"Well, September," I say. "We're leaving. I won't live there anymore. So, you know, they like having me at home, and they don't know we're leaving soon, so I should…I don't know, I should sleep at home, just until we leave."

He sighs again and rubs the back of his hand across the stubble on his chin.

"I guess," he says.

I think about earlier this evening, splayed out together on the floor, his skin so warm and soft. The vulnerability of his heartbeat in my ear. Only a few more months of leaving him at night, and then we'll wake up together every day for the rest of our lives.

He walks me to my door and we stand there hugging. 10:59. I can hear the credits of a TV show in the living room and the sound of running water, my mom washing dishes. Jake pulls back and kisses me gently.

"I love you, Caroline."

"I love you too," I say.

"September," he says.

"September."

I walk inside and close the door behind me, feeling warm from his body and cold from the blast of air conditioning. Mom turns around and smiles as I walk into the kitchen.

"Caroline! How was your day?" she says, drying a soup pot in her hands. She smiles really big and I register, briefly, the lines around her eyes and the step she takes forward to greet me.

"Good," I say. "I'm really tired, though. I'm gonna go to bed."

"Oh, okay," she says, and she starts to say something else,

but I'm already out of the room and up the stairs. I take off my clothes and get into bed naked without brushing my teeth. I try to imagine rolling over and finding him there instead of the wall. The backs of my eyelids are etched with the constellations above Arizona. In my mind, the lines between the stars draw themselves into brilliant shapes. September.

I walk into the aquarium gift shop at 8:58 a.m. It's empty except for Jenny, who is lounging against the display of animal-themed chocolate bars behind the counter.

"Hey," she says. "We got a thing today."

"Oh yeah?" I drop my backpack and lean beside her.

"Yeah. The kids, the fuckin', whatever it is"—Jenny snaps her fingers—"Junior Aquarium Camp, they get to come in today and pick a figurine. It's included in the price of tuition."

She gestures at the clear bins of small plastic sea creatures that line the back of the store. At two dollars each, they are some of the cheapest things we offer. They're big enough that you can't eat one, which is a selling point for parents, but they're not very well constructed.

"What do they do with them?" I ask.

"Who knows," Jenny says. "But listen." She turns toward me, her eyes serious behind her glasses. "No substitutions, okay? This isn't a goddamn restaurant. They can't have a stuffed animal. They can't have a poster. They can't have chocolate. They can't—listen, even if it's cheaper, it doesn't matter, like, they can't have a pen. Or a sticker. They can have one figurine." She leans back and exhales. "The director was very fuckin' clear on that point."

"Okay. I mean, that shouldn't be that hard," I say.

"You'd be surprised. They can be sneaky." She extracts herself from behind the counter. "Anyway, you're here now. I'm heading back to my office. Got some"—she waves her hand in a lazy trail—"stuff to do."

I reach under the counter to the drawer with the phone book and brush my fingers around the back until I find my chocolate bar. Yesterday I saw Jenny take one from the wall behind us, which is bullshit because she gave me a big lecture about theft in our hour of training on Friday. When I saw her take it, I asked if I could have one too. She said yes as if it was no big deal, but I'm pretty sure she had to take them out of her salary. Or mine.

My chocolate bar has a panda bear on the wrapper, which is now crinkled and folded in half, and contains little dried cranberries. I take one square, fold it back up, and replace it in its hiding place. I'm guessing Jenny would eat it if she found it, out of spite.

I pull out my phone and text Jake:

hey

He doesn't reply. He's not up yet.

People drift in and out for hours. Moms with babies and toddlers. Nannies with older kids. The occasional elderly couple, or a group of fourteen-year-olds, parents having dropped them off in front of the building.

I was hoping Jake and I would be able to text more in the morning. During the school year, he used to always text me at this time, when the grocery store was nearly empty. It's looking like the aquarium will be similarly slow. In school, I could never answer—my teachers were really strict about phones. I could talk to him now, but he won't respond.

As I'm checking my phone for the thirtieth time, the doors to the aquarium area open from the inside and four blue-shirted, khaki-panted Junior Aquarium Camp counselors slip out. The same girl from yesterday is among them. She's speaking quietly but rapidly to one of the guys, her hands gesticulating in big loops that are impossible not to watch. The guy shrugs, and she hangs her head in an exaggerated signal of defeat as the conversation ends. I find myself smiling, watching her.

The four counselors position themselves in a wide, loose arc across the lobby, starting at the door to the aquarium area and ending at the activity room. In their matching uniforms, hands clasped behind their backs or resting on their hips, they look sort of like bodyguards awaiting celebrities—almost, but not quite, cool.

Then they all take out their phones. It ruins the illusion. One of the guys shows his screen to the girl. She leans over to look, her ponytail swinging to the side, and I see her laugh. I can hear the sound of it, barely, through the open door to the gift shop. The glass between me and them makes it feel like a silent movie.

Then the aquarium doors crack open. "Incoming!" someone bellows, and the counselors straighten up. The doors burst open from the inside and a flood of six- and seven-year-olds run out. Some of them go the wrong way, try to run outside or toward the gift shop. The arc of counselors gently nudge them back into position, and they change direction as easily as if it had been their intent the whole time. They look like a school of fish, small and sparkling.

The guy at the end closes the door of the activity room after the last kid. "Clear!" the first guy yells, and all the counselors laugh. They head toward the activity room in a clump, moving slowly and talking.

But the girl breaks away from the group and jogs toward the gift shop. I stand a little straighter and brush a stray hair out of my face. She grabs the glass door frame and swings her body around it, looking right at me. I haven't noticed until now just how small she is, not even five feet tall.

"Hey," she says, walking over to me and sticking out her hand. "I'm Georgia. With the camp." She cocks her head to the right, toward the now-packed activity room.

I shake her hand. Her palm is as dry as her shoulders are damp.

"I'm Caroline," I say. "I...work at the gift shop. Which I guess you know."

She laughs. "No worries," she says. She spins around, displaying the COUNSELOR lettering on the back of her shirt, and looks over her shoulder at me. "My job's pretty obvious too." My phone buzzes in my pocket.

"Anyway," she continues, "we're gonna be bringing in the kids for the figurines pretty soon. In about twenty minutes. I talked to someone about it earlier, I think your boss? Jenny?"

I nod at Jenny's closed office door. "Yeah. She got in before me this morning. She told me you'd be coming."

"Cool. So you know the whole thing. One figurine, no more, nothing else, et cetera."

"Got it."

Georgia rolls her eyes. "It's ridiculous, I know." She smiles, and I smile with her without meaning to. "Anyway, we should be in and out in fifteen minutes max. I'm gonna give you a sheet, and you put a check in the box at the intersection of their name and their animal. Then we're going to the pool and we'll be out of your hair."

"Gotcha. I thought you went to the pool in the morning?

That's how they always did it when I was in camp," I say, and immediately feel silly. I don't know why I want her to like me, but I do, and I doubt she cares that I went to her camp when I was little.

"No, yeah, we usually do, but the local swim team had a meet today. They're using the aquarium pool this summer while they're renovating the pool at Central. When they have morning meets, we go in the afternoon," she says. "Personally, I think I'm going to like going in the afternoons better. Sometimes they're sleepier in the morning. Easier to deal with in our other activities. Then when they really ramp up the energy, if it's an afternoon session, we get to stay at the pool longer. There's a lot less shit for them to mess with there."

"So, if it's afternoon today, why is your hair wet?" I ask. Another inane question. My phone buzzes in my pocket for a second time. I want her to leave so I can stop ignoring Jake. I hate it when he ignores my texts, and I don't want to do the same thing to him.

"Oh," she says, touching her head. "That's just from my shower this morning."

"Oh, okay," I say. "Cool." The gift shop is silent for a few seconds. From Jenny's office, I hear a familiar burst of sitcom music. She watches TV at lunch. And the rest of the day. She told me when I asked that it helps her focus, which I'm not sure I believe.

"Well," the girl says, "I'm gonna go check on the kids."

"Georgia, right? It was nice to meet you," I say quickly, now suddenly wanting her to stay as much as I wanted her to leave a moment ago. "I think I'm the youngest person working here, and I don't know that many people, so…I guess…yeah. It was nice to meet you."

"You're not the youngest," she says and smiles. "I'm sixteen."

"I'm sixteen too," I say.

"Oh, hey! Two of us. Nice meeting you too, Caroline," Georgia says. She flashes me a smile and jogs back to the activity room.

My phone buzzes insistently and I pull it out of my pocket. I have two texts from Jake and one from my dad. I tap Jake's name.

hey baby

what's up

where were you when I texted?

don't you have work

The symbol that means he's typing appears and disappears. I look at the texts from my dad.

Hi Caroline. Wanted to check in

hope you're having a good day.

Takeout Chinese 4 dinner tonight if u want.

I sigh inwardly. I already told my parents I'd be out until curfew tonight. I think they understand that I want to spend time with Jake, but they still want to lure me home.

Thanks Dad. I think I'll be out tonight.

But I appreciate it. My day's good. Hope yours is too.

Jake responds as I hit send.

called in sick ;)

are you kidding me

you need the money

actually WE need the money

relax baby

I needed sleep

gotta be ready for you tonight ;)

Against my better judgment, I smile and look around at the shop. It's empty, but I still feel like someone's watching. I pull my phone closer as he continues.

anyway I was tired

I'll go tomorrow it's cool

and I'm making a surprise for you tonight

what is it?

I can't tell you!

wouldn't be a surprise ;)

don't be mad baby

I'm not

I'm excited for tonight :)

gotta go tho

ok love you

love you too

I have to type my last message fast because the counselors are lining up in the same graceful arc, this time from the activity room to the gift shop. Georgia stands closest to me. The guy at the end shouts, "Incoming!" The activity room door opens, she turns around to wink at me, and the children come running in and collide with the plastic bins of sea creatures, hands scrabbling.

"Clear," yells Georgia as she ushers in the last kid, a blond-haired girl with a shirt covered in fish. *Good luck*, she mouths across the room to me, her lips forming the words big and exaggerated. But I don't have time to dwell on that because a little boy is standing in front of me, his head level with the top of the desk, and he is waving a small plastic whale.

The next twenty minutes are a blur of names—four Madisons and three Connors—and sea creatures. I shoo a kid's hand away from the jewelry display as a blond girl, who appears to be the only other female counselor, briskly picks up a boy who is trying to run out of the store and deposits him back inside. I decline another child's sincere offer to purchase a chocolate bar with a handful of dimes. Two kids start sword-fighting with rolled-up posters, and one of the male counselors yells "I'm so sorry" in my direction as he runs to separate them. It's absolute madness but kind of nice—working with all the counselors makes me feel like part of their team. When I finally get a chance to breathe, the counselors are forming their line again, which culminates at the front door this time.

Georgia comes over to the desk as I'm registering a stingray to a redheaded boy with a stuffy nose.

"All done?"

"This is the last one," I say. I mark an X at the intersection of Connor M. and stingray.

"Great. I'll see you later," she says. She grabs the little boy's hand and leads him to the door where the other kids have collected in a clump. Some of the boys are making their animals fight. A shark and a starfish are locked in deadly battle near the stuffed animal display. She herds them, in clumps and one by one, out to the front of the building where the rest of the counselors are waiting to lead them to the pool on the other side of the complex.

Jenny pops her head out of her office. Her TV's laugh track is conspicuous in the sudden silence.

"What was all that?"

"The camp kids getting their figurines."

"Oh."

"Wanna know what animal got chosen the most?"

She shuts the door.

"Dolphin," I say to no one.

I look at the clock. It felt like no time at all, but the campers were in the store for almost thirty minutes. And I still have hours left in my shift.

An old man buys a stuffed seal and asks for it gift-wrapped.

I have to tell him we don't do that. He purchases a tote bag with cartoon seaweed on it, places the seal inside with no tissue paper, and leaves. A group of teenage girls come in, pick things up, put them down again. I watch their purses closely. They're the kind who would try to steal candy or a pen. I know because my friends used to do that kind of shit, and they look a lot like my friends. But they don't steal anything. After a few minutes, they leave and amble outside to the parking lot where they lean against a car and pass around a single cigarette.

I text Jake.

what is your favorite sea animal?

This time, he replies immediately.

what? why

the kids had to choose a sea animal

the camp kids at work

dolphin whale shark starfish or stingray

eel

not an option

I like eels

you're gonna like the surprise later

what is it???

can't tell ;)

maybe it's eels

I laugh aloud and Jenny, leaving her office to go to the bathroom across the lobby, looks at me suspiciously.

"What's going on?" she says.

"Nothing," I say, and tuck my phone into my back pocket. I coast until five, when a few moms and kids come in to buy trinkets after camp dismisses, and close the shop at exactly 5:30. My closing work is supposed to take until six, but today and yesterday it only took me a few minutes. Georgia and the counselors are still counseling when I leave at 5:45, chatting with kids whose parents are late. But Georgia looks up at me as I leave.

"See you tomorrow, Caroline," she says.

"Bye, Georgia," I say. It's nice that she thought to say goodbye to me, and I feel light and happy as I walk outside to Jake's car—he is early today, thank goodness—and climb in.

"What's the surprise?" I ask him after we kiss. He grins and starts to drive, one hand on my thigh, the other resting loosely on the wheel. I roll down the window as the radio bursts into song.

When we get home, I find out: flowers and the promise that his roommates won't be back until eleven.

"So we can be loud," he says and grins. My guts twist into a knot and untangle themselves just as quickly, my body's now-familiar response to being wanted. Before we started dating, it was a foreign sensation. Now I feel lucky every time, but worried, as if I am equally likely to lose it as I am to feel it again.

He turns me around gently and starts kissing my neck, my stomach pressed against the kitchen counter. The flowers peek out of a water glass in front of me. Their petals are bright pink and yellow, and they look like they've been pulled right from a garden. Fresh. Sometimes the store manager lets him bring home the old flowers, still pretty, but wilting and browning at the edges, the ones that no one will buy even on triple markdown. I've gotten used to seeing them around the house one day, then throwing them out the next. But these are brand new.

"Do you like 'em?" he whispers in my ear.

"I love them," I say and turn around. "I love you."

We have sex in the living room, and I'm loud like he likes. I like it too. He doesn't do anything different from usual. It's not as if I'm normally holding back screams. But this feels more adult somehow. Freeing. No one around to tease us when we shut the door to the bedroom or pound on the wall during.

After, we lie on the couch. I watch him play video games, and he feeds me crescent moons of clementines. I get home at eleven o'clock exactly.

That night I dream of Jake, and in the dream, we're in a cabin somewhere cold, the edges blurry. We're sitting on his couch, staring into a fire as if it's TV. I think he's angry at me, but I don't know why. I relented and went to the Northeast with him, and in the dream, I love it. It is better than I could have possibly expected, but he is somehow disappointed. I feel strange and guilty at how straight he's sitting against the couch, the firelight reflected in his irises.

I move closer to him. He feels far away and cold, like a statue. We are alone here. We will never have to speak to anyone again. The thought should be a comfort, but it feels all wrong. I try to lean my head on his shoulder; his bones are sharp, and I can't find a comfortable place. He is still staring at the fire, and the walls are dissolving, something throbbing inside me or knocking outside of me, I can't tell, everything getting colder—

I wake up hyperventilating.

When I was little, I used to have nightmares all the time. Monsters under the bed, kidnappers outside my window, burglars in the closet. After I screamed for my mom, too terrified to get out of bed, she would come into my room and turn on the lights.

"Now," she'd say. "What's scaring you?"

If there was a ghost waiting under the mattress, we'd lift the bed skirt together and touch the floor and the wood of the bed frame. If there was a ghoul outside the window, we'd put our hands on the windowpanes. If I feared a murderer bursting out of the closet, she would part my jeans and dresses so I could touch my fingers to the painted wall behind them.

"When you have a nightmare, it all feels real. But it isn't real," she said to me those nights. "When you touch something, you know it's real. You know it's only what it is. Your window's just a window. There's nothing there."

I lie down and try to go back to sleep, but my heart is beating too fast, and I see the firelight every time I close my eyes. I am shivering.

So, foolish as I feel, I get up and turn on my lamp. I touch the wall beside me, solid and smooth. I walk to the laundry room, next to my room, where the dryer is bumping against the wall like a stranger knocking on a door. I touch it. It is warm beneath my palms. I turn it off and the thumping trembles, quiets, stops.

I open the window in my room as wide as it can go and stick my body out into the night. The air is like the water left over after you make pasta: hot and sticky and rich. I start sweating on contact with it. I touch my own arms and my T-shirt and my bare legs. My skin is warm as ever, blood flowing safely beneath.

I leave the window open and climb back into bed. The ghostly blue light of my phone takes away all the firelight from behind my eyes. I text Jake, but he's asleep, of course, and doesn't reply. He always swears that he'll leave his phone on loud so it wakes him up, but it doesn't. I try not to text him at night anyway. I want him to get a good night's sleep.

I fall asleep to the sound of frogs and crickets, the humidity drifting through conditioned air to my body. In the last moments before unconsciousness, I reach out to touch Jake—but he is not there, and so I do not know if he is real.

3

The next day, Toby wanders into the gift shop and jumps up to sit on the counter, nudging over a bucket of shiny pencils. They clatter and roll on the floor like pick-up sticks.

"Hey, Caroline," he says, adjusting his skinny ass on the countertop.

"Toby, what the fuck? Clean those up," I protest. "Jenny's gonna be pissed." I put down my phone. Jake and I were texting about places, and I'm making a concerted effort to keep the discussion away from the Northeast. I suggested the Pacific Northwest. Seattle, maybe. I read something online about how it's not so expensive if you live in the suburbs, and you can go hiking and white-water rafting in the summer.

Toby leaps off the counter like he's making an Olympic

dismount and starts gathering the pencils. "One thing you gotta know about Jenny," he says, "is that it's best to leave her to her. She has her own deal."

"Her deal is watching TV."

"She won't mess with you if you don't mess with her," he says, straightening up.

I look toward Jenny's door. It's closed and quiet, like usual. "But she's my boss. Asking questions isn't messing with her."

"That's where you're wrong," Toby says. "The best thing to do here is whatever you want. Jenny's better at it than anyone. She's been here almost as long as I have, so at this point, she's probably the aquarium's second best employee." He looks at me expectantly, waiting. I roll my eyes.

"And you're number one?" I say.

"Indeed I am." He grins, and I feel a flutter in my stomach. Jake sometimes talks about Toby's girlfriends: there are too many to keep track of. I can see why.

"Anyway, Caroline, I came here with a purpose," he says. He places the container of pencils back on the counter. My phone buzzes underneath it. I glance down. *San Diego? We could swim in the ocean.*

"Yes?" I say. San Diego. God, that'd be amazing. I've never been to California.

"Yes. Now, you get a lunch break, correct?"

"Uh-huh."

"At what time?"

"One."

"For an hour?"

"Yeah."

"And you usually stay here and don't take a break and don't eat anything, right?"

"Well, I bring my lunch."

"Whatever. My cousin Jake instructed me to take care of you when you got this job, and thus far I feel I have not fulfilled my duty."

"It's been three days," I say.

He ignores me and continues. "So," he says, "most days at one, I, like you, have my lunch break. As does the better half of the camp counselors, because they eat in shifts so the kids aren't left alone. Today we are ordering pizza. Normally I would be first out the door, but Liz is sick today, so I'm leading her half-hour tour at one. I think you should come on the tour and then eat lunch with me and half the counselors."

"But I've already been on a tour. I had to when I got the job."

"Ah, but who led your tour?"

"Um…" I try to remember. "Mary?"

"Sure. Mary may be a cougar, but her tours lack a certain pizzazz. You've not yet had the full Tobias Markham Aquarium Tour Experience." He winks. "It's a whole different ball game."

"But who will run the store?"

"Jenny, obviously. You're legally required to have a break."

"I don't know if she'll be okay with that. She never actually runs it. She works in her office."

"Caroline." He shakes his head. "You've only been here a couple days. The time to set a precedent is now. You gotta stand up to her."

"I thought you said I had to leave her alone."

"Well, you know. It's a balance." He starts walking away, backward. "Come out to the lobby at one, we'll do the tour, eat some pizza, whatever. See you then?"

"Yeah, sure," I say, because there seems to be no other option. My phone buzzes again as he walks away, strolling through the lobby, aquarium doors swinging open and shut behind him. *San Diego, baby,* Jake says, and I text back simply: *yes.*

Three hours later, I knock on Jenny's door.

"Come in," she calls from within. I open it. She peeks out from behind her computer. "Yes?"

"I was thinking I'd take my lunch break now?" I say, my voice turning into a question, though I don't mean it to. She looks at me skeptically and says nothing. "For an hour, right? At least I thought that was what you said when you hired me…"

She sighs. "Yeah, okay. Are you gonna take it at one from now on?"

"I was thinking so, yeah."

"Okay. Just make sure the sign on the door says we're closed and you'll be back at two."

"You aren't going to take over the register for me?"

She looks at me blankly. "I have things to do."

"Got it," I say, although I have no idea what those things are. I close her office door behind me. At the door to the shop, I turn the OPEN sign to CLOSED and hang the little vinyl clock sign underneath it, pushing the hands to 2:00.

"I will," I say, stepping out of the doorway so she can come through to my usual spot behind the cash register.

Then I hustle out of the shop to join the group that has gathered in the middle of the lobby. Some of them see my aquarium shirt and ask me when the tour is starting, or whether they'll get to see the great white shark. I tell them one o'clock and our shark is on loan to an aquarium in Maryland, but I just work in the gift shop and the tour guide will be here soon. They turn away, disgruntled. We get the shark thing a lot; Jenny prepared me for that question. The shark is a lie. We have never had a shark.

Toby strolls out of the double doors at one exactly. The crowd quiets.

"Welcome!" he yells. "To this, the second aquarium tour of June the twelfth, one o'clock on this glorious summer afternoon, the most thrilling, the most heart-pounding, the very *best* tour of the watery underworld you shall *ever...*" He leans down to a bemused five-year-old and cuts his voice to a whisper, "experience."

The five-year-old puts his thumb in his mouth.

I slowly pull my phone out of my pocket.

I'm about to go on a tour with toby

hahahahah

oh man

what?

They're ridiculous

one time I went on one

I was drunk it was great

ok well I'm sober

still gonna be great

gotta go someone wants to know where the hummus is

After a prolonged staring contest with the child, Toby straightens up and claps. "All right, ladies and gentlemen. Let's go. This way, please, follow me." He turns toward the swinging doors, and the crowd follows. Some of the mothers are murmuring to each other. I put my phone in my pocket and stay in the back. One small girl looks up at me with round brown eyes.

"I know," I say to her quietly. "He's a lot."

We walk through the swinging doors, and my eyes have to adjust. The gift shop is normally flooded with sharp summer sunlight, and I've gotten used to squinting at anyone walking in from the lobby. The aquarium is dark and cool. The carpet underneath my feet is blue, and it seems damp. The little brown-eyed girl hugs her mom's calf.

We're in a tunnel, both walls long and curved, made of thick glass. The water inside is fluorescent and murkier than it should be. Our cleaning crews aren't on top of their game. A large sea turtle glides silently through the soft, cloudy blue, moving close to the glass and then drifting up to where the air and water meet. In the far back of the tank, another shelled form drifts aimlessly back and forth.

"Now," Toby begins, with a sweep of his arm, "these are our leatherback turtles, Banjo and the Admiral. The Admiral is the one you saw diving in front of us. Banjo's in the back there. These are actually the very first animals this aquarium acquired more than fifty years ago. They were already adults when we got them, so there's every chance they might be up to three hundred years old."

"I thought the oldest turtle in the world was only like a hundred and twenty," one man says, furrowing his brow.

"Common misconception," Toby says with a straight face. "Liberal media, et cetera."

The children ignore his words. They press close to the glass and gaze upward, where the Admiral's pale belly is just barely visible from his floating position near the surface.

"How many of you have found a turtle in your backyard?" Toby asks. One child turns around and raises his hand tentatively.

"Right," Toby says, "well, did you ever see it tuck its head into its shell? Like this?" Toby shrugs his shoulders up around his ears. It's a little freaky how high he can make them go. I wonder if he's practiced.

The kid stares at him blankly. The others are still looking up at the Admiral and whispering.

"Well, so, if you did see a turtle in your backyard, it would probably be able to tuck its head in. Like turtles in cartoons. But leatherback turtles—hey, let's please not tap on the glass, they don't like that—leatherbacks can't do that. They can do some other pretty cool stuff, though. Like migrate hundreds of miles between nesting grounds to find the right place to raise their kids. That would be like your mom moving to Alaska to have you!"

A few moms are standing in a line in the back. Their arms are folded. None of them laugh.

"Okay, not a crowd-pleaser. Here's a good one: leatherbacks can stay underwater for as long as five hours, and they can actually slow down their heart rate to conserve oxygen. How long can you guys stay underwater? Do any of you know? Do you want to all try to hold our breaths now?"

He sucks in a deep breath and holds it, his cheeks puffed out. No one else follows suit.

A few of the kids turn around. "I can count to fifteen," one of them says.

"I got to twenty once," says another.

Toby exhales dramatically. "That's pretty great. I can't do that," he says. "But the leatherback's got you beat. Another weird thing is that if they're left alone for too long, their shells actually become translucent—that's another word for clear—so you can see right through them. But it's much healthier to have a hard, green shell, like you see these turtles have. That's why the aquarium has always kept Banjo and the Admiral together, so they don't get lonely and their shells stay healthy."

The Admiral has drifted away, and now all the kids turn to face Toby.

"Why do they get clear?" one girl asks.

"I've never heard of that," her mom says.

"It's actually to make them easier to see in the water," Toby says. "They absorb more light so other leatherbacks can see them from farther away and realize that they're alone. It's basically a mechanism to make friends."

"So…it's a mating thing?" one mom says.

"You could say that," Toby says, raising his eyebrows slightly.

"I'm not sure if—" the woman starts, but Toby interrupts her.

"Let's move on!" he exclaims brightly and starts walking into the next room. The group trails behind him.

I run ahead to where Toby is striding forward, long arms swinging.

"Is that really true? About how old they are? And their shells?" I whisper.

"I mean, maybe," he says. "Who am I to know the mysteries of turtles?"

"So you're lying to these people."

"I like to spice things up. Keep 'em engaged with the material," he says, and then he turns around and raises his arms in a dramatic *V*. "The rainbow fish," he proclaims. "Peaceful schooling fish, which means, like you, they gather in big groups called schools. But unlike you guys, they stay in schools during the summer!"

The kids giggle at this one. I walk closer to the edge of the tank and put my hand on the glass, lukewarm and dry. It's marked with thousands of tiny handprints around the height of my thighs. Inside, the rainbow fish dart by so quickly that I can't distinguish one from another. They are too fast and tiny, like individual sparks of a firework that someone exploded in the water.

The children follow the school back and forth as they whirl around the tank, jump to touch the glass where the fish just were. For every lap they take, one trips on the uneven carpet, but apparently, falling such a short distance isn't even painful. They immediately get up and keep running—back and forth, one school chasing another.

While they run, Toby tells us there are more than seventy species of rainbow fish, and the more males you keep together, the more colorful they get. To show off for the ladies, he says while winking at one of the younger mothers, who blushes and frowns simultaneously. In fact, he says, there's one documented case of a school of rainbow fish, composed almost entirely of males, which never stopped changing color, but constantly shifted through all the tones of the rainbow.

As we move on to the next hall, I'm not sure which of these things are true, if any. My hand feels greasy where it touched the glass. I look back once before we pass through the door and see the school whip toward the left side of the tank in one coordinated motion, like dancers.

We walk through a few more fish tanks and the alligator's area. The kids can barely see the alligator, so small and bumpy that he blends in with the rocks where he's sleeping. Toby tells a story about how the alligator, as a baby, attacked an aquarium staff member and lost. His pride was so hurt that he'd never grown any bigger.

"That's a lesson to you. Don't get in a fight, and if you do and you lose, don't be a sore loser," Toby says. The kids are getting antsy, and their parents are checking their phones.

Toby leads us into the next room, and I actually gasp because this room's tank is resplendent with jellyfish. It looks like hundreds of them, but it can't be; I know we don't have facilities big enough. The water is a little cleaner here and still that crazed, false blue.

The jellyfish float up and down, sideways and diagonally, propelling themselves with muscle contractions I don't understand. They bump into each other and bounce away. When I took the introduction tour last week, the jellyfish tank was being cleaned. I've never seen them before. We don't sell much jellyfish paraphernalia at the store.

These are not like the animals I used to see in National Geographic TV shows and picture books when I was little. Not the Portuguese man o' war, with its long trailing tentacles, or the sinister jellies with yard-wide tops that descend into rainbows of color. These jellyfish are small and unintimidating. Their white bodies blue from the water, their edges pale pink and brown like they've been burned.

Toby comes over to me and says quietly, "I'm about to take 'em to the touch tank. Usually it's only about three minutes before someone pokes something sharp and starts crying, so the tour should be over soon and we can grab some lunch."

"I think I'm gonna stay here until you're done," I say.

"Are you okay?" he asks. "I know my tour sucks, but it's never been bad enough to actually make people ill."

"I'm good," I tell him. "I think it's the water. Everyone looks kinda sickly."

"Yeah." He glances at his tour group, who are mostly playing freeze tag. "Time to go."

He herds them through to the horseshoes and starfish, and I sit on the floor. I watch the jellyfish swim gracefully across the tank, float into the distance and back again. They move from corner to meaningless corner like they're tracing the edges of their world. I run my hand along the line where the glass meets the wall. It is straight and cool. On the floor beneath it, there's a little pile of dust and a green rubber band from someone's braces.

I don't know how long I sit there. Until the jellyfish look like the snowflakes, whirling and twisting into nothingness.

"Caroline," Toby says loudly, making me turn fast. "Lunch? Pizza? Yeah?"

"Yeah," I say, rubbing my neck. "Let's go."

He leads me through the touch tank room, where a father is comforting a sniffling child, and through a door marked STAFF ONLY that leads to a long white hall. The rest of the aquarium tries its best not to look bleak and institutional, but this hallway isn't even pretending. The signs next to the doors have official-sounding titles—SENIOR MARINE SPECIALIST, ASSOCIATE MANAGEMENT—and all the offices are empty.

When Toby pushes open the door at the end of the hall (EMERGENCY EXIT, DO NOT OPEN, ALARM WILL SOUND), I find myself on a wide stretch of concrete, beyond which are trees, brown grass, and, far to the right, the back edge of the parking lot. The building might offer a little shade in the morning, but not now. The sun is high in the sky, and it is oppressively hot.

The JAC counselors have spread out pool towels in a haphazard square, and five of them are clustered around five boxes of pizza right in the middle. Their COUNSELOR shirts are flung in a pile off to the left. The girls are in bikini tops and the guys are shirtless, their boxers barely showing above the waistbands of their khaki shorts. Their skin is alternately tanned or red with the sunburn that comes before tan, all shining with sweat.

"Everyone," Toby says, "this is Caroline. Caroline, this is Matt, Dave, Serena, Devin, and Georgia." He points around the circle as he talks. I recognize most of them from the figurine chaos yesterday, but I know I'm going to forget their names as soon as his finger passes. Georgia, though, I remember specifically. I didn't recognize her at first, her head laid sideways on interlaced hands while one of the guys—Matt? Dave?—talked to her.

When Toby says my name, her head pops up, black hair piled in a shaky bun on top of her head. She licks her fingers and grabs another slice of cheese from the box directly in front of her.

"We met yesterday," she says, swatting away a hand that has crept toward her pizza box. "Caroline?"

"Yeah," I say, awkwardly folding my arms over my chest. I wonder if I'm supposed to take off my shirt too. I wore a lacy black bra today, something only Jake has ever seen on me.

"Matt, scoot over," she says.

"Hi," he says to me, sticking out his hand, which has a not insignificant amount of red sauce on it. I shake it anyway, which is awkward given that he's reaching up from the ground and I'm still standing.

"Hi," I say. "Caroline."

"Matt. Welcome."

"Matt, *move*," Georgia insists. He scoots over a few feet. "Do you like cheese?" she asks me.

"That's really nice of you, but I'm not that hungry."

"Well, you should still sit down." She pats the ground next to her.

I walk around the circle and lie down on my stomach like the rest of them. Down here, the air smells like pizza grease and chlorine.

"Morning pool time?" I ask.

"Yeah," Georgia sighs, taking a bite of her pizza. She chews and swallows. "It was great. They've all made friends already. They've invented this very elaborate game where half of them are mermaids and half are pirates, and basically it can keep them occupied for hours. Most of the time they're fighting against each other, but any time we try to make them do something, we're sea monsters and they team up against us."

"I'm a shark," Matt adds, raising his eyebrows. He gestures toward the only other girl in the circle, who is lying on her back, wearing sunglasses and headphones and holding a thick book open above her head, its library plastic shimmering in the sun. "Serena over here is the whale, which is—"

"Offensive and inaccurate," she cuts in without looking at us. Her voice is surprisingly low.

"The most beautiful whale that's ever lived," Matt says affectionately. She ignores him.

"I'm the kraken," says one of the guys across from me. "My kraken name is Glorb. But my actual name is Dave."

"And I'm a walrus of some type," says the guy next to him. "Devin."

"Nice to meet you both," I say.

"I'm...a giant octopus. I think. It's sort of hard to tell," says Georgia.

Toby, who has squeezed in between Serena and Dave, sighs. "If only the children on my tours gave me the same kind of honorific," he says. "I swear, kids these days have no interest in learning."

"Maybe it's your teaching methods," Georgia suggests.

"Nonsense. Yo, Serena, move so I can stretch out." Serena closes the book without speaking and delicately scoots farther away from the circle, combing her fingers through her pale hair as she goes.

Toby rolls his eyes and unfolds his long legs. He opens the only box still closed, revealing a large pepperoni pizza. "Oh my God, yes. Now, Devin, what is this I hear about you going to the beach with your parents instead of attending the excursion to Great Adventures at the end of the summer? You may not know this, being new, but that simply won't do."

As they start to talk, Georgia ducks her head and turns over onto her back, squinting up at the sun. She puts one arm over her face and looks at me.

"One of the guys told me that Toby and Serena used to date," she says quietly. "That's why she seems like such a bitch. Supposedly he cheated on her."

"I'm not surprised," I say. I turn over on my back too, and close my eyes. The sun warms the cotton of my shirt. After the stale cool of the aquarium tour and the sharp air conditioning of the gift shop, it feels good.

"Did you know him before you started working here?" Georgia asks.

"Toby?"

"Yeah."

"Yeah. He kind of got me this job. I'm dating his cousin. Jake? You know him?" As always when I talk about Jake to someone new, I feel a tiny thrill traveling from my toes to the top of my head: the fact of us being a couple.

"Nah. But that's cool. With Serena, though...why not surprised?"

"Oh, Jake says Toby cheats on his girlfriends all the time."

Georgia sighs. "He's an asshole," she says. Behind us, Toby's voice is rising louder and louder, something about Great Adventures, tradition, on and on.

"I don't think he's an asshole," I say. "I mean, he's a good guy."

"How? He cheats," Georgia says, and I can hear her

readjusting herself, turning on her side to face me. I turn too, and her dark eyes look right into mine. "Asshole."

"Maybe you're right," I say.

"Well," she says, "maybe you are. You know him better than I do, anyway." She grabs another piece of pizza. "Want any?"

"I'm good," I say.

"Are you sure?"

"Oh…" I hesitate. "Sure, I guess. Yeah. Thank you." I take it from her, warm and slippery with cheese. I haven't had pizza in ages. For a second, I am on the porch with my parents, some late summer Saturday last year, our family night.

Then I open my eyes and see Georgia, smiling at me. Her eyes are bright and curious, and even though she's eating most of a box of pizza, shirtless in front of a bunch of people, she doesn't look ashamed or self-conscious in the least. I can't tell whether I'm envious or confused. Maybe both.

"You're welcome," she says and laughs. "Any time. You looked like you needed it."

"Are you a rising senior or junior?" I ask as I slowly eat.

"Senior," she says. "Late summer birthday."

"Yeah, me too. It sucks. Last year my mom and I planned this whole party, and then no one came except my boyfriend."

"Shit. That's horrible." She's silent for a second. "When's your birthday?"

"August twentieth. Usually right before school starts."

"Hey, mine's the thirteenth!"

"Oh yeah?"

"Yeah. We'll make them have a party for us here," she says. "Like we have for the JAC kids, with the little hats and dolphin plates and everything."

"That'd be great," I say, imagining—for one embarrassing moment—the counselors toasting us with glasses of juice. "What school do you go to?"

"Eastern Academy. You?"

"Jackson. That explains why I haven't seen you around."

"Yeah, Eastern kind of sucks, but it's also nice. It's pretentious as hell, but I have friends there, you know? That's something. Although," she adds, looking around the circle, "Katie and Priya are both at camp or visiting family practically all summer, so for the most part I'm stuck with this crowd of jokers for the next few months. Hey, Matt, can I trade you a pepperoni slice for some sausage and mushroom?"

I don't say anything. I don't really have friends at school, not anymore. Ever since I started dating Jake, all the girls who used to come over to my house for sleepovers have stopped talking to me as much. They're still nice to me, but we're not as close. They grew closer to each other and found other people, so slowly I didn't even realize it was happening, until one day in March I didn't understand the inside jokes they were making at lunch. I didn't even know some of the girls at the table.

I'm not sure why it happened. When Jake and I started dating, they squealed and giggled over him as much as I did, and now they barely pay attention to me. But Jake never liked them—said they were superficial and boring—and now I guess he's proven right.

"Whatever, though. I'm out of here soon," I say.

"I know," Georgia sighs. For a second, I panic. I shouldn't have said that. Even Toby doesn't know about our plans to leave. So far it's only me and Jake. We want to keep it an absolute secret, just in case. But then, Georgia speaks again. "College. I can't wait. I'm so excited."

"Oh," I say. "Yeah. Me too."

"I can't even decide where to apply. I've got like twenty schools on my list. There are so many factors to consider, you know?" As Georgia talks about research positions and major fairs and SAT scores, I turn onto my back and stare up at the sun until I have to close my eyes. I pull up my T-shirt to the bottom of my bra. Her words turn into a soft blur in my ears while the heat presses down on me, warming me from every angle, until I hear her say, "Anyway. There's a lot to think about," and the two of us are silent together.

Jake has the late shift at the grocery store on Wednesdays and Thursdays, so today, at 5:55, I'm lying on the sidewalk near the curb with my eyes closed, waiting for my dad to pick me up. Normally I would worry about someone seeing me, but it's been a long day, the sidewalk is warm, and there are no benches. Besides, no one has come out of the aquarium's double doors since I got outside. Jenny left abruptly around three o'clock, saying she had to go home early without an explanation, and the last few JAC babies were all picked up ten minutes ago.

My phone buzzes. It's Dad.

Got caught at office. Testers found another bug!!!!! leaving in 5. be there son

If only his company knew that their best software developer could barely operate a phone keyboard.

I close my eyes again and run my fingers along the crease between sidewalk panels. Twenty, thirty minutes of learning the way the grass grows from the dirt in the cracks. I text Jake *hi?*, but the evening is always busy for him, and I don't expect a response.

A door slams and I sit up quickly. Georgia is standing over me, thumbs hooked into the straps of her flimsy JAC backpack. She squints down at me.

"You okay?"

"Yeah, I'm...well, I'm waiting for my dad to pick me up, and he probably won't be here for a little while, so I was just... resting," I finish feebly.

She cocks her head. "Where do you live?"

"Meadow Valley."

"Off Millhouse?"

"Yeah."

"I can take you home, if you want," she says, extending a hand to pull me up. "My parents are out at some charity dinner tonight anyway, so I don't have to be home any particular time."

"That would be so great," I reply, a little surprised. "Really? Are you sure?"

"Yeah, don't worry about it. It's not far from my house."

"You have a car?"

"Yep, over there," she says, tilting her head to the last

remaining car in the parking lot: a gleaming black sedan with a blue paint scrape on the fender.

As we climb into the car—which is boiling hot—I text my dad.

Girl from work is taking me home.

Don't worry about picking me up.

Are you ok? Does she have a license?

I can still pick you up. Really sorry I'm late

He always takes longer to type than I do. I wait for him to read what I've written.

Ok. Tell her to be careful driving.

I do not tell Georgia, turning on Top 40 radio full blast, to be careful driving.

She's a counselor for the camp, don't worry. All of them have to have licenses.

"Thanks again for driving me," I say to Georgia, who is humming along to the music. "Jake would pick me up, but he works a lot of evening shifts."

"You're welcome," she replies, smiling. "But it really is no big deal."

My phone buzzes with Dad's response:

Is she a new friend?

Does she want to come to dinner?

I can't decide whether to grimace or smile. My parents want me to make more friends, ever since the girls from school stopped coming over. They say they like Jake, and though I know they're not a fan of his age or his smoking habit, I think they're at least okay with him. But Mom told me in halting language as we washed dishes after dinner a few weeks ago, "We just want to make sure you have people to talk to who are, you know, *not* boys, and maybe closer to your own age." At the time, I told her Jake and I were only two years apart, and I sulked until we finished the dishes, but she wasn't wrong. It would be nice to have someone to hang out with in the evenings when Jake is working. And it would make my parents happy.

"Do you wanna stay for dinner?" I ask Georgia. "After you drop me off?"

"Yeah, sure!" she says, eyebrows arching up. "Oh, wow, thank you. I was gonna order in pizza again, but I've had pizza for lunch every day this week and last week, and I'm trying not to get sick of it."

"How—" I start, but then I stop. It would be rude.

"What?" she says, glancing over at me.

"I mean, how do you eat pizza all the time and not, like, gain a ton of weight?"

"Well, I'm kind of fat already," she says all matter-of-fact, "but I'm on the swim team at school, and we're basically on our feet all day at camp, so—"

"You're not fat," I say quickly.

"I am, kind of. It's cool. I like how I look. My mom worries about it more than me."

She turns into my development, past the faded *Meadow Valley* sign and the tiny pool swarming with kids and teenagers. The neighbor boys who were my childhood friends are all lifeguards now, swimsuits slouched low on their skinny frames, jaws working around their gum. I stopped going to the pool last summer, when those boys' gazes would linger on me and my friends a little too long.

"Turn here," I say, and Georgia curves the car onto my road. The houses line up neat and orderly, alternating the colors of their doors: red, blue, green, red, blue. Not for the first time, I try to imagine a life in which I do not come back here at night, leave here in the morning. But the future is foreign to me, and so bright I can't make out its shape.

"Which one?"

"Right here, 1621. You can park on the curb."

Georgia is over a foot from the curb when she turns off the car, but I don't say anything. I only got my license a month ago, and since I don't have a car, I rarely use it. I'm not that great a driver.

"This seems like a really nice neighborhood," she says. "Really friendly."

"It's all right," I say. "It was fun when I was little because there were a lot of other kids to play with."

"It seems like it would have been nice," Georgia says and unbuckles.

The door to my house is unlocked. "Mom?" I call as I walk in. "I brought home someone for dinner, did Dad tell you?"

"In here," she calls from the kitchen at the end of the hall.

We walk in. Mom has the curtains thrown all the way open, and the sunlight is streaming in, coating the whole kitchen in a soft yellow glow. The somber voice of the classical music DJ drifts from a radio in the corner. She looks up from a cutting board overflowing with broccoli, and a big wide smile—the one my dad always talks about when he tells the story of how they met—washes over her face.

"Caroline! This is your friend from work your dad was telling me about?" She sticks her hand across the kitchen island. "I'm Cathy. You can call me Mrs. Weaver if you want, but Cathy's okay. Or Mrs. Caroline's Mom, if you want." She winks. Georgia shakes her hand. In the two days I've known her, I haven't gotten the impression that this girl is particularly shy, but next to my mom she seems almost meek.

"Georgia," she says. "It's very nice to meet you. Thank you for having me for dinner."

"Oh, you don't need to be so formal," Mom says, brushing the chopped broccoli into a pot. "We're not fancy here. Do you like chicken and pasta? I like to put some veggies in there too. Complete the bowl of nutrients, if you will. I'd offer to leave them out if you don't like broccoli and peas, but honestly, I think y'all eat too much crap as it is, so you're gonna have to suffer through it."

"No, I love broccoli. That sounds great," Georgia says. She shoots me a look. It's one I'm used to. I get it every time I bring home new friends. The last time I saw it was on Jake's face a year ago, the first time he met my parents. Part scared, part amused, and part amazed, it is the standard reaction to my mother: *This is too much.* I used to find it embarrassing, but I've come to accept that anyone I bring home has to have a strong constitution.

Which doesn't mean I can't help out my guests a little. Mom has launched into a slew of questions about where Georgia goes to school, what grade she's in, and what she does at the aquarium, but I interrupt her.

"Mom, I think Georgia and I are gonna go upstairs. I want to shower before dinner and, you know, show her the house and stuff."

"Oh!" Mom exclaims. "Well, of course that's fine. Dinner should be ready in half an hour or so—"

"It's okay. I can stay down here while you shower," Georgia says. "Keep Mrs. Caroline's Mom company." She leans against the kitchen counter and peers at the cutting board. "Can I help at all?"

I go upstairs, happy but baffled. As I leave, Mom starts her questions again, and I wonder what kind of person would want to extend a conversation with my mother at their inaugural meeting. She mellows out after a while, but I've never introduced her to anyone who has willingly stayed for that first interrogation.

And sure enough, when I walk back into my room, wrapped in one towel and drying off my hair with another, Georgia is sitting on the bed and inspecting my pictures.

"Oh, sorry—I would've changed in the bathroom if I'd known you were in here," I blurt, grabbing a pair of shorts and a tank top from the pile of clothes on my dresser.

"Well, I meant to stay downstairs, but I couldn't do it," she says. She grins ruefully. "Your mom talks a lot. She's really into the Fourth of July, did you know that? Event planning generally. I got a full recap of the brunch she hosted for that volunteer society, the Better Bonneville Group? I think my mom's in that technically, but she never goes. But mostly she wanted to talk about me. She had a billion questions about my job. And she wanted to hear all about my classes next year."

"I am so sorry," I say, wincing. "She never stops talking…" I step into my closet and close the door, maneuvering around the piles of clothes to find a spot where I can pull on my shorts. "One sec, I'm gonna change."

"I don't hate it," Georgia responds, her voice muffled by the door. "It's just a lot to take in. I told her I wanted to wash my face but came up here instead."

I put on the tank top and open the closet door. "Are you sure you don't want to shower? You have time. You could borrow some of my clothes."

Georgia looks down at her khakis and bright blue counselor

shirt, sweat stains fading but visible beneath her arms and breasts. "That would be great, actually. If you have anything that would fit me?"

"Um..." I look in my closet and regret making the offer. I don't know how to estimate other people's clothing sizes, but compared to me, Georgia is rounder all over—hips, boobs, thighs. Still... "I think I have some T-shirts that would. And this skirt, maybe?" I grab one of my sleep shirts and pull the skirt from the back of the closet, a neon-green elastic-waist nightmare that goes all the way down to the floor. My aunt bought it for me a long time ago. I hesitate with the hanger in my hand. I don't want Georgia to make fun of me for it. But when I turn around, she's already standing in the doorway of the closet.

"Oh, I love that," Georgia says sincerely.

"Really?" I say, surprised. I've never seen anyone at school wear anything like it, which is part of why I have never worn it in public.

"Yeah, absolutely. What a great color." She takes the clothes, folds them carefully, and holds them in a pile against her chest. "Towels in the bathroom?"

"Yep, underneath the sink," I say, and she steps into the bathroom and closes the door. I hear the fan cut on, and I lie down on my bed. A piano sonata begins on the radio downstairs. The pictures on my wall are split into light and shadow from the sunshine drifting in through the window.

My parents bought me the bulletin board for my birthday the year I started middle school. It was a gigantic thing, well over three feet wide and almost as tall. It's something every teenage girl should have, they said, even though I wasn't a teenager yet. They said I'd need it for keeping up with homework and tests, so I could maintain a good GPA. At the time, I didn't understand grades, and they didn't yet know my middle school didn't use GPAs, but it all made me feel awfully grown-up. They hung it on the wall beside my bed. They completed the gift with a box of pink and purple tacks and a calendar of beach pictures: blue water, white sand, green palms, twelve times over.

I don't like taking things down. It feels like I'm finalizing the end of something, and I don't like thinking that way. So, over the years, I've pinned new memories over the old to-do lists and photos and ticket stubs. Now it's mostly Jake: a photo booth strip that we got at the mall last year, pictures of us at the park and in his backyard, a card with a sketch of the sky he bought for me last Christmas that says *I love you more than all the stars*. There's also the aquarium logo, which I tore out of their brochure when I got the gift shop job; a program from my end-of-year choir concert; and a postcard from my aunt from her trip to Italy earlier this year.

Then there are the pictures of destinations. When I started pinning them up, Mom asked me what they were, and I told her they were places I wanted to go. Which was partially true.

Really, they're ideas for September. Whenever Jake and I talk about a place, I find a picture online and print it out. San Diego, yes, and Arizona, Texas, New Orleans, Massachusetts, Vermont, New York City. Places we've talked about visiting someday: Rio de Janeiro, Sydney, Paris. I've written airport codes in permanent marker over a picture of the Pacific.

We talk about these things when we're lying in bed together, waiting for my curfew to come. How after we settle down and earn some money for a couple of years, after we have our first baby, we'll tour the world together: a little family of three. We'll be travelers, washing windows to earn enough to get to the next place. We'll stroll on boardwalks and dip our toes in foreign oceans. We will never talk to anyone else. We will only need each other.

Georgia opens the bathroom door and releases a cloud of steam. She absently ties up her hair in an elastic band. The green skirt puddles around her feet and trails on the floor, and the T-shirt is tight across her chest.

"So what is all this stuff?" she asks, sitting on the edge of the bed. "All these pictures? And that guy, is that your boyfriend?"

"Yeah, that's Jake," I say. "And they're nothing. Just ideas for…for after graduation, I guess."

"Good ideas," she says softly, and we sit like that for a while, looking at visions of the future, until we get the call to come to dinner.

The next day, Thursday, Toby swings by the gift shop at lunch-time to tell me to come out for pizza. Later, Georgia helps me close, and when Dad texts me to tell me he'll be late again—the bugs they found yesterday have mutated into different and more difficult bugs today—Georgia offers to drive me home.

"You know," she says as we get into her car, "your house is right on the way to mine, and my parents are almost always at work until late. So I can drive you any time." We get into such a good conversation in the car, her telling me a story about an absurd swim meet trip last year, that it seems only natural to invite her in for dinner again. And then, in what seems like no time at all, it's 10:00 p.m., and her parents are texting her to come home.

I spend Friday night and the weekend with Jake and my family, and on Monday when I start to lock up the store, Georgia is waiting with her keys without me even having to ask.

"I really appreciate this," I tell her after texting Dad to let him know he can stay at work later. "My parents do too."

"No worries," Georgia responds easily, then hesitates. "You know, I can just drop you off. I don't have to stay for dinner tonight."

"No, I want you to," I say. She doesn't say anything, and I worry I've misinterpreted her. "I mean…if you want to," I follow up quickly.

"I do," she says, smiling at me, taking her eyes away from the road for a little too long. "There's nothing going on at my house anyway."

"If you're sure," I say, but I'm glad. I feel at ease with her in a way I can't explain, and the few evenings we've spent together were more fun than I've had in ages.

In this way, the summer settles into a quiet rhythm that carries me through my days like a tide. Breakfast with my parents, ride to work, watch the store until lunch, when I cultivate my tan outside with Georgia and the counselors. I started bringing salads for lunch after Toby spent several days haranguing me about not eating pizza. My mom puts sliced-up fruit into the Tupperware with spinach and arugula, and I taste mango, strawberry, apple on my tongue as the sun warms the top of my head.

At first, lunch with the counselors was more than a little overwhelming. They talk over each other constantly and are forever getting into playful arguments over nothing at all. But as I've started to get to know them a little better, I am beginning to feel as if I belong. Georgia and Toby go out of their way to welcome me. Matt barely stops talking long enough to take a breath, but he involves me in conversation as much as he does anyone. Serena doesn't really speak to me, but then again, she rarely speaks to anyone. Dave and Devin remain as interchangeable as they were when I first met them, archetypal bros who seem more comfortable talking to Toby and Matt than me, Georgia, and Serena.

After work on Tuesdays and Fridays and sometimes Mondays, Jake picks me up, and we go to his house. Wednesdays, Thursdays, and other Mondays, he has the late shift at the store. Then Georgia takes me home, and we lie on my bed or on towels on the porch, talking until dinner and after, until Mom gently pokes her head around the door frame to say, "Georgia, honey, don't you think it's about time to be getting home?" She jumps up, apologizing, and I spend the rest of the evening watching TV with my parents or lying in bed, staring at the brightness of Jake's texts on my phone. When I close my eyes to sleep, all I can see is that square of light. It burns blue and purple on the backs of my eyelids.

It's a good and comfortable pattern, so when I got a text from Mom disrupting it one Wednesday during lunch, I am more disgruntled than I might be otherwise.

hi caroline

Ac is out @ home

guy couldn't come to fix until tomorrow

"Ugh," I groan, falling back onto the cement. Georgia peers over me, her head blocking out the sun.

"What's up?"

"Our air conditioning stopped working, apparently."

"Fuck that," Matt pronounces from the other side of

Georgia. He takes a bite of pizza and speaks around it. "You know, if you need somewhere to cool off, the aquarium kiddie pool's open to you. I mean, I know you don't technically have a pool pass, but I'll make a special exception. For, uh…" He waggles his eyebrows. "A favor."

"Absolutely not," I say while at the same time Georgia says, "Ew."

"Offer's on the table," he counters, grinning. Matt's one of those guys who's always been the funniest guy in the room, but because of that, he's not necessarily the nicest. He's stocky and tan, with long, thin hair that balloons into impossible spikes after he comes out of the pool in the morning. I've never seen him without sunglasses.

"Anyway," I say, turning back to Georgia. "You probably shouldn't come over tonight. The house is going to be miserable."

She makes a sympathetic face and is about to respond when my phone starts to ring. It's my mom. I get up and move away from the crowd of counselors, scuffing the edge of my flip-flops into the dry dirt where concrete meets grass.

"Caroline?"

"Hey, Mom. I got your texts."

"Oh good. I never know if they sent or not."

"You can tell by if it says…never mind. Air conditioning's out."

"Yes, well, so it is, and apparently it's been nonfunctional since early this morning, so the house is really starting to heat up. I'm going over to Vivian's house now, since her house is a reasonable temperature, and your father is going to join us for dinner. That way we'll only have to come back here to sleep. I wanted to see if you'd like to come too."

"Can—"

In the background, Toby's voice explodes loud enough to make me turn around: "I swear on my fish's grave, Devin, if you skip the end-of-the-summer Great Adventures trip to go on a *family vacation*, I will fucking *end you*."

"What?" Mom says. I shake my head.

"Sorry. Can Georgia join us?" We have plans to hang out tonight, and I don't want to abandon her.

"Well…" She hesitates. "I would think so, but I'd have to talk to Vivian first. Can you—"

"Hold on a sec," I say in a flash of inspiration. I jog back over to the group and touch Georgia on the shoulder to get her attention. "Georgia, can we hang out at your house tonight?"

Her expression is unreadable: not angry, but not quite happy either. But I really don't want to spend the evening with Vivian. She is one of my parents' oldest friends, a coleader with my mom at the Better Bonneville Group for years now. But she's also the least interesting person I've ever met, and the most soft-spoken, so you always have to ask her to repeat her meaningless statements. "We don't have to," I tell Georgia, "but it would be fun, right? I've never met your parents. Or seen your house, even."

"Okay," Georgia replies, and quickly adds, "tentatively, though. I gotta check with them first. But I think they'll say yes."

"Yes, thank you. You have no idea what you're saving me from."

I put the phone back up to my ear. "Mom, Georgia and I can go to her house. Would that be okay? I'd be back by ten."

"Oh, sure. That's fine." She actually sounds relieved. I do complain about Vivian a lot after every time we see her, so maybe she's happy not to deal with it. "Will her parents be home?"

I relay the question to Georgia, who shrugs. "Yeah," I say, interpreting her gesture.

"Good, then. But make sure to be home by—"

"Ten, I know."

"There's no need to interrupt."

"Sorry."

"I'll set up some fans before I leave, and maybe it won't be too hot by the time we all get back. I love you, Caroline."

"Love you too, Mom."

I hang up the phone and fall back beside Georgia, nudging her lightly with my knee. "Thanks," I say.

"Mm," she replies, in the middle of a bite. She swallows. "My mom responded. She said it's okay, as long as I can still be in bed by eleven. Also, she says she left us dinner, but it probably sucks so we'll have to figure something out on our own. Also, she and my dad may not be there."

"Okay," I say, a little taken aback. "I mean, is it actually all right? I kind of figured you come over to my house all the time, so it would be cool, but I can go hang out with my parents at their friend's house if it's going to be trouble."

She makes an unhappy harrumphing sound and leans on her elbow, turning to face me. "I'm sorry, it's not a problem. They're fine with it. It's just, my parents…" She looks up and squints into the sky above me. "Well, they're not like your mom and dad."

"What do you mean?" I ask.

"You'll see," she says, sounding weary.

It is at that moment that Toby yells, "Back to the work pits, scoundrels," and I look at my phone and see I'm actually a minute late already.

When I get back to the store, there are a couple of people in line, and Jenny behind the register stares daggers at me as I dash in. The rest of the day is busy enough that I don't have time to dwell on Georgia's weirdness. I do text with Jake in a few free moments, trying to figure out if he can get off work early so we can hook up in my empty house instead of me apparently imposing on Georgia. But one of his coworkers started throwing up and had to go home, so there is no chance of him faking sick.

Which means that when 6:00 p.m. rolls around, I grab my bag and meet Georgia in the parking lot, where she seems to be in better spirits.

"Anything good happen today?" I ask as we climb into her car.

"Oh, such a great afternoon," she sighs, rolling down the windows. "There's this girl, Olivia, who hasn't really engaged with camp the entire time. Every single day, when her mom drops her off, she starts crying. For three weeks. It's the saddest thing. And also, on a cynical level, pretty frustrating, because it requires a lot of time and effort, and we still never make her happy. We've gotten used to it, though, so it had kind of stopped bothering me.

"But today," she says as she pulls out of the parking lot, "we did an activity with clay, and she absolutely lit up. Hasn't cared about painting. Or swimming. Or any of the animals. Or construction-paper masks or paper-bag puppets or *anything*. The clay, though, she loved. And she was good at it! I mean," Georgia amends, "for a four-year-old. She made a very passable manta ray. So, all in all, a pretty great afternoon, despite us having to return to my house tonight."

"About that," I say.

She looks over at me as she turns, right instead of the left that would take us to my house. "Sorry about being weird earlier," she says. "I really don't mind. I mean, I come right home most nights you're hanging out with Jake, obviously. It's just…" Her eyes are fixed straight ahead now. The houses passing are getting bigger and fancier, set farther back from the street, all the cars parked in long driveways and the streets smooth and clean. "Your parents are so nice. They're so welcoming."

"And yours aren't?"

"I mean, you probably won't even see them."

We reach a cul-de-sac and Georgia turns into the driveway of an honest-to-God mansion. Three marble steps lead up to a pair of double doors edged by intricate stained glass. I can count at least nine windows in the front alone. The lawn is bright green, sprigs of white lilies lining the pathway to the door. My eyes must be popping out of my head because Georgia lightly taps my temple as she turns off the car.

"Stop staring. You're making me feel weird."

"This is *your house*?"

"Yeah."

We get out of the car. The neighborhood is utterly silent. No kids bicycling, no ice-cream truck, no motorcycle kickback from the college kids down the street. Our footsteps echo as we walk up to the door and Georgia unlocks it.

The house is just as impressive inside as it is outside, and equally silent. Georgia leads me through a two-story entrance hall and a massive den with shining velvet couches before reaching the kitchen, which actually takes my breath away. My mother would faint if she saw it. It is huge and pristine, everything in its place, and the appliances gleam in the afternoon light. Like our kitchen, it opens onto a back deck, but unlike ours, this deck has a set of lawn chairs with an umbrella and—down a few sets of stairs—its own pool.

"Holy shit, Georgia," I finally say. She fidgets next to me. "Why don't we come here all the time?"

"I know what it looks like," she says. I step closer to the back window and look down. The pool is a perfect rectangle, its edges squared off in blue tile. She stays standing behind me. "But my parents get really mad if anything's messy. They prefer everything to be…as it is. We couldn't hang out here like we do at your place."

"We could clean up after ourselves."

"They would find something. Trust me." She walks over to the fridge and opens it, peering inside. "I would ask if you want some dinner, but there's nothing good here. My mom started buying me these premade meals from some fancy-ass weight loss company, and they're the worst."

As she holds the fridge open, I can see two items pinned on the door: a blank office calendar and a thin, long line of magnetized color that looks a little like a thermometer. The very top is green, a little piece underneath that is yellow, and the rest is red. A small silver magnet sits in the middle of the green zone.

Georgia closes the door and notices me looking. "That's the Chart," she says, capitalizing the word with her voice. "Green, I get to do whatever I want. Yellow is the danger zone, early curfew, no allowance. Red is grounded. Updated weekly." I must look confused because she rolls her eyes and says, "During the school year, it's about grades. My current average across all my classes. Ninety-five or higher is green. My parents used to let me give it up in the summer, but now it's based on my most recent SAT practice score. I take them every Sunday."

I pause for a moment, taking all this in. "Jesus," I say as I start to do the math. "An entire test? But those things take... what, four hours?"

"Yeah," she says, gloomy. I look around. The calendar and the Chart are the only things on the fridge. But hung on the walls all around the kitchen—and, now I think about it, the entryway and living room we walked through—are small canvas paintings, none larger than a poster.

They aren't exactly fine art. The brushstrokes are either tentative and awkward or bold and careless, the colors are occasionally muddy, and the scenes aren't anything to write home about. Some are generic landscapes of mountains or beaches, neither of which exist near our town. Others are images of Bonneville's most iconic landmarks: a church, a statue, and a downtown office building constructed by a semi-famous architect in his fading years.

There's something else weird about the paintings that I can't put my finger on until I do a full scan across the room, think back through the rest of the rooms we walked through, and realize that there are two of every single scene.

Georgia notices me looking. "Ah," she says, "you've seen our art."

"What the hell is all this?"

"The results of approximately a year and a half of weekend couple sessions at the Bonneville Bev'n'Brush," Georgia says. "It's this place where you go and drink wine for two hours while they teach you how to paint. Except they don't teach you how to paint, exactly, they teach you how to make one specific painting."

I walk closer to the nearest canvas, an eleven-by-seventeen portrait of a pine tree. "Your parents do this together?" I ask.

"Fuck no. My dad would hate it. He goes out with his running group while I go there with my mom."

"But you can't drink wine."

"That is true. But Mom makes me come with her anyway, and we pay the child rate for me. It's weird because everyone else is actually a couple, we're the only mother-daughter pair. But a friend of hers did a birthday party there a few years ago, and Mom totally fell in love with it. She says it's the most relaxing thing ever. And she works so much that she really does need to relax."

I move across the kitchen to the identical copy of the tree. Where the first tree's needles were small and precise, with several shades of green and brown, this one is rendered in big, sloppy strokes, like a child painted it. "Let me guess," I say. "You did this one?"

"Nope," Georgia says, "I did the one you were looking at first."

I look at her, questioning. She shrugs.

"Mom always gets kinda tipsy. Whereas I actually find it stressful. I want to get it right, you know? But she loves it so much, and it's one of the biggest ways we spend time together, so I still go with her."

"Huh," I say, looking at the paintings again. Georgia shifts her weight, following my gaze.

"Let's go up to my room now," she says. She scampers out of the kitchen and up a set of back stairs I didn't notice.

I'm expecting a hallway or maybe a playroom at the top of the stairs. But instead, Georgia turns at the landing, throws her arms open, and says, "Welcome." The staircase enters directly into her bedroom, which is as big as our den, wall-to-wall windows facing out onto the pool. Unlike the rest of the house, which is so clean it's almost eerie, this room looks like a pack of feral dogs has run through it. Clothes, books, and papers are everywhere, covering the carpet so thickly that there have been actual paths carved through it: stairs to bed, bed to desk, desk to bathroom, bathroom to closet.

The walls are just as messy, in their own way. She has taped things floor to ceiling: photographs, posters, notes, pictures torn out from magazines, and then weirder stuff—business cards, menus, advertisements. Some of those Bev'n'Brush canvases hang crookedly from nails among the papers and photos taped to the wall. She does not have a bulletin board. The room is the bulletin board.

"It's the blessing and the curse of the Chart," Georgia says, looking at me to see my reaction. "As long as I keep my grades up and I don't leave clutter around the rest of the house, my parents don't care if I clean in here."

"Georgia, this room is unbelievable," I manage. "Your house is unbelievable."

"Well," she says, awkward, "it's not all that great." She cocks her head down the way we came. "No door." Then she nods to the other side of the room, where there *is* a door set into the wall beside the bed. "And that leads down the hall to my parents' offices and their bedroom. But it doesn't have a lock. So, lots of space to do whatever I want with, but no privacy." She shrugs, self-conscious, and goes to sit on the bed. She tangles her fingers again, grabs a pillow and presses it against her chest. "I guess you see why I didn't want you to come over."

"Are you kidding? This place is great," I say, moving farther into the room, turning to take in everything on the walls and that stunning view out the window. "When are your parents coming home? I wanna meet them."

Georgia sighs. "Oh, it depends," she says. "Sometime between seven and ten thirty. It varies. This is a busy time for both of them. I'd guess we probably won't see them tonight. They work late during the week so we can hang out all together on weekends. That's why I never see you on the weekends, by the way. I mean, I know you're hanging out with Jake most of the time, but still. Gotta spend *some* time with my parents."

I am not sure what to say to this. It makes me think of the house as an enormous, beautiful box with Georgia rattling around in it alone, like a firefly cupped in someone's hands. I wish my parents were less overbearing about Jake, but I still like seeing them before I go to bed. It is unfathomable to me to come home to someplace so quiet.

Georgia fills the silence by flopping back on her bed and pulling out her phone. "Even if they do come home, though, those weight-loss meals are the worst, so we should probably order some food," she says.

"I cannot see another pizza," I say, thankful for her ability to change the subject. I feel awkward and guilty and like I want to hug her. I lie on the bed beside her and watch her flip through her contacts. Beside us, a stack of SAT and college reference books teeters on the nightstand.

"I don't understand that about you, but I respect it. How about that Italian place off Highway 80? They deliver."

I give her a look.

"What? They make more than pizza. You can get a salad. I'll get pasta. All good."

She calls Buona Tavola and places our order. You can tell she's a regular—she asks the person on the other end how their dog's surgery went.

I walk around the room, looking at the walls, while she talks. There are pictures of Georgia as a baby, as a child, as a slightly younger teenager with braces. Pictures of her wearing medals at swim meets and with her arms wrapped around girls I don't know, her friends from school. I see her parents for the first time too: the three of them laughing at Christmas, her mom standing behind her as she holds up a spelling bee trophy, her dad with his arm around her shoulder as they dangle their legs in the pool. There's one of Georgia and her mom in an art studio that I can only imagine is the Bev'n'Brush, both beaming and holding their paintbrushes in front of them like crossed swords.

She hangs up and says, "Forty minutes." She gives me an exaggerated sigh. "But I'm starving now. Do you wanna play foosball?"

She leads me down the hallway to the game room, and I get a peek inside her parents' offices and their bedroom—each its own ornate, orderly world, crystalline in its cleanliness. We play foosball and she beats me easily, though I start to get better with each passing game.

"It's really hard to play this by yourself," she says breathlessly, having whooped me a sixth time. "I've tried. Way better with another person."

The doorbell rings with our food before I have a chance to respond.

At my request, we sit outside by the pool while we eat, dangling our feet in the water. I'm around water all day, but it feels different here, with no screaming kids or smudged glass separating us. Even Georgia admits it's nice.

I tell her about how weird it was to date Jake during the school year when he wasn't in school anymore, how my friends would get quiet and judgmental when I told them he wasn't a college student. She tells me she's never had a boyfriend, never even gone on a date, and when I say the guys at Eastern don't deserve her, she laughs and says, "True." She discusses her frustrations with her best friend at school, Katie. She only talks about herself, Georgia says, and she is too competitive about grades. I try to explain the way my friends have drawn away from me over the past year. I feel like an open door, as if I can say anything at all and it will disappear safely into Georgia and the clear turquoise water beneath us. Anything except the biggest thing—September.

We talk until it gets dark and then keep talking, lying down with our feet still in the water and staring up as the stars come out. Only when all the blue and purple light has drained from the sky do I hear a car pull into the driveway, then see the lights come on inside the house.

Georgia and I dry our legs with the remaining napkins from the to-go bag, and she leads me back up the stairs. She opens the sliding door just wide enough to slip through, and I follow, closing it behind me.

"Hey, Mom," she says.

I turn to my left, toward the end of the kitchen, and see a woman straighten up from the sink. Georgia's mother: a perfect simulacrum of Georgia, if she were a supermodel. The woman is tiny, even shorter than she looked in the pictures on Georgia's wall, and remarkably thin. She's wearing heels and a gray pantsuit, and she walks swiftly over to us. You can tell she started the day wearing a lot of makeup, but it's faded, and there are purple loops underneath her eyes that make her look a couple of steps beyond exhausted.

"Hey, Georgia," she says to her daughter as she approaches. She gives Georgia a big, tight hug, then holds out her hand to me. "Jessica Lee. Pleased to meet you…"

"Caroline," I fill in the blank quickly. Her grip is strong and hard, all bones, and her eyes are so intense I have to focus on a spot just beneath her chin. "It's nice to meet you too, Mrs. Lee."

She does not correct me back to the informal *Jessica*, like my mom always does. Instead, she says, "Georgia tells me you work at the aquarium with her?"

"Yes, ma'am," I say. "In the gift shop, though. I'm not a counselor."

"You like it?"

"Yes, ma'am."

"From what Georgia says, those kids are hellacious. Must be nice not to deal with them." She smiles a little, but in my peripheral vision, Georgia looks uncomfortable.

She turns and goes back to the refrigerator, pulling out a silver container. She is about to close the door when she does a double take, and her gaze flickers over the items inside.

"Georgia," she says, sounding openly exasperated, "you know we had plenty of those NutriPlus meals. Did you get delivery again?"

Beside me, Georgia shrinks into herself. Her lips start to form the lie, and I know she's no good at it. I jump in.

"Mrs. Lee, I've actually been craving Buona Tavola all week. I asked Georgia if we could order in. I'm really sorry."

Her gaze switches from Georgia to me. "No problem, Caroline. Next time, you're welcome to anything in the fridge. No need to spend money on takeout. We could all stand to eat a little healthier." She sighs and puts the container into the microwave. "Georgia, your dad should be home in half an hour or so. He had a client dinner. I know it's late, but he wanted to watch an episode of that new show we were talking about, the nature one? The episode about the peregrine falcon?"

I sneak a glance at Georgia. She's wearing an expression I've never seen on her before: part shame, part love, part exhaustion.

"Mom," she says, "you know it's your rule that I'm supposed to be in bed by eleven. Plus, I do actually love sleeping."

Mrs. Lee releases a breath, opening the microwave to poke at its contents, then closing it and setting it for another minute. She turns around.

"I know," she says. "Maybe just the first half, then."

Georgia throws up' her hands. "But then how will I know what happens to the falcon?"

Her mom gives us the first real smile I've seen on her. "Fair. We'll save it for Saturday."

"Much better. Besides, I have to drive Caroline home now. If that's okay."

Mrs. Lee glances at me. "Caroline, you live pretty close, right?"

"Just ten minutes or so."

"Then that's no problem. Thanks for coming over, Caroline. Georgia spends so much time at your house, it's nice to meet you." She motions Georgia over to her, and Georgia gives her a perfunctory hug. "Drive safe. I love you."

"I love you too, Mom," Georgia says. "Be back soon." She catches my eye and cocks her head toward the doorway sharply.

"Bye, Mrs. Lee, it was nice to meet you," I say as we leave the kitchen.

"You too," I hear her call, as if from far away.

We're both silent as we walk out the door, our footsteps echoing in the tall foyer. The silence continues as we get into her car and pull out of her driveway. I gaze out the window, sneaking glances at Georgia as often as I can. She looks tired.

When she switches on the turn signal to leave her neighborhood, she finally speaks up.

"So now you get why we never go to my house."

"It really was not bad," I say. "Your mom seems nice. And your house is an actual art museum. I felt like I was among the old masters."

"It's just," she starts, ignoring my joke, and then stops for a moment. Her headlights trace a steady path down the dark road. "I know the house is nice. I know I'm really lucky. I really truly do know that. But my parents are just so…much. They expect too much. They have all these rules, and they expect me to break them for them, but not for myself. They can be so *mean*. About whatever. School. Messiness. Food, like tonight."

"She didn't seem mad," I ventured. "Just annoyed. About the food."

"Oh, trust me, she's mad," Georgia says. "We fight about it all the time. My dad is even worse about it, actually, because he used to run track in college and he's always been thin. The only other fat person in my family is my mom's mom in Washington, and she lives in a nursing home, and my parents think she's sick because she's fat. Which isn't true, but whatever, that's not the point. So, when you started inviting me to your house in the afternoons… I mean, your parents are so nice. They're happy all the time, and they care about you."

"Your parents care about you too," I say tentatively. "I mean, your mom's not…the warmest person, necessarily, but she clearly loves you."

"But your mom," she starts again, "I know it pisses you off

when she talks about college, but...she would probably be happy with anything. Not to say," she follows up quickly, "that you couldn't get into an Ivy League. But my parents are so intense about it. I mean, I had to *beg* for them to let me work this job this year. Last year, I spent half my summer at this gifted-and-talented camp and the other half volunteering at the library. It was fine, but I felt like I was in school all summer. This summer, I just wanted a normal job. Especially since I have to do all the SAT practice tests."

"Well, I'm glad you're working at JAC," I tell her quietly.

"I am too."

"You know, your parents should be happy. You're basically surrounded by academic superstars at the aquarium," I say. "I've been meaning to tell you that I got early acceptance to Harvard. I'll be leaving for the fall semester." That makes her crack a smile.

"Really, though," she says, "your mom just wants you to go to college, which you are." I fidget in my seat, but Georgia doesn't notice. "I don't think it matters to her so much where you end up. All she wants is to be involved and make sure it's not, you know, some sketchy unaccredited hole in the wall. And I know it bothers you, I'm not trying to say that's not legiti- mate, but my parents are so much more aggressive about it. It's so much pressure."

We slow and reach the stoplight right before my neighbor- hood, and she looks at me.

"They're like that all the time," she says.

I put my hand on her knee lightly, her skin warm against my palm. I let it stay there while she pulls into my neighborhood, passes the dark and gated pool, and arrives in front of my house, and then I give her an awkward hug across the middle of the car. She laughs a little—my head is sort of resting on her shoulder and I can't quite reach across—and that makes me giggle too, and soon we're just sitting in the dark car, laughing together, me leaning against her. Then the porch light switches on, my mother's face appearing in the window, and we break apart.

"So my house next time, then," I say.

"I think so."

I get out of the car and pause, my hand on the door. "I'm really sorry, Georgia," I say, and I don't know exactly what I'm apologizing for.

"It's okay," she says. "They love me. We're a family. We're good. I'll see you tomorrow."

"See you tomorrow," I say, and I close the door. As I walk up the sidewalk, my mother peering out at me from beside the door, I feel guilt and gratitude in equal measure, and I cannot bring myself to examine why.

I talk to Jake about Georgia all the time, and vice versa. But they keep just missing each other: I'm at Jake's on the weekends, and Georgia leaves work a little earlier when she's not waiting to take us to my house. It is, needless to say, awkward.

"You've gotta let me meet him," Georgia says finally. "I feel like I know him already, and I've never even seen him in person. It's very weird."

I tell her she will meet him soon, but I'm worried. They are two separate worlds. Georgia is lunchtime, and making faces at each other through the gift shop window, and Wednesday and Thursday nights with a background of my mom's classical music. Jake is clementines and butterfly kisses and sex. And though they are the two melodies in the song of my June, they alternate; I fear they won't fit in the same time signature.

It's a Monday evening, and I'm waiting for Jake to come get me, arms sore from lifting the heavy boxes of penguin notebooks we just got. It's the most humid day of the summer so far. A storm came through this afternoon, sweeping in rough and loud, and we had to move our lunch to the miniscule staff room in the back. I watched the rain from the window there as I ate blueberries and hearts of romaine. It hit the sidewalk like it was pounding on a locked door.

Now, I'm sitting on that sidewalk and my butt is thoroughly wet, and I'm trying to figure out whether Jake will think it's funny or gross, when Georgia bursts out the doors, yelling, "I have had it with this fucking place. I cannot deal with it any more. I am done."

"What's the deal?" I say, arching my head up to see her. She flings down her backpack and sits beside me. Her cheeks are flushed, and she's tangling her fingers together, making her hands look like soft pretzels.

"Just the permission forms," she says, quieter now. "For the natural history museum trip we did last Friday. They said they didn't have all of them, and I know for a fact I put every single one in the folder, just like I do every time we go anywhere new. I know how to do my job. Now they're talking about getting sued, and how much trouble I could be in. But nothing's gonna happen. It never does, because I always do what I'm supposed to. They'll find it tomorrow, and they won't even apologize."

I scoot behind her and rub her back. Her shoulder blades jut softly through the cotton. She sweeps her ponytail over her shoulder and sighs.

"It'll be okay," I say.

"I know. I love this place. I love it so much, but some days it just really sucks. I can't wait for the Fourth of July break." We sit for a moment in silence. I consider telling her that she will probably get roped into my parents' enormous Independence Day party—which will make the long weekend anything but a break—but I don't want to make her mood worse.

And then I'm inspired. "Hey," I say, "do you wanna come to Jake's place with me tonight?"

She twists around to look at me, and I gently push her head straight, rubbing small circles on her back with the heel of my hand.

"Seriously?"

"Yeah, seriously. You guys have been waiting to meet each other for forever."

"Huh." She winces as I make my way down her lower back. "But won't you guys be hooking up or whatever?"

"We don't have to do that every time we're together," I answer, feeling mature. Jake and I are more than our chemistry. We'll have to be, being together for our whole lives.

I still haven't told Georgia about our plans for September. But I did tell her that I'd had sex. We were lying on my bed making fun of old issues of *Cosmo*, and she didn't believe me at first. Then I think she judged me a little. Then she had all these questions. What hurt, what felt weird, what felt good.

"But have you ever…I mean, have you, like…had, with him…"

"An orgasm?"

"Yeah."

"Nah. Well—" I thought about it for a moment. There was once, almost, but… "Not really. At least I don't think so."

Her eyes got big, and I felt ashamed of myself and defensive of Jake all at once. "I mean," I said quickly, "sex is great. He's really good at it. I just think there might be something sort of wrong with me. Or something. I'm sure I'll figure it out."

"But wouldn't you know for sure if you've had one? From, you know…" She tilted her head down at the article in the magazine: "31 Ways to Spice Up a Solo Date Night."

"I mean," I started, and then stopped. "I do know. It's not that I don't know. It's just that…it's not always so cut-and-dried. Whether you have one or not."

Her cheeks flushed and she flipped to a fashion spread. "Seems pretty straightforward to me," she said, her voice half-amused and half-annoyed. And then, normal again—"Look at this hideous fucking skirt"—and we moved on to celebrity style, a topic about which we disagree vociferously.

We haven't talked about sex as much since then. But now, she laughs.

"Well, if you're sure you won't be overcome by your cavewoman urges, then yes, I'd love to come over," she says. As if on cue, Jake's pickup turns into the aquarium parking lot. I hop up and pull Georgia with me.

"Are you sure he'll be cool with it?" she asks. We watch him swing into the circle, and I feel vaguely uneasy. I didn't think to ask him if Georgia could come. But I'm sure he'll be fine. He has been wanting to meet her for a while, after all.

"Definitely," I say. He pulls up and puts the truck in park.

"Hey, baby," he smiles. "Ready to go?"

"Yeah," I say, "but hey, this is my friend Georgia I've told you about. Georgia, this is Jake."

He leans way over and sticks his hand out the passenger side window. Georgia shakes it firmly.

"Nice to meet you," she says. "Caroline's told me so much about you."

"All bad things, I hope," he says and grins, and my stomach turns over.

"Hey, love, I was hoping that maybe Georgia could come over to your place with us tonight? And maybe have some dinner with us? She has her own car and everything, so…"

"Yeah, come on over!" Jake exclaims, waving his arm abstractly toward the road. "My roommates'll appreciate the company. We don't get a lot of girls around the house. With the notable exception of Caroline, of course."

Georgia half laughs and tucks her thumbs into the straps of her backpack.

"So...I'll follow you there?" she says.

"Sounds great," Jake says cheerfully. He reaches across the car again and opens the door for me. "Caroline?"

"I'll see you there," I say to Georgia. As I get in the pickup, I watch her in the rearview mirror, jogging across the parking lot. I try to tell how she's feeling from the cadence of her run—is she nervous, excited? Does it even matter to her, meeting my boyfriend? As she opens her door, Jake leans over the divider and pulls my attention away from the mirror with a long, wet kiss. His hand roams over my thighs, searching.

"Not tonight, Jake," I whisper. "Not with Georgia around."

"Oh, she won't mind," he says, so soft and low I think I might dissolve in his voice.

"Just one night, love. Just not tonight. No big deal."

"If you're sure," he says. He straightens up and checks the side mirror. I look in the rearview again. Georgia's car is idling, and she's staring absently out the window at the sparse forest across the street from the aquarium. She doesn't look nervous or excited, just lost in herself, un-self-conscious in a moment alone. I watch her until Jake puts the truck into drive and pulls away, the view in the mirror twisting abruptly into a blur of concrete, trees, and sky.

On the way to his house, Jake rests his hand on my knee

and spends too long looking into my eyes between glances at the road. The wind brushes my hair back from my face, and the guitar on the radio twangs its way through a familiar melody.

He asks me how my day was, and I tell him about the boxes and the storm.

"I'm glad I'm finally meeting Georgia," he says. "You talk about her so much, she's gotta be pretty cool. Do you think she'd be into Craig?"

"Maybe," I say, thinking of Craig's perpetually snotty nose and wrinkled polo shirts. "Probably not, though."

"Ah, well," Jake sighs, "worth a try. Anyway, cool that she's hanging out with us. What do you want to do?"

"What we usually do, I guess."

"Minus sex."

"Minus sex, yeah."

"Well, what do you guys do when you hang out?"

I think about Wednesday and Thursday evenings. The hours pass slow and fast at the same time, the way you don't think the clouds are moving, but they're in different shapes the next time you look up. Magazines, movies, the back porch, and our hands red with strawberry juice.

"Anything. We can watch a movie, I guess. That'd be nice."

"A movie it is!" Jake declares and puts both hands on the wheel in a gesture of finality.

"How was your day?" I ask.

He launches into his favorite story of every day, the tale of the weirdest purchase. Today, it's an elderly man buying apple-cinnamon cereal, pink princess cupcake holders, and rat poison. He's speculating about what this guy might be doing. But as much as I want to, I can't focus, because the sky is so blue, and Georgia is bobbing her head back and forth in the car behind us. I want to freeze this movement—the world so warm and every-one I love here with me, all of us in motion.

At the house, Jake throws open the door and ushers in me and Georgia first. He gives her the tour. It's brief: "Here's my room, and here's Craig's room, and Joe's room—I wouldn't go in there—and here's the bathroom—I try to keep it clean for Caroline—and here's the kitchen, and there's the porch, and here's the living room. You cool with hot dogs for dinner?"

Georgia stands between the two couches, slowly turning in a circle, looking. It's the same way she looked around my kitchen when I took her home the first time, as if to her, every new place holds secrets worth finding out, even if it's just a decaying little ranch house like this one. The sun drips yellow and gold through the mosquito screen on the porch. Jake turns on the radio as he pulls a pan out of their cluttered cabinets. I want to give her a different tour, show her the house as I saw it the first time Jake opened its door for me.

It was our fourth date in as many weeks. The first date was coffee. The second was also coffee. The third was a movie.

The fourth started with dinner at the Italian place where Craig worked and could get us a discount. It was the beginning of the summer, just after school had let out, when the heat was only starting to make itself known.

We finished dinner early. The sun was still going down, and as he drove me to the house, we talked about the colors of the sunset, and I tried to keep my voice from wavering.

"And this is my place," he said casually, as he pulled into the gravel driveway and turned off the car. The house was dark, flat, and quiet, red brick and a scratched front door painted green like a Christmas tree.

I had never dated a guy with his own place before. I'd never even dated a guy with a car. The only real boyfriend I'd ever had, a guy named Ethan I'd gone out with for a few months freshman year, always got nervous at the beginning and end of our dates; his mom would drive us to the movie theater, and his hands would shake when he was buying the tickets. But there was nothing shaky about Jake. His chest was wide and his wrists were strong, and in his car, outside his house, he was looking at me with something in his eyes I'd never seen before.

He leaned over and kissed me until I had to break away to breathe. It wasn't my first kiss, or even my first kiss with him, but it was the first one in my life that felt serious—not like Ethan's slimy tongue and tentative touches, but something confident and commanding and new. His hands roamed over my torso, tracing the underwire of my bra and wrapping around my back, drifting down my spine.

"Wanna go inside?" he said softly. I did.

Jake had just moved in, so there were a few boxes still scattered around the doorway. But otherwise, it was almost the same then as it is now. The kitchen was big and mostly clean, the living room carpet a rusty orange stretching from couch to sagging couch. Through the door to the back porch I could see the last rays of the sun stretching over the tops of the trees. Jake waited for me to put down my purse and poured me a cup of water from the pitcher in the refrigerator. It struck me as so genteel—the car and the house, the furniture and the dishes on which he had made and eaten meals for one, the water pitcher, all these trappings of adulthood.

But I didn't drink the whole glass, because almost as soon as I had taken a sip, Jake was kissing me again and pushing me down the hall. I walked backward until my back bumped into a wall, and then he turned my body to move me into a dimly lit room, and as I fell on his bed, he pulled away from me. I thought I had done something wrong until I saw he was lighting a candle, and then, so fast, he was back with me again.

That first night I mostly saw his bedroom from my back, his tiny television and bookshelves filled with shoeboxes filled with who knows what, skewed horizontal from the bed. The movie posters on his walls and ceiling flickered with the light, coming in and out of focus. They were a patchwork quilt of stories I didn't know, familiar faces and peeling corners.

We didn't have sex that night. He didn't even take my top off. We just made out for a long time, his hands slinking beneath my shirt, and when I saw the clock tick to 10:45, I said we had to go. As he was driving me home, I asked him if he would show me all those movies. He's tried, but we usually only watch them halfway through before we start hooking up.

So, I guess I don't want to show Georgia the place as I first saw it, not exactly. But I wish I could tell her, easily, how good I feel when I walk in the door. How perfect this place is.

And right now, she is unreadable. I start to worry she isn't impressed. I see, as I come to stand beside her, the flickering bulb above the stove, the dust bunnies under the easy chair, the stains and scratches on the table. It's not a flawless place. It's nothing like what she's used to, the impeccable arches and sparkling floors of her home. But it's a house, and it's his—well, as long as he and Craig and Joe pay rent—and that independence is precious.

"Pretty great, right?" I say, and I kick myself inwardly for the defensive edge in my voice.

But I guess she doesn't hear it, because she turns and smiles real wide, and she says, "Yeah, this is incredible." She sounds sincere. And that's good enough for me.

"Y'all can sit down," Jake says, so I flop onto the couch, pulling Georgia with me. The material sinks in underneath us, and I slide toward her, the two of us squished together in the middle. You need at least three people to balance this thing out.

Georgia wraps her arm around my shoulders and calls out, "So, what kind of hot dogs are you making?"

"Oh, the usual. Ketchup, mustard, slaw. Nothin' but the best for my girl. Well, girls, tonight."

"Georgia's not your girl, she's mine!" I cry out in mock offense. Georgia lolls her head dramatically.

"It's true," she says. "We're meant for each other."

"Well, Georgia, you can have her during work hours, but she's mine at night," Jake says. "And personally, I like Caroline a lot better at night."

I can feel myself blushing. Georgia gives me a look that says: *What am I supposed to do with that?* So I just say, "I'm fun all the time," and Jake says, "Yes you are, baby," and we turn on the TV. There's a shitty action movie from a few years ago just starting, and even though Jake has seen it three times already, he insists it's a good choice.

We spend most of the night like that. I snuggle into Jake and Georgia snuggles into the other side of the couch. I feel bad for making her the third wheel, but it was unavoidable. And once Craig and Joe get home, they keep her occupied. They're neither smart nor cute, but they're funny, and we laugh at the jokes they make about commercials.

Sometimes I wonder why Jake lives with them. He doesn't

dislike them, but they're not close friends either, and if I had a choice of roommates, I don't think I'd want to live with anyone I didn't really like. But this place is temporary, and it makes sense. You do what you can with what you have.

The movie finishes, and we watch a couple episodes of some terrible sitcom before Georgia leaves to make her ten o'clock curfew. Jake convinces me—without much effort—to go back to his room, and then he takes me home and kisses me goodnight.

I get a text from Georgia as I'm brushing my teeth. Which is weird, actually. We don't talk much at night, and she is not part of my bedtime ritual, which Jake and I spend together through my phone. Georgia usually goes to bed early. She likes to swim laps before work on morning pool days.

You up?

Yeah, of course

I wash my face and change into my pajama pants before she texts back.

So meeting Jake was awesome

☺☺☺ he's so great

yeah he definitely is

his roommates are nice

it was a little weird tho

right? idk

I look at the screen for a long time, the side of my face pressed into the pillow. She texts back before I respond.

ugh idk

forget about it

no no no

it is a little weird

I mean basically different friend groups right?

yeah

he's really really great

good night Caroline

night Georgia, sleep well

you too

I don't fall asleep, though, not for hours. I try not to think about what Georgia was thinking, sitting there beside me on the couch all night. *A little weird, right?* I try not to think about how she might judge Jake—for his lack of higher education, his shabby house, his crude jokes. I try to empty my mind until it is a calm, dark ocean, lulling me into sleep.

I fail.

At 2:00 a.m., I give up and go outside to the back porch. In other, older summers, Dad and I would camp out here together, setting up the tent and reading stories by flashlight. In the past few years, I've come out by myself some nights with a sleeping bag. This is the first night I've been out this year.

I lie on the splintered wood, looking up at the sky, watching the trails of late incoming planes. I try to imagine myself into the future: Jake's arms around me and the cool of the truck bed on my legs as we rest together somewhere in the desert. But it's like finding the last puzzle piece when it's fallen under the table. I know what it should look like, but I can't place it.

So I count the stars instead, squinting at the sky. I don't know the planets, so I count them all the same. I don't remember reaching a hundred, but my mother finds me there in the morning, curled up with a crescent moon of mosquito bites down my thighs. When I wake, I don't know where I am. All I see is her silhouette and the pale morning sunlight behind her, making her skin glow like an angel's.

"Oh, my baby," she murmurs. "You gotta bring out something to sleep on next time, you'll get splinters." I lean on her as we go up the stairs together, and she puts me to bed for a few more hours of rest.

JULY

Jake and I decided to leave back in April. It was unseason-
ably cold, nearly freezing, a Saturday. Mom dropped me off at his
place after lunch. His roommates had turned off the heat after a
recent warm stretch, and the house was damp and chilly. Jake and
I snuggled together in the sunken couch and watched cartoons.

We'd talked about leaving before. Phantom plans, spun-sugar
nothings, while we lay on the back porch or texted between my
classes. We used words like *someday* and *maybe* and *after I gradu-
ate*, and we never talked about where I might apply for college.
We sought our future lives like you look for shapes in the clouds.
Like everyone does.

And it bothered me, being so ordinary in our dreaming.
When I told my friends at school about how Jake and I talked, all

the things we planned, some of them laughed; others just smiled sympathetically. "But after college, right? And there will be so many college boys... I mean, you won't be with Jake forever," Chandler said to me. Fury bubbled up inside me; I turned away, said, "You never know."

That day in April at Jake's house, a tourism commercial for Minnesota came on. We were laughing at it—what do you tour Minnesota for, anyway?

Then Jake said, "You know, we could just go and live there."

"Minnesota?"

"Anywhere."

"Oh, we should live in Paris. I would love to see the Eiffel Tower."

Jake muted the TV and twisted his body to face me. "No, Caroline, I'm serious. Why don't we just go? To Minnesota? Or wherever, not Minnesota. Anywhere. Anywhere in the States, at first, I guess. Anywhere we can drive to."

I looked at him for a long time. His face was inches away from mine, and his eyes were earnest and determined. In that moment, I could feel the future unraveling and reshaping itself.

"When?"

"Now."

"We can't. I'm in school."

"Oh..." Jake sighed and started absently cracking his knuckles. "After the end of the semester, then."

"Not after graduation?"

"What's the point of graduation?" he said. "Just another bullshit year in school. You can get your GED, and it's exactly the same as a diploma. It's not that hard. Do you even like school?"

I thought about the long, lonely seven hours of moving from class to class. Broken pencil stubs and repetitive math problems. Report cards and parent-teacher conferences. I liked reading and my English classes, but that was about it. "No," I admitted.

"Exactly."

"But what about money?"

"I have money."

"You haven't been saving it, though." He looked like he was about to get defensive, so I quickly added, "I mean, you're doing great, but you haven't been *really* saving to the point where we'd be able to live off it. And I haven't saved much either. I think we'd need a little more if we wanted to leave." My heart expanded in my chest as I said the words—*if we wanted to leave.*

"But *do* you want to?" he said, and he grabbed my hand. "Do you want to go somewhere and have a life with me?"

I tried to memorize the asking of this question. The exact soft tone of his voice, the cool dusty scent of the room around us, the sound of the rain as it began to fall on the roof.

"More than anything," I whispered.

And so we worked it all out, there on the couch as the rain turned from a drizzle to a thunderstorm and the skies got dark.

I would get a full-time summer job, and he would try to take some extra shifts, and we wouldn't get fast food so much. We'd leave at the end of the summer: September 1, the first day of senior year.

That night, I got home fifteen minutes after curfew. Earlier in the week, Mom and I had fought about my grades. I'd gotten a C– on a chemistry test, which barely mattered because it only brought my average down to a B, but still, she was furious. The week before, she had made me cancel a date with Jake to have dinner with her and my dad and Vivian, claiming she'd told me about it in advance when she hadn't. And now, she gave me a lecture on personal responsibility that lasted what felt like hours. Through every word, all I could think was that soon I would be free of it all.

I'm thinking about it now because I have to lie about it. It's July 3, just past the two-months-'til mark, and my legs are still itchy from the rash of mosquito bites I sustained after sleeping on the porch a few nights ago. Scratching is a welcome distraction from the dinner table, where Georgia and my parents are talking about college.

"Well, I took the SAT for the second time in May, and I did well—really well—but there were some points left on the table," Georgia is saying, "so obviously I've been practicing, and I'll be taking the test again in October. My ACT score is great, so that's done, thank goodness. And I haven't started my essays yet, but I have a bunch of topics I'm sketching outlines for, that kind of thing. Most colleges haven't released full applications yet. But if you read the books, you start to find patterns in the kinds of questions they ask. So, I'm not, you know, resting easy or anything, but I'm not *too* worried about it." She takes a moment to catch her breath.

I'm a little irritated, but mostly I'm thankful for Georgia's enthusiasm. She draws my parents' attention, which is welcome— their faces are turned toward her as if in worship. I know they would love to hear all that chatter from me. I used to read all those college books, when I was a freshman, already thinking about what would come next. But for obvious reasons, I haven't picked them up recently. If I do go to college, it'll be later, after Jake and I have settled down.

My parents have trouble understanding. Mom especially. She's read all kinds of studies about the importance of a college degree, and she sees it as a hard requirement for me. I used to think so too. But there are so many different paths she can't see, ones that don't involve four more years of academics that aren't necessary in the life Jake and I are choosing.

She talks about it all the time. But I can't bring myself to concoct some elaborate lie about where I'm looking and what my goals are, so I just shrug and deflect whenever those questions come up. After I made a good-not-great score on the SAT at the end of last year, she started leaving SAT prep books on my bed, which actually works out okay because Georgia likes me to quiz her. Georgia's never asked why I don't ask her to quiz me back. When we're out on the porch, lying on our stomachs with the college books in front of us—in front of her—my mom smiles at us from the kitchen.

Dad is a little calmer about it. When Mom starts to nag me, he just says, "Come on, Cathy, she has time." Then he gives me a hug. "You have time, Caroline," he says to me. It hurts more, not telling him.

Right on schedule, as Georgia takes a bite of her asparagus, Mom sets her gaze on me.

"Now I *know* Caroline's been looking at colleges, but she's been very secretive about it," she says, her eyes flicking between me and Georgia. "When we did our tour of in-state schools earlier this year, she wouldn't even tell us which one she was most interested in. Has she said anything to you?"

Georgia glances at each of us in turn, as if she's prey trapped among predators. I take a long drink of water. That trip was awful. The campus tours were all the same, and a series of thunderstorms followed us around the state, so we were always slightly damp.

"Um," she says, swallowing her food, "I don't think she's decided yet."

"Yep, haven't decided yet. Sorry," I say, attempting nonchalance. Mom sets down her fork and looks like she's about to really launch into it, but Dad gets there first.

"Georgia, how are you feeling about attending your first annual Weaver Fourth of July party tomorrow?"

"Oh, great," she says, perking up. "I'm really excited. Caroline says it's huge."

"A little bigger than our house can allow at this point, I think," Dad says, and Mom butts in.

"It's fine," she says. "It's going to be great. Georgia, we're so excited to have you. I really think it's going to be the best party ever; you two have been so helpful with the decorating."

The annual Fourth of July party is one of my mother's finest achievements. It's her favorite holiday by a mile. She's already festooned the house in classic Americana. Red, white, and blue paper decorations cover every available surface. Fairy lights—separate strings of the same three colors that Georgia and I helped braid together a few days ago—are draped around the back porch, though my mom's elaborate rules say we can't actually turn them on until tomorrow.

Tomorrow is for baking. Cupcakes with American flags on top, a huge white cake with blueberries and raspberries, pigs in a blanket, homemade cheese crackers. Georgia's sleeping over tonight, and since JAC takes the holiday off and Mom made me ask for the vacation day early, we've been enlisted to help.

"Yeah, Caroline says it's a really big deal. I'm thrilled," Georgia says between bites. "We've never done a whole lot for the Fourth, so this is new to me."

"Well, your parents are welcome to come!" Mom exclaims. "I can't believe I didn't think of it before. You should invite them. I'd love to meet them."

Georgia reaches up to tighten her hair tie, a nervous tic that leaves the back of her head looking like a rat's nest after a long day at work. "That's really nice of you, Mrs. Weaver, but they're visiting my grandparents."

"Without you? Not much fun to be apart as a family on America's birthday."

"It's not a big deal." Georgia fidgets, and I wish I could help her, but I have no clue how to jump in. "I always used to go with them, but it's a superlong flight, and it's always really boring. Independence Day parties at nursing homes aren't that exciting. So," she says, smiling, "I managed to convince them that all the travel would make it too stressful to go back to work on Monday. And y'all were kind enough to invite me here, and this party looks like it's going to be beyond incredible."

My mother considers this information, clearly torn between reprimanding Georgia for abandoning her family and accepting the pre-praise for her event. She chooses the latter. "Thank you, honey," she says. "But please tell them they're always welcome to come over if they're in town."

"Thanks, Mrs. Weaver. I'll let them know."

"We'll invite them for dinner," Mom says, starting to clear the plates. "I just think it's not right that their daughter is over here all the dang time and we've never laid eyes on each other."

Georgia makes a noncommittal noise and scoops the last piece of lettuce from her salad bowl.

"Mom, I think we're gonna go up to my room and work on some of those tissue flowers," I say.

"Sounds good," she says, "but make sure you alternate red, then white, then blue. Last year you made them all one color, and they didn't live up to their potential."

"Got it," I say, and Georgia and I hustle out of the kitchen and up the stairs.

"Are your parents really visiting your grandparents?" I whisper as we leave.

"Yeah," Georgia says under her breath. "I've gone with them every year too, and it really does suck. All their food recipes are from the fifties. The serving tables are basically an endless plain of Jell-O."

"I'm kinda surprised they let you stay."

"Well, I still have to take my SAT practice test on Sunday."

Red, white, blue. We aren't very good at it. I turn on the radio, and we wrap and fold until we're drowning in crumpled tissue paper and a few halfhearted flowers. Georgia teaches me a different technique than the one my mom showed us. It works okay, but the colors cluster, not alternate.

I lose my phone under a pile of blue and scramble to find it when it buzzes. It's a video from Jake—he and his roommates and Toby are at the beach. I scoot closer to Georgia, so she can see my phone. The video opens on black and Jake's voice saying, "Here we go!" and then there's a blinding purple flash and hoots from the boys. The camera tilts up to capture fuzzy explosions of light.

"That's so cool," I whisper, half to Georgia and half to myself.

I wanted Jake to come to the party. I invited him, obviously, for the second year in a row. He hadn't been able to come last year—he got hooked into a double shift at work—and as silly as my family's traditions are, I wanted him to be a part of them this year. I wanted him to see how we decorated the house and for him to shield me from the worst of our neighbors. I wanted to kiss him under the fireworks.

But Craig and Joe beat me to the punch. I walked into Jake's house one day in May after school, and they were all talking about the trip to the beach. This was their tradition, apparently, going on four years. This year, they'd invited Jake and Toby, who had enthusiastically accepted. Later that night, I asked Jake if he would go to my family's party instead.

He was taken aback. "I'm sorry, babe, but I already said I'd go with Toby and them."

"It's a big deal," I said, my voice wavering.

"Well," he said, looking down, his shoulders falling, "if it really matters to you…"

I didn't want him to be sad. "No," I said, "no, it's okay. It's just a party."

"But you could come with us!" he said. His eyes lit up. "The guys wouldn't mind."

All May and the beginning of June, I fantasized about the possibilities. We could play in the water, have sex on the sand. It would've been our first road trip together, a whole day of driving, which would have helped prepare us for September. After I started hanging out with Georgia a lot, Jake said she could come too. Craig's stepbrother's house even had an extra room for me and her—well, for her, and for me to tell my parents I wouldn't be sleeping with Jake.

But when I finally worked up the courage to ask my mom, she didn't even blink before she said no. She said she wasn't comfortable with me sleeping over with Jake, and she needed me to help set up for the party.

I was pissed at first. Really pissed. But after two days of ranting about it to Georgia at work, and two correspondingly grumpy nights of cuddling with Jake on the couch, the vitriol was draining out of me. Anyway, Georgia said her parents would've forbidden it too.

"Have you even asked them, though?" I said over pizza one day at lunch.

"Not worth it," Georgia said, shaking her head. "Dating isn't really on the table."

"But you're not dating any of those guys..."

"Yeah, but they're still guys. I'd be staying overnight with them. Anything could happen." She waggled her eyebrows. "I mean, *we* know what Jake's roommates look like, and that you're dating Jake, and that I wouldn't touch Toby with a ten-foot pool cleaner. But my parents don't have that information."

"That sucks."

She shrugged. "It's unsurprising, given how strict they are about everything else. And I don't really mind. All the guys I know are boring and shitty anyway." She nudged the pizza box toward me. "It'll be a good Fourth of July."

"I guess you're right," I sighed. "It was a fruitless endeavor."

Now, Jake's video ends abruptly as the phone swings toward him, and I catch the blurry edge of his jawline. I'm left staring at a blank screen.

Georgia moves away and starts tugging a new set of tissue paper into a clumsy flower. Halfway through, she stops. I'm still looking at my phone, thinking about how to respond to Jake. She gently takes it from my hands and puts it on the opposite side of her.

"I have to text him back," I tell her, reaching for it.

"No, you don't," she says, scooting it farther away. "He'll be fine on his own. He's with his friends, you're with yours. You're good."

"Georgia."

"I'm serious!" I'm surprised by the sharpness in her tone. She drops the flower. "Look," she says, "I know you love him, and he's a really great guy. But you're always texting him. Literally always. Can't you just stop and hang out for a little bit just with me? I'm not saying you have to stop all the time. Here"—she hands me my phone—"text him back if it's important. Just… maybe put your phone away sometimes?"

I look at my phone, look at Georgia. She's never texting anybody when she's with me.

"I'm sorry," I say. I quickly text Jake, *that's so amazing! i gotta go but i'll talk to you later*, and slide my phone across the floor. "No more texting for the rest of the night."

"Seriously?"

"Seriously."

"It's only ten, that's like…four hours if we stay up late. Are you sure you'll survive?"

I'm offended at first, but then I see she's trying not to laugh. I throw a crumpled flower at her head.

"You're horrible," I moan. "You're awful. You're the worst."

"You're stuck with me." She giggles. She puts down the flower she's holding and reaches up to untie her hair. It shakes loose across her back, and she falls onto the piles of reject paper, black sweeping over the colors in long, thin lines. "For the night, anyway."

"I'll run away to the beach," I say.

"No, you won't," she says, and she turns toward me and props her head on her arm. In this light, her dark eyes are shimmering and her skin is golden brown, round and full in her cheeks and chest and arms. I lie down and lay my arm next to hers. You can see my veins, blue and purple, through the skin.

"Will I ever get tan?" I ask her.

"You'll never get skin cancer."

"Not good enough. I wanna tan like you do."

"You don't wanna look like me. I'm fat."

"You're not fat."

"It's fine, I am, and I am also unspeakably beautiful," she says, smiling. And she is.

We watch the ceiling fan spin in lazy circles, pick up tissue paper and drop it again. With the light showing through the colors, falling on our bellies, they could be the sparks of fireworks.

7

The next day, I wake up earlier than Georgia and untangle my feet from hers. Light is only barely visible outside my window. Georgia's breathing is deep and even and soft. Her hair is spread out over my pillow, and her hands are twitching in a dream. For a minute, I try to pretend it's Jake next to me. But his sleeping breath is loud and deep with the rumbling edge of a snore.

I turn away and close my eyes again. Thinking about Jake in bed next to me while Georgia is there makes my stomach hurt, and I don't know why—though my mom did bring us a huge bowl of leftover cookie dough last night, so come to think of it, there might not be any weird emotional shit. I force myself to stop thinking and fall asleep again.

When I open my eyes, it's after 9:30, and Georgia is

looking at herself in the full-length mirror, twisting her torso to see the back of a frilly red-and-white skirt. "Fuck it," she mutters. She struggles out of the skirt and pulls on the same ratty cut-offs she wore yesterday. She catches my eye as she tugs up the zipper.

"You gotta get up. Your mom's been calling us for breakfast," she says, pulling her hair into a ponytail. "Don't wanna incur the wrath of Cathy."

I groan. "This day is going to be fucking ridiculous. I hope you're prepared."

"I'm pumped," Georgia says. "The Fourth always sucks at the nursing home. I've been looking forward to this for weeks."

I roll over toward her and shove my pillow farther under my head, propping myself up with my elbow. "You and Mom both," I say.

When I was little, we would make a countdown like other people keep an Advent calendar before Christmas. Starting on the last day of school, Mom would read to me from a history book about the Revolutionary War every night before bed, and we'd cross off the day together. I learned all about the Founding Fathers, and for a while she taught me about the Marvelous Mothers, but then I referenced them at school and everyone teased me because she had made them up.

"I'm with your mom on this one," Georgia tells me, smiling. "You can't bring me down."

"It might be fine. I guess we can wait and see," I say to Georgia as I try to muffle a yawn. "I'm glad you're here. Last year, all my friends were out of town and my parents' friends kept asking me how I was doing in school, and it was awful."

"I love that shit," Georgia says. "I always brag a ton when it's people I don't think I'll see again. I'll say I'm taking ten AP classes this semester and I edit the school newspaper, or something like that."

"What?"

She shrugs. "I lie. White lies, little things. Why not? It's a completely meaningless interaction. And it's not as if these are total fictions or anything. Like—I *was* assistant editor of the newspaper sophomore year, and I *do* always take a bunch of AP classes. I never make up anything really absurd. I just exaggerate to the point where it's *almost* unbelievable, and then people don't know what to do because they know it's bullshit, but they aren't sure how much is bullshit, and they don't want to be the stranger calling out this teenage girl, so you can just run with it. Try it, I'm telling you."

I ponder it for a moment, trying to think of minor accomplishments I could exaggerate and coming up empty. It strikes me, not for the first time, how smart and driven Georgia is in comparison to me, and I shake my head. "It wouldn't work," I tell her. "They've all known me since I was a kid. Which makes it even worse. They always ask me if I'm going to sing."

Georgia stares at me for a moment. "What?"

"I used to sing at the party."

"Wait, seriously? As...entertainment?"

"Kind of. My mom made me sing the national anthem."

When I was little, I loved to sing. Everyone clapped at the performance, the last event before the end of the night. I adored the attention. It got uncomfortable, though, as I got older and a cappella renditions of "The Star-Spangled Banner" weren't so cool. The older neighbor kids smirked at me behind their parents' backs. When I was thirteen, I had a mild cold and used it to get out of singing. Mom's asked every year since, but she's always accepted my excuses.

"Huh." Georgia ponders this, leaning over to grab a white T-shirt from her duffel bag. "Weird. Well, you're still in chorus, right?"

"Yeah, but I stand in the back. I'm not that great."

"But you're singing tonight, right? I mean"—she looks at me dead serious—"it's *America's birthday*."

I bury my head under the blankets. I can hear her giggling. When I peek out, she's sitting on the floor in her sports bra, holding her shirt in her lap and shaking with mirth. The sunshine from the window drapes over her, lighting her up, and it's impossible not to smile at the sight of her laughing there. I give her an exaggerated sigh and throw the blankets off me.

"I will never sing that awful song again," I say.

"I bet you were great."

"I was not."

"Girls!" my mother yells from downstairs. "Happy Fourth of July! Now get your tushes down here!"

I look at the clock: 9:55. We're almost late. I jump out of bed and throw on a tank top and shorts.

"I thought you had a whole outfit planned," Georgia says.

"Yeah, but we have baking to do. Whatever clothes you wear now are gonna be totally messy when the party starts. You just gotta save time to change."

"Fuck," Georgia mutters, throwing the pristine white T-shirt back into her bag.

"*Girls!*"

From ten to noon, we work a cupcake assembly line with factory-level precision. Mom mixes the batter; Georgia puts it into the pan, works the oven, and licks the bowl; and I make and apply the frosting. Cupcake frosting annoys my mother—the recipe takes no skill, she says, while the application is harder than it should be—and Georgia is too impatient to get it right. But I love it. My favorite part is adding the food coloring. Georgia puts the red into one bowl, and I put the blue into the other. We only add a few drops, but the color suffuses cleanly through the butter and sugar.

From there, we sprinkle parmesan on homemade cheese crackers, gather and organize about a hundred cases of beer and soda, and cut up enough salad vegetables for an army. And then the pièce de résistance: a gargantuan vanilla sheet cake, which my mother lets no one touch until it's out of the oven and cooled in its pan. She tells us to spread it with white frosting and gives us a large place mat of the American flag and two big bowls of blueberries and raspberries. Our instructions are to make an exact model of the stars and stripes using fruit.

"Make sure you leave fifty *obvious* white spaces between the blueberries," she says from the other end of the kitchen, where she hovers, craning her head to see our work, while pretending to clean.

She finally releases us at 3:30, half an hour before the party starts. In the shower, I have to scrub to get the stains off my hands: blue, purple, and red from the food coloring and the berries.

I also accidentally spend ten minutes in bed texting Jake. I've barely talked to him all day—my hands have been too full, literally. But he remembers how much food my mom bought for this event last year. He was working at the store that day. It was four full shopping carts, and I was embarrassed to be seen with my mom and so much junk food, frustrated to have him selling us food for a party he couldn't attend. But he told me my blushing and my scowl only made me look cuter.

The first ring of the doorbell makes me scramble up to find my hairdryer. I hear Mom greeting Mr. and Mrs. King at the bottom of the stairs, and I get ready in a record twelve minutes. But when I come downstairs to run the gauntlet of guests, I see Georgia through the back window. She's leaning against the porch railing, still in her jean shorts and frosting-stained T-shirt, munching potato chips from the bag and talking to my dad.

"Excuse me," I whisper as I move through the kitchen, giving polite smiles in place of greetings, and open the back door. "Georgia?"

"Yeah?" Georgia says, her mouth full of chips.

"People are getting here. You wanna change?"

"Balls!" she exclaims, dashing into the house and toward the stairway. She narrowly misses the Thompsons as they set down a six-pack of beer. Dad chuckles and flips a burger.

"I like that one," he says.

"Me too," I say, smiling in spite of myself.

"You wanna help me with these burgers?"

"I don't know how to grill."

"Yeah, but you know how to not stand inside with the rest of those clowns."

"That's true." I sigh, closing the door behind me. Outside, the silence stands in stark relief to the increasing noise in the kitchen. All I can hear is the hiss of meat and the faraway yells of the kids down the street, playing in someone's backyard.

"Why do you and Mom still throw this party every year?"

"Your mother likes it."

"Yeah, but you have to like it too. It can't be all her."

"I like it all right. I like the food, and I like that the three of us spend the whole day together. But mostly, I like how happy it makes your mom. You know, I don't go to enough of those events she throws with her volunteer group. She puts a lot of work into those things. So, I try to get excited about this party, to make up for it."

I groan. Through the window, I can see the Yearbys have arrived. Every single time I see them, Mrs. Yearby corners me to tell me about an article she read involving turtles. Turtles were my favorite animal when I was a kid, but I've moved on. And Mr. Yearby always says how much I've grown, but these past few years he's started adding a wink, and it makes me feel gross.

"Caroline?"

"It's the Yearbys."

"Ah. Yes. They're not my favorite either."

"I think we should cancel it next year."

"The whole thing?"

"The whole thing."

My dad flips a burger. "You know, here's the other thing. There's value in having a community around you. A community of friends. That's especially important for your mother and me because we don't have very much family."

"We have Uncle Frank. And Aunt Nancy."

"But they're not within easy traveling distance, you know that. And besides..." My dad makes a face and lowers his voice. "They're not that great, right?"

I can't help laughing. Frank and Nancy, my mom's only brother and his wife, are devout members of their country club, and their kids are brats.

"And with my parents and your mom's parents both gone," my dad continues, "it can be easy to just hole up as our own little family and never see anyone else."

I cross my arms. "I guess," I say.

"All I'm saying is, if it weren't for your mother, I would be the world's worst hermit." Dad looks up at me with a grin. "At least with these parties, I'm reminded that we have a good community, even if we don't see some of them very often."

"But at Fourth of July, you always just find your friends from grad school and drink with them the whole time."

"Well, true. But I don't see them very often, so I think that's fine. As for the Yearby clan and their ilk," he says, "they help me remember why I like you two so much."

I lean against the porch railing. Sometimes my dad sneaks in his advice like this—slowly, veiled in camaraderie. It's different from my mom's ready-to-go aphorisms, her let's-sit-and-talk lectures. It's harder to ignore.

Inside, Georgia has come downstairs wearing a white dress. I recognize it from the bottom drawer of my dresser. My aunt bought it for me last year, several sizes too big, and I was too pissed off to tell her to take it back. It hung on me like a white sack. But Georgia fills it out just right; she looks beautiful.

She's talking to a couple I only vaguely recognize, beaming and gesturing with one hand while she dips a tortilla chip in guacamole with the other.

"You gonna go in there and be nice?" Dad says without turning his head.

"I guess," I say.

"Well, help me load up some of these burgers, and you can take in the first plate. You'll be greeted as a heroine."

Mom opens the screen door for me as I walk in, back-first, tray of burgers heavy in my arms. They go in the middle of the table on a cake stand she modified and strengthened for this very purpose.

"Folks, time to eat!" she yells, and the chattering chaos of friends and neighbors begins to collect itself into a line. I walk quickly to Georgia, who is still talking to the couple I don't know.

"Caroline!" she exclaims as I come up, cutting herself off mid-sentence. "Do y'all know Caroline?" she asks the couple.

"I don't believe we've met," the woman says, sticking out her hand. "Tasha Nolan. You're Cathy's daughter?"

"Yes, ma'am," I say, shaking her hand. "Caroline."

"Bill," says the man, who also shakes my hand.

"Cathy and I are in the same aerobics class at the gym," Tasha explains with a smile, "and she was kind enough to invite us today."

"And then we get here," Bill picks up, "and find that somehow Georgia is part of the crowd as well! Small world!"

"Tasha and Bill have a kid in JAC," Georgia says. "Gretchen's great. She never causes any trouble, even when all the other kids are being loud and disruptive." I search my mind to attach a face to Gretchen, but all the kids are the same to me—an anonymous stream of giggling, three-foot-tall babies with colorful swimsuits and curious smiles.

"Well," Tasha beams, "Gretchen just loves you. She says you're her favorite of all the counselors. At home, it's 'Miss Georgia' this and 'Miss Georgia' that all evening."

Georgia blushes deeply and there's a beat of silence—the clicking of plastic forks and other people's conversations. Bill steps in to ask me if I also work at the aquarium, and we maintain comfortable small talk as we move slowly to the front of the line. I like this better than the usual bullshit, actually, talking to people who haven't known me since I was a baby. To this couple, I am nothing but the friend of their child's favorite person; daughter of the no-doubt helpful and enthusiastic Aerobics Cathy.

When we reach the table, I pause for an instant, overwhelmed by the options. There is far too much food here for any group to ever finish. But Georgia nudges me forward, and I grab a little of everything.

It's then that Mr. Yearby strikes. He slides right in front of me, an unfortunate apparition, as I'm reaching the end of the table.

"Caroline!" he roars, patting me heavily on the back. "Lookin' real grown up now."

He winks. I wince.

"How old are you this year? Heading off to college soon, huh?"

"Not yet, sir."

"Aw, man. You'll love college. I can tell you some stories," he says. He folds his arms and looks at me intently. "I was in a fraternity, you know, and I'd highly recommend you join a sorority. The parties, let me tell you, they—"

"Caroline?"

I take a step to the side. Georgia, plate piled high with food, is standing right behind Mr. Yearby. He turns around to see her and is opening his mouth to speak, but she beats him to it.

"We have to talk."

She looks serious, and for a moment I'm honestly alarmed, but then the corner of her mouth twitches and she tilts her head back toward the porch.

"I'm sorry to interrupt," she says, "but I really need to borrow Caroline. It's important."

"Well, certainly," Mr. Yearby bumbles. "I'll speak with you later, Caroline."

"Yes, sir," I say and slide past him to follow Georgia.

She opens the porch door, sun striking against the glass. When she turns back, her face is delighted. "You're welcome," she says with a smile. I follow her outside.

"I really should be inside, though," I say as Georgia sits on the porch, and I take a bite of my burger.

"Why?" Georgia rolls over on her back and dramatically throws one hand over her forehead. "I'm your guest. You need to take care of me. God forbid I get bored or upset. I just might need you to stick around."

I sit down cross-legged beside her and look up at my dad, who is shaking his head with a small smile. "Sorry, Dad."

"I'll forgive you someday," he says.

Georgia makes a face. "Whatever, your mom's too preoccupied to notice you're not making the rounds."

We lie like that in the hot July sun, eating in silence to the sound of the birds and the kids down the street and the burgers on the grill. And it's only when I roll over onto my back, belly so pleasantly full, that I remember I left my phone on my dresser. I think about going to get it. But Jake is having a good time with his friends. I'm having a good time with mine. It's like Georgia said last night. We're doing just fine.

When my mother calls me in an hour later, half scolding me for hiding outside but half just happy, her curls escaping her ponytail, it isn't even hard to fake interest. I move through it all with ease: the questions about college, Jake, the future, the aquarium job. Through the rote exclamations of how thin and grown-up I am or have become. Through even the un-asked-for suggestions about how I should be preparing for my senior year, even the veiled insult about my boyfriend's lack of higher education. Maybe it's the half a bottle of champagne that Georgia stole from the kitchen and split with me outside. Maybe it's the sun. But whatever it is, I am above it all, unbothered. I float.

The guys in the cul-de-sac down the street, home from college and restless at their parents' houses, light fireworks as the air starts to get thick and purple. The party wanders outside to watch. Little kids squeal, and Georgia wraps her arm around my waist, and my parents are tipsy and laughing. The sky lights up, the air shrieks. But we all, including my parents, walk away fast as we hear the police a few streets over. Their sirens and the red and blue lights mimic the fireworks. In a blissful daze, I drift back home, holding Georgia's hand.

The cops didn't catch Jake and his friends after they set off the fireworks last night. They ran. All down the beach, by the ocean, into the dunes.

I find my phone halfway through the night and text Jake between talking with Georgia. He's happy-drunk too, Craig's friends having bought them two cases of beer. He tells me they played music on the beach and put up some cheap tiki torches from Walmart and people just flocked to them—that now it's this huge party, strangers dancing and laughing and drinking. Half of me doesn't believe him and half of me is jealous, praying he didn't kiss anyone.

But

i love you

i love you

i love you

he texts me, over and over, and I know he wouldn't touch another girl. His love burns into my eyes with the brightness of the phone until he says, *i'm passing out, babe, i love you*, and I have outlasted him in wakefulness.

Georgia and I lie next to each other in my bedroom, staring at the ceiling and talking. We stop mid-sentence every time we see the flash of fireworks outside my window. I feel myself coming down from being drunk. My whole body is tired, and a headache is blooming like a flower across my forehead and down into my face and neck. We make shadow puppets on my wall: bunnies, dogs, wolves chasing each other across pictures of younger me.

"Have a good Fourth?" she says to me finally, turning toward me at 4:00 a.m.

"The best," I say, turning to her, and we sleep like that, facing each other, two halves of the same crooked heart.

With my mom's patriotic obsession, the Fourth of July has always felt like the turning point of the summer. It's only a third of the way through, really, but it seems like half—we build up, we come down. Now, I'm falling toward September.

And it's not just me. The whole sound and mood of the house changes. Every year on the last day of school, as soon as I arrive home, Mom's conversation turns to the Fourth. July fifth, she starts in on school supplies, new clothes, classes. And now, college.

She's only bugged me a little so far this summer, and I was foolish enough to think that was as bad as it was going to get. Not so. After brunch at noon, Georgia goes home—yawning and carrying a platter of leftover cupcakes—to finish sleeping off her hangover in her own bed. As I push my plate away, Mom slaps down the big book of higher education: a seven-hundred-page tome describing the pros and cons of the top five hundred colleges in North America. I know the look of it well. Georgia often borrows our copy and flips through it as we lie outside on the porch. Its pages are filled with her notes.

"Mom," I protest.

"Nope," she says, whisking away my plate. "You've put this off far too long already. The college counselor at school sent us a mailing that said top candidates should have started looking last fall."

"I'm not a top candidate, Mom, what does that even mean— and wait, was that the envelope addressed to me the other day? You told me it was a PTA thing!"

"Well, you didn't care about it," she says. "And you are a top candidate. A few Bs here and there won't ruin you. You've been on the dean's list three times, and you're an excellent choir singer. I just wish…"

"Mom."

"Just spend half an hour, sweetie. Half an hour. Until"— she checks the clock—"12:40. Okay? Half an hour of looking at colleges, and after, maybe you can tell me if there are any you want to apply to."

I take the book outside and sweat over the pages. I text Jake, *my mom's making me look at this stupid college book and it sucks,* but he's not awake yet. Probably hungover. It occurs to me that I, too, am hungover. My stomach is twisting itself in circles and last night's headache is now pulsing in my left temple. I go back inside and return to the kitchen table, facing away from the window. The heat of the sun feels good on my back, but outside, the crisp white pages of the book were too bright.

It's in alphabetical order. It has dollar signs for cost and stars for quality. On the inside of the cover my mom has scribbled her own notes:

$ limit = $$

Star limit = ∞

Georgia's notes, scattered throughout the pages next to my mom's, are more interesting. They're on what seems like every other page, everything from doodles to whole contemplative paragraphs.

Swimming + warm! But how much party school = too much?, she wrote on the page for a university in Florida next to a childlike drawing of the sun. On a page about a small liberal arts school in the Midwest, she simply said: *Never.* A university in New York City yielded a wide ring of question marks around the entire perimeter of the page; our local state school, only an hour away from the aquarium, got a huge frowny face. Underneath Georgia's pencil, I find evidence of Mom: a hopeful highlight of the location and cost markers, close and cheap.

When I come across an Ivy, things get really exciting. There are so many words on those pages that I can barely keep track. Clearly, this book isn't the only place Georgia has looked for information. *SO BEAUTIFUL*, she's written at the top of the Princeton page, with *but NJ sucks* tucked down at the bottom. *Mom's #1 for me* arcs over Harvard in a graceful rainbow. On Brown, she's circled "independent class structure" and scrawled *Yankee hippies* beside it. It's unclear whether this is good or bad.

There are notes on every section. "Living:" She prefers dorms for underclassmen with off-campus housing for juniors and seniors. "Sports:" She doesn't give a fuck about which league the college is in, but she makes positive notes next to strong intramural programs, especially swimming. "Academics:" She only takes the school seriously if it's strenuous. Notes about her parents dominate in those sections.

"Culture" is the least consistent. I know Georgia drinks, but I've never thought of her as a party girl. I can't picture her wasted off cheap beer in somebody's basement. And yet whenever the big book notes a school's opposition to drinking or its lack of a vibrant campus social scene, she makes an X or a frowny face of disapproval. *Meh*, *urgh*, and *no* all adorn the page of a Christian women's college in Nevada.

I spend my mom's required half hour reading Georgia's comments and ignoring any substantive information about the colleges themselves. But against my will, I do manage to internalize the basic categories of their comments—the jargon of choice around universities. There is incessant talk of class size and professor-to-student ratio, unique majors and research opportunities, Greek life and housing. The same words appear on every page. As if they're trying to express limitless possibility, but with an intensely limited vocabulary.

From Georgia's comments, I can tell she's into it. She gets it. She sees the differences between the endless options; for her, the choice is so multifaceted it's nearly impossible. But to me, they all look the same. The choice isn't between one place or another. It's whether to enter that world at all.

Mom finds me staring absently at the book, open to a page about a small university in Oregon. *Cousins in Portland*, Georgia's scribbled down the side in purple pen. *Do I like them? Can't remember.* I am tracing the curves of her handwriting with my pencil, my mind on Jake and what opting out of college might mean. But Mom sees me looking, I guess, and so she comes over and places her hand on my back.

"West Coast colleges!" she exclaims. I look up to see her smiling. Then she bites her lip. "That's awfully far away. And without in-state tuition…but if it's what you want—"

"No, Mom, I wasn't really…" I close the book. "That was just where I stopped. No particular interest."

"Oh." She touches my hair lightly, tucking a strand behind my ear. She used to do that when I was a kid. In the summers, I'd sit in this chair reading, because the sunlight came through the window and warmed just this spot. She'd marvel at how hot my hair had gotten. Back then, it was so blond it was nearly translucent, and the light would filter through it like it was nothing.

"So, anything good in there? See any places you like?"

I look up at her again. She is so expectant, so excited for me. I don't want to make her unhappy. I almost wish I was as interested as Georgia about this stuff, though I know I never will be.

But her eyebrows are raised and her smile is big, and I can't bear to disappoint her. "Lots," I say. "Lots of good stuff."

She grins even wider and awkwardly hugs me from behind.

"I'm so glad," she says. "Do you want to keep it in your room?"

"Let's just put it back on the bookshelf. I'll look again tomorrow. If that's okay?"

"Of course," she says. She slides it between *300 30-Minute Recipes* and *Living Health* on the kitchen shelf. She moves over to the sink and starts on the pile of platters and serving utensils from yesterday. "Got any plans today?"

I don't. I haven't had time by myself in a while. Weeks, actually. I'm always with Georgia or Jake; now, she's napping, and he's not responding to my texts.

"I guess not," I tell her. She turns and brightens.

"How about a family day? It's Saturday! It'll be just like old times. I think we all had lunch already, but we could start with froyo."

When I was little, family day was every Saturday. It entailed lunch, generally at a chain restaurant in a nearby strip mall, followed by frozen yogurt at Frozen Palace, an ancient yogurt emporium that my mom discovered when she was pregnant with me. We traditionally followed this with a board game, some alone time for a few hours, and then takeout dinner and a rented movie.

They were great when I was nine, but I've grown out of them. A few years ago, I started going to the mall with friends on Saturdays, spending the whole day nibbling at a shared soft pretzel and trying on things we didn't have the money to buy. Then when Jake and I got together, he would take me out on Saturdays for day-long dates, to the park or the pool and then, eventually, just to his house. And the thrill of being out without my parents, independent, made it easy to phase myself out of family day.

But now I am facing a day of sitting alone with the college book, Jake busy, and Georgia asleep. And maybe it's the hangover and maybe it's the way Mom bit her lip when she saw me looking at a college thousands of miles away, but I just feel tired, and a day of my parents treating me like a kid sounds pretty nice.

"Froyo would be good," I say.

"Really?" Mom raises her eyebrows as if she can scarcely believe it.

"It's not a big deal," I say. I can hear the defensiveness in my voice, and I hate it, but I can't help it. It pisses me off when my parents act as if I've abandoned them. I still come home to them every night, after all.

I won't forever, though, I think to myself, and then push the thought out of my head with superhuman force.

"Well, we haven't had time with just the three of us in quite a while, and I think it'll be great," she says, missing my bitterness completely. "Tom," she yells around the corner, "we're having a family day!"

"Oh, wonderful," he says from the living room. "Will we be having second lunch?"

"Starting with froyo," Mom yells back.

He ambles into the kitchen, book tucked under his arm, and smiles mildly. "This will be nice," he says. "Haven't had a family day in a while."

It's true. Our last family day was the day I met Jake, over a year ago. It was spring near the end of school, after I had already started spending Saturdays with my friends. But on this particular Saturday, Chandler was visiting her grandparents, and Erin was busy on a science project, and Lauren was babysitting. So, I was with my family.

We got pizza and strawberry froyo, and then we had to stop at the grocery store to pick up supplies for a fruit salad my mom was making for dessert that night. My parents dropped me off in front with a twenty-dollar bill because the parking lot was too crowded. Big sale at the department store in the same strip mall, I think, but whatever it was, it was a blessing. I picked up strawberries, blueberries, and a pineapple and went to the quick check-out aisle, which was empty.

I saw him from the back at first. He was texting, and he didn't notice me when I walked up with the fruit. I grabbed a tin of mints from the stand next to the conveyor belt, shaking them loudly to get his attention, and he turned toward me, ducking his head. When he saw me, he smiled. It was an utterly disarming move, and I smiled back without even realizing it.

Then he looked at me—skimmed my body all the way down to my toes and back up to the top of my head—and I didn't know what to do with my hands.

No one had ever looked at me like that: completely. Mom and Dad could sometimes look into me, like they knew what I was feeling and thinking. Ethan, my one ex-boyfriend, had looked at my boobs with that kind of intensity, but only my boobs. And boys at school mostly didn't look at me at all.

This was different. It was deep and long and intimate and sexual all at once. It made me feel like the most beautiful woman who had ever lived. Helen of Troy in Ten Items or Less.

Then it ended. He dropped his eyes to the fruit, scanned it with big, sturdy hands, and put it in a bag. He looked up at me, expectant.

I thought, for a second, he was waiting for me to talk, to continue the conversation he'd started with that look. Then he nodded toward the screen and said, "Ten dollars even," and I realized he was just waiting for me to pay. I felt my face getting hot as I handed over the cash. He gave me my receipt, and I was stepping away when he said, "Wait."

"Yeah?" I said, timid. A line of shoppers was growing at the end of the aisle. An old woman nudged her cart forward an inch.

"Yeah," he said. He tore off a slip of blank receipt paper. "Sorry for the holdup. I just need you to do something for me."

"Um…" Now the woman was glaring at me. "What's up? Is the money okay?"

"Oh, yeah, the money's fine," he said. He passed me the slip of receipt paper and a pen. "I'm gonna need you to write your number right here."

There were no words.

I wrote my phone number on the paper and passed it back to him. His hand brushed mine, and he smiled.

"Gotta go," he said, cocking his head toward the old lady.

"Me too," I said. When I got into my parents' car, idling in the fire lane, my hands were still shaky.

He texted me almost immediately, as we were unloading the groceries and Mom was asking what board game we should play. I didn't expect him to text right away. According to my friends, most guys wait a few days, and I get that—kind of a power play. I'd do the same thing if I had to make the first move. But he didn't.

is this the girl from the store?

I stood in the kitchen, one hand on the box of strawberries, the other holding my phone. My mom shooed me out of the way, and I sat on the couch, still staring at the screen. After a minute, I texted back.

yeah

But it was just one little word. It didn't seem like enough. Feeling bold, I added:

what's your name?

He responded fast. I pictured him standing at the checkout counter, ignoring a customer in favor of me:

ok great didn't want to text a fake #

Jake, you?

Caroline

do girls usually give you fake #s?

no one ever has

but your so beautiful I bet you get asked all the time

thought you might have a fake one ready for such purposes

And if he didn't have me already, he had me then. All of me, immediately, in that perfect misspelled compliment. Beautiful. Beautiful. Beautiful.

anyway so Caroline

pretty name for a pretty girl

wanna get coffee sometime?

I nearly fainted.

yeah sure :)

next Saturday?

so far away?

yeah I have school :(

high school?

I panicked. In the kitchen, Mom was unpacking the grocery bags and talking to me about an orange glaze for the fruit salad, but I couldn't pay attention. I hadn't even considered that he might not know I was in high school. But there was nothing to do about it. You can't take that back.

yeah I'm gonna be a junior next year

but very mature for my age :)

I believe it ;)

I'm 18...not too much older

your 16 right?

will be in a few months!

It would have to do. I was trying to think long-term. He'd find out eventually. But still, he took a long, long time to respond. When he did, it was worth it.

you look so mature

in a good way

still up for that coffee?

saturday, 2?

at stomping grounds? it's near the grocery store

absolutely :)

can't wait

Mom shook the Sorry! box, startling me into dropping my phone.

"Caroline?" she said, looking at me over the game. "Caroline, who are you texting? Is everything okay?"

I picked up my phone from the floor and dusted the crumbs off it as if it was a treasure. "No one, Mom. Everything's good."

"It had to be someone."

"The kid Lauren's babysitting is acting up. It was funny."

The lie slipped out of my mouth so easily it surprised me. I didn't usually lie to my parents. They never disapproved of my choices, so there was no point. Maybe it was his age, or the fact that we'd only just met—for a few minutes, no less—and I'd agreed to go out with him. They wouldn't love that. But mostly, I felt like it was a miracle to keep all on my own: if I spoke it out loud, it would disappear.

Now, Mom dries the last plate and puts in the cabinet with a clatter. "Shall we get going, then?" she asks. Dad wanders back into the living room to put away his book, and I go upstairs to get my purse. I text Jake, *i miss you*. He doesn't respond.

Getting in the car with my parents, my mom prattling on about how our old yogurt place has gone downhill, I can't shake this feeling of missing something more than his presence. Missing my stomach dropping out from under me whenever I see him. I still feel like that sometimes. But not all the time, not anymore.

Mom moves on to her standard post-party recap, which she does after every major holiday, the Fourth most of all. She will accept responses from either me or my dad. Both of us staying silent is not an option.

"...and I really think the party went well this year." She finishes a sentence, takes a deep breath, and launches into the next one. "Brian Michaels was a little uptight, but then again, that's just his nature. And Doreen is so fun. I don't know how those two have been married for so long. I shouldn't question other people's relationships. But those two. Whew! It's just hard for a girl to understand."

"Brian and I had a nice conversation," Dad says. "I think Doreen is a bit loud for him sometimes."

"Well," Mom sighs, "I prefer her to him, but I'm glad you entertained him. I hate seeing wallflowers."

She meets my eyes in the rearview mirror. "Speaking of, Caroline, you and Georgia spent a lot of the party outside. I was beginning to get worried you wouldn't come in. But I appreciate you spending all that time talking to Mr. and Mrs. Harold. They've missed going to your choir concerts, you know. But he travels so much for work, and she doesn't like going out alone."

"It was no problem," I say.

The world outside the car window is as familiar as it is boring. Green grass, white houses, clean but dilapidated strip malls. We pass the shopping center with the grocery store where

Jake works and the coffee shop where we had our first date and the old yogurt place, Yo-Life.

"Did Georgia enjoy the party?"

"Yeah, I think she had a good time."

"Good," Mom says, contented. "I'm glad. We've enjoyed having her around this summer. I think she's really good for you." She looks back at me. "And she goes to that small private school, right? Eastern?"

"Right." I look at my phone. The screen is black—Jake still hasn't said anything. I debate whether it's too much to text him a third time without a reply. Probably.

Mom keeps talking about Georgia, and I tune her out. They were never this enthusiastic about Lauren or Chandler, even though I've known those girls for years. I think my mom likes Georgia's girl-next-door, make-yourself-at-home shtick. She's never even met Georgia's parents, which is probably for the best. From my brief interaction with Georgia's mom, I don't think they'd get along particularly well.

We pull up at the new yogurt shop. I haven't had frozen yogurt in months. Mom tells us she goes here with Cynthia after power yoga every Wednesday.

The walls are a neon yellow, and the oldies' mix station is blaring from a boom box—an actual boom box—in the corner. My mom gets strawberry-chocolate blend with chocolate shavings and whipped cream. "Just one more day of indulgence," she says. My dad gets vanilla with M&M's. I get a bowl of fruit with a perfunctory swirl of raspberry yogurt on top.

"You can have more than *that*," Mom says when she sees my bowl, but Dad quietly shushes her, and we sit there with the old music blaring. The fruit is fresh and good. My parents both eat their yogurt carefully, spoonful by small spoonful. If I close my eyes and forget the yellow walls, it's actually kind of nice. The three of us here together, our small family, just like it used to be.

The rest of the day is quiet. I watch a movie with my parents; we eat leftover burgers and salad for dinner. Jake finally responds to my texts, apologizing for his silence and blaming his hangover. Later that night, I am in bed, texting and halfheartedly painting my toenails when Mom pokes her head in the door.

"Hello?" she says, knocking. "Can I come in?"

"Yes," I say. There's no point in knocking if you've already opened a door, but I don't think she would listen if I told her that.

She sits on the bed next to me, and I move my wet toes carefully away from her. My bedspread would not be forgiving to the purple glitter polish Georgia lent me.

"I wanted to talk to you," she says. There is something a little odd about her tone, and I realize she's nervous. I stop painting my nails even though I'm only half done. I don't think my mom has ever been nervous about anything in her life.

"Yeah?" I say.

"Yeah," she says. "About college."

"Mom, I looked through the whole book this morning, I marked the places just like you said, I thought—"

"I know," she interrupts me. She pauses for a beat. "It's not about college exactly. It's also about Jake."

She knows. How does she know? She's been reading my texts. She's eavesdropped. Jake told Toby and Toby told Georgia and Georgia told her mom and her mom called mine. My brain stops working, and for a moment I can't breathe. I should be figuring out a game plan, but coherent thoughts are impossible.

But then she exhales and puts a hand on my knee, and my room comes back into focus. I start breathing again. The rational part of me knows if she found out, she'd be furious, and she's not angry at all. She's just looking down at her hand on my knee as if she almost can't believe it's there.

"Yeah?" I press, tentative.

"Yes," she says, shaking her head as if to clear it. "Did I ever tell you about any of the guys I dated before your dad?"

I shrug. I know she and Dad met when they were both twenty-four at a party thrown by a mutual friend, and I had not considered she might have had boyfriends before then. I'd never contemplated my parents' relationship in any depth at all, come to think of it.

"Well," she says. "There were several."

"Okay." I don't know where this is going, but I desperately hope it isn't going to turn into a sex talk. We did that when I was fourteen, and it left me scarred for life. Besides, Jake and I always use condoms, so I don't need the lecture. Not that I can tell her that.

"But my high school boyfriend was the only serious one before your dad. Henry."

I don't respond, and she continues. "We started dating when we were in middle school, if you can believe it. Seventh grade. And we were still together when senior year came along. I had always kind of thought we would go to the University of Alabama together and then get married. It was that serious.

"But you know, when you're applying to colleges, you're supposed to send in more than one application. Just in case." She pauses for a moment, but there is no way I'm taking that bait, so she keeps talking. "So that's what we did. We each applied to three or four schools. All of his were in Alabama, and most of mine were too, but I also applied to Vanderbilt. I had gone with my mom for her reunions a few times, and I had always thought it was such a beautiful campus. And I loved Nashville. We wouldn't have had the money for it without scholarships, and I thought I'd never get in, but I applied anyway."

I nod. Mom went to Vanderbilt, I know this. She still watches their football games on TV sometimes, even though their team isn't that great and she doesn't keep up with football generally.

"Well, so, March rolled around, and Henry and I had both gotten into the University of Alabama. Which I was very happy about. It's a good school with a lot of great programs. He sent in his acceptance letter the first day he could. And he kept asking me when I was sending in mine. But I wanted to wait until I heard from Vandy, even though I thought it was really unlikely. And then I heard, and I'd gotten in. Not only that, but with the financial aid combined with scholarships, I'd actually be able to go.

"So I was overjoyed, obviously, and the first person I told was him. We had never talked about what we'd do if I got in, because I never thought I would, but I assumed he'd be happy for me. It's only a three-and-a-half-hour drive between the two colleges, and he had a car. I had some older friends who were still dating their high school boyfriends across much longer distances."

She pauses and looks at me, as if I'm supposed to respond.

"He wasn't happy for you," I guess.

"No, he was not. We got into a huge fight about it. He said if I didn't go to Alabama, it was over. And not only that. He said lots of nasty things." She shakes her head.

"So you broke up with him?"

"Well, no. I said I'd go to Alabama. And I told him I'd sent in the acceptance letter. But I hadn't. I couldn't make myself put it in the mail. It was the biggest lie I had ever told."

I shift in the bed. I suddenly want to start painting my nails again so I have something else to focus on, but I feel like it would be rude.

"I just kept waiting and waiting. And then, the week it was

due, I had put the stamp on the envelope and everything, and my friend Lindsey called me and told me Henry was cheating on me."

My mouth drops open. "Seriously?"

Mom nods, and what had been an uncomfortable, contemplative expression on her face shifts into something like victory. "Yep," she says. "For months. With a girl he'd met at the YMCA. Two years younger than me and much bigger boobs."

"Did you know her?"

"Vaguely. She went to the same high school. Her name was Alexandra."

"So what did you do?"

"I broke up with him, shredded the Alabama envelope, and sent my enthusiastic acceptance to Vanderbilt."

"But wasn't he mad?"

She looks at me, her expression unreadable. "Yes, he was," she says. "But I was mad too, remember. And personally, I think I had more of a right to be angry."

I look down again. There's a smudge of purple drying on my pinky toe where I missed the nail. "Yeah," I say. "Fair. So..."

"Well, then I went to college, and we talked a couple times that first semester. But soon enough we lost touch, which was for the best. I dated a few different guys in college. And then later, a couple years after graduation, I met your dad, and we got married and moved here and had you."

"Okay."

I want to ask her why she's explaining this now, but I also don't want to know.

"I'm telling you all this," she says, as if reading my mind, "because I think Jake is one of the reasons you're not as interested in college as I was."

"Mom, that's such bullshit," I protest. "Jake would never cheat on me. He's super supportive." The truth of our future grows in my stomach like a hot air balloon, pushing organs uncomfortably out of the way, threatening to burst me from the inside out. I imagine the leaving in vivid clarity—waking up in a bed that isn't this one, my mother infinitely far away—and I feel as if I'm going to choke.

Mom holds up her hands. "I know he'd never cheat on you, Caroline. That's not what I'm saying. And please don't curse," she adds. The familiar request breaks some of the tension in me, enough to help me breathe. "Jake is a good guy. We like him. I just don't want you to limit yourself to stay closer to him." She puts her hand on mine.

"I'm not asking you to break up with him," she continues. "All I'm saying is that if I had stayed with Henry and gone to college with him, my life would have been very different. Honestly, not as good as it is now. And I want you to have all the opportunities you can. As much as I would love if you were always here with us, I want you to have the chance to go somewhere else. I don't know if you're getting any pressure from Jake to stay here, but..."

"I'm not," I say flatly. The truth feels like a lie. "He's not pressuring me at all. He's a really good boyfriend, Mom. He's great, actually. My high school boyfriend is not your high school boyfriend."

She pauses for a moment, her hand still on mine. Then she takes it away and stands.

"Okay," she says. "I'm sorry for upsetting you." She walks to the door and looks back at me. She looks tired and sad, and somehow, older than usual. "I love you," she says.

"I love you too, Mom."

She closes the door behind her. In the time we've been talking, the light from the window has faded into dusk, and with the door closed, my room is a dark, bruised purple. I pull the covers up over my body, my one glitter-nailed foot sticking out of the blankets like a diseased limb. I'm shivering a little, even though it isn't cold at all. I look at the glitter on my big toe, a murmur of sparkle in the darkening room, and then I close my eyes and try not to think about anything.

Going back to work feels, appropriately enough, like jumping into a pool the morning after a thunderstorm. First, the cold is a shock, and then you swim around for a while and it's comfortable again. It's funny how nice it is to have that extra day in a three-day weekend. I wonder if my job in Arizona or Connecticut or Washington will have three-day weekends. If it'll have weekends at all.

The aquarium was closed on the Fourth, but open on Saturday and Sunday. Usually, Jenny only works on weekdays, and Naima runs the store on weekends—she's a year-round schoolteacher who uses the aquarium gig to pick up extra money. But she asked off a long time ago, so Jenny had to work. I think Jenny would've made me be here with her anyway, even though

Naima normally only runs the cash register and doesn't do any of the administrative work that supposedly takes up Jenny's time during the week. But from the moment of my hiring, my mom made sure the aquarium knew that Fourth of July weekend was nonnegotiable vacation time.

Anyway, the upshot is that Jenny is really pissed this morning. I come in one minute late, and she gives me the dirtiest look I've ever seen. Slams down the phone from some conversation about the event space (which, to be fair, isn't her job), says, "Hope you had a nice weekend," and walks into her office without another word.

The door closes behind her. Almost immediately, I hear the dulcet tones of sitcom voices on her computer. Then she turns down the volume, and the store is silent.

I sigh and lean against the back bookcase. I check the secret chocolate bar drawer, where I've kept a stash of chocolate ever since my first day working here, and am dismayed to discover that the candy is gone. Jenny probably took overtime to look for it, just to spite me. Not that I need any more sweets after this weekend. The leftovers, as always, were prodigious. At my mom's insistence, I left two trays of blue-and-red cupcakes in the cramped JAC break room this morning.

I text Georgia to tell her about the cupcakes, and she responds with twelve smiley faces. Then I check my texts with Jake. He hasn't messaged me yet this morning, and I'm not sure what to do. I want to talk to him, but I don't want to make the first move. I'm mad at him—or if not mad, upset, or if not upset, frustrated—and I want him to apologize.

Last night, Jake got back into town, and I was so fucking excited, so happy to see him and snuggle and have sex. But first, his roommates wouldn't leave to give us privacy, which annoyed me. And when they did leave and we finally had some time to ourselves, he told me about his weekend. That made everything worse.

It sounded perfect: the fireworks, the beer, the party in the sand. He talked about the guys and girls who came stumbling down the beach from the other houses, and I could see them in my imagination—the kind of boys who wouldn't have given me the time of day, the kind of girls who are prettier than me. The night after the party, they slept until noon and got pancakes and bacon at a diner down the road. He let it slip that he was awake when I was texting him that afternoon. Turns out he was just ignoring me.

He told me they ran into the ocean and swirled their hands around in the water and saw bioluminescence. I didn't know what that was. He told me it was tiny particles of seaweed that glow in the dark, bright green if there's no moon. It collects around the motion you make. We don't have any of it at the aquarium, I'm pretty sure. I think I would have noticed.

He told me all of it, and I listened. But as I listened, I also thought about my Fourth of July weekend, lying on my bedroom floor making paper flowers with Georgia, frosting cupcakes, getting tipsy on champagne. At the time, I had felt so open and free and happy. I had been okay with Jake being far away. Our phones connected us like a thread across the miles. We echoed each other: When he had to go hang out with his friends, I had to go be with mine. When he was drunk, I was drunk. We were with each other, were each other, even though it was the longest I'd gone without seeing him since school let out.

But now my entire weekend seemed so childish. Family day. Drinking in my parents' house, the pimple-faced boys who had set off the fireworks. It was high school, it was stupid, it was nothing like the freedom to which Jake was accustomed. The kind of life he had at the beach, without parents supervising him, without my too-young presence dragging him down.

He talked about the girls taking off their T-shirts to go into the ocean, and I was not sure anymore if he wanted to share that freedom with me.

Many minutes later, after the sun had set and the only light coming in through the porch was dim and gray, he finished his story. There was a long pause. He sighed contentedly, a sigh that turned into a yawn.

"Great weekend. Really great," he said, wrapping up. I didn't say anything.

Then, after all that time, he asked me how my weekend

was. In retrospect, maybe he didn't say it dismissively. Maybe he really did care about the frozen yogurt with my parents and the college book and the cake. But it didn't feel like it. It felt as if he had moved beyond me, like he had walked into the dunes and left me staring out the window of some spindle-legged beach house, alone.

So I just shrugged and said it was fine. We sat in silence for a minute, staring at the blank TV. Someone had left the game console on. It whirred quietly, maintaining the stasis of some shitty video game so the boy playing it could come back any time and pick up where he left off.

His arm felt heavy around my shoulders. I didn't know what I wanted. I wanted to cry. I wanted him to have asked me how my weekend was first. I wanted him not to have left me to the unfettered mediocrity of my family's traditions. It was a long time before I said anything, and when I did, it wasn't nearly enough.

"I missed you," I said.

And he, thinking that was all, cuddled me into his arms and said he'd missed me too, and started talking again about that long beautiful series of sea-salt moments and the places where he thought I might have fit into them. It made me feel a little better. But only a little. Because I had not been there, and someone else had filled the space I could have taken.

We had sex, and it was nice. He whispered to me how sexy I was while the tension built between my legs and then dissipated after he was done, and he held me close and told me he had missed me so much. Still, though, when he took me home and kissed me at exactly eleven o'clock, I closed the door behind me feeling as if something vital and elastic had snapped between us, leaving a lot of little strings frayed and wanting, waiting to unravel.

I got out my phone in bed that night. The last thing I'd texted Georgia just a few hours earlier was: *JAKE'S HOME THANK GOD*, to which she had responded: *cool!* I wanted to talk to her now, but I didn't know what to say. She didn't have a boyfriend, had never been in a serious relationship. She wouldn't understand.

Besides, with JAC launching back after a three-day weekend the next day, she was probably asleep. I knew she would wake up for me—we had made a pact with each other, to always turn on text sounds instead of vibrate before we went to sleep, in case one of us needed the other—but I didn't want to make her. Nothing was wrong.

So I didn't text her. I didn't text Jake either. I lay in bed, staring at the ceiling, watching the light fade slowly from the glow-in-the-dark stars my mom had put there when I was seven. I lay there thinking and not thinking, getting sadder and sadder. I felt somehow already tired from the week ahead, until I turned and saw the clock click to 2:00 a.m.

When I saw the time, three numbers lining up so neatly and simply—two zero zero—sensibility kicked in, and I tried to turn off my brain. I pictured erasing it like a whiteboard. I didn't think it worked, but it must have because I woke up at eight with a headache and the sun was out. It's 10:30 a.m. now, and I still haven't texted him. He hasn't texted me. I don't know if he's mad at me. I don't know if I'm mad at him.

But I don't have a ton of time to ponder because apparently everyone chose the Monday after the Fourth to expose their kids to the wonders of the ocean. I hear the familiar sound of approaching laughter, and the doors to the aquarium open and unleash a flood of freshly toured families, all of whom head straight toward me.

Simultaneously, an enormous group of children are giggling their way to the activity room: the JAC kids, back from their long weekend. Georgia brings up the rear, as always, chatting with a dark-haired little boy. She catches my eye and grins before returning her attention to the kid, who is fully absorbed in whatever he's telling her. But then the first child walks through the doors of the store, and I don't have time to wink back at her.

The sudden influx of customers means I can't catch my breath for almost two hours. As soon as one group leaves, another comes in. They buy chocolate, posters, books, and postcards, and they ask questions about what animal this is or why we don't have that thing in stock, and I'm too busy to be bored or sad.

At one, my lunch break hits, and Jenny emerges from her

office to reluctantly take over the cash register. I walk through the tour group, looking alien in the filtered blue light of the aquarium, and past the sad, locked offices of the administrative hallways, all the way down to the concrete patch behind the building.

I'm the first one there. Sometimes this happens. They have trouble corralling the kids, or the pizza hasn't come yet, or the other half of the JAC counselors were taking too long to return from their daily trip to the sandwich shop.

So I lie down on the ground and savor the warmth. Jenny keeps the store at a reasonable temperature, but there's nothing like the heat outside, relentless and consistent, to wake me up from a stupor. I hold up my phone to block out the sun and squint. Jake still hasn't texted me. Maybe he's just been extra busy—he mentioned last night that they'd be short-staffed as people call in sick with hangovers. Either way, I'm feeling okay about the whole thing, and I miss him a lot. So I text him *hey love, how's your morning* and instantly feel relieved, as if my chest had been tight all morning and it's easy to breathe again.

He replies almost immediately with a comforting buzz: *super busy baby cant talk now! txt you later.* I close my eyes. The sun is warm on my eyelids and my chest and the tops of my feet. The mosquitoes haven't gotten to me yet. Jake's not mad at me.

I hear a door slamming and a burst of familiar laughter. I crane my head up to see Toby walking through the door, his face obscured by a stack of pizza boxes piled dangerously high. My usual lunch crew follows close behind. Georgia is already holding a slice.

"Caroline!" Toby exclaims, setting the pizzas on the ground. The counselors sit in a circle around the boxes and pass them around. "What the hell is up, you beautiful creature? Oops, don't tell Jake I said that."

Serena peels off her T-shirt to reveal her bikini, lying on her stomach and adjusting the straps. She arranges her book in front of her—this time it's a different hardback, even thicker than the last—and props herself up on her arms. She's the only other person who doesn't eat pizza every day. I feel a strange mix of envy and companionship around her. I have no idea why she became a counselor, though; she seems singularly unsuited to the job. When I look away from her, Toby has already started talking to someone else.

"How's the first day back?" I ask Georgia. She's just taken a bite of pizza that comprised about half the slice, and apparently it's too hot, because she groans in response and flutters her hands around her face. Tomorrow she'll complain about the roof of her mouth hurting. Matt, who is just opening his box of pizza, butts in.

"Well, Georgia here has quite the admirer," he says, grinning at her.

"Oh yeah?" I take out my container of blueberries. Georgia

attempts to swallow and speak, but there's still too much food in her mouth. All I get is a muffled *ughhh* sound.

"*Oh*, yeah. He's very into her. Quite the gentleman. He is, ah..." He turns to Georgia in mock puzzlement. "Has he yet reached the age of five?"

"Fuck you," Georgia spits, wiping her face with the back of her hand and blowing on the remaining half slice of pizza. "God, the poor kid. I feel bad for him, but he's also the worst."

"He..." Matt dissolves into laughter. "He brought her flowers. From his mom's garden. Except obviously he wanted to keep it a secret, because, you know, forbidden love—" Georgia attempts to swat him, and he dodges away. "So in the middle of pool time, he gets out of the pool and goes to his backpack and takes out these flowers that have been all crumpled up at the bottom of the bag, so they look trashy as hell. And he brings them to Georgia, all serious, and he gazes up at her—and she's on the lifeguard deck so he can barely even see her—and he says—"

"'You're the most beautiful girl in the world and I would like you to be my girlfriend,'" Georgia finishes. She shrugs helplessly. "The fuck do you say to that? I couldn't take the flowers, that would have made things even worse. He had to go throw them away. And then you could tell he was trying not to cry. He's such a sweet kid."

"Sweet kid, huh?" Matt says, raising one eyebrow.

"I cannot stand you."

"So wait," I say, "is there a policy for that?"

"How to talk to a four-year-old with a crush on the hot counselor?" Matt says, laughing. Georgia rolls her eyes, but blushes a little too. Serena looks up briefly, her expression unreadable, and sets her head down again. "No. No, there is not."

"I felt so bad for him. So bad," Georgia sighs. She turns to me, waving a piece of pizza in my face, and I shake my head. "Suit yourself," she says, taking a bite. Her mouth full, she adds, "Distract me from this humiliation, Caroline. Tell us about your day."

"It's been really busy, actually," I reply after swallowing a mouthful of blueberries. "I don't know what it is, but there were way more big tours than usual today, and everyone wanted to buy shit. Some of them were real assholes," I say, remembering a guy at the back of the line who had yelled at me to move faster, and then, when it was his turn at the front, argued about the price of his plush turtle. "It probably would have freaked me out a month ago, but today there was so much happening that it was just like, well, so it goes."

"That happens to us all the time," Georgia says. "Specifically with this one guy, actually. Older dad. He really hates Matt—"

"Because of my long hair, probably."

"—and he really likes Serena—"

"Because of my tits, definitely," Serena adds from beside us.

"Right, so, the guy always wants his kid to work with

women. Who knows why. I'm sure because he just sees us as babysitters. But his kid responds much better if a guy tells him to do something—probably because his dad accidentally taught him not to listen to women—so usually we have him work with guys, because it's not my burden to bear to dismantle everything he's learned in his four and a half years in this world. And it just so happens—" Georgia pauses to take a breath and Matt jumps in.

"That every single time we have any kind of parents' event, I'm the one this kid asks for. Or I'm helping him in some way. Or whatever. Every. Fucking. Time."

"The kid actually really likes Matt."

"Because of my long hair."

"Sure. But anyway, this dude will see Matt helping his kid color a picture or whatever, and he always gets pissed and invents some bullshit lie, like he heard Matt cursing or shit like that. So, he pulls Matt aside and yells at him—"

"Like, 'I don't want you around my child, you're a bad influence—'"

"So, you've never actually done anything to upset this guy?" I ask. They have it much worse than I do.

"Well." Matt smirks. "One time I cussed at work, and apparently the kid came home and started yelling 'fuck' at the dinner table. But I denied that."

"Recently," Georgia continues, ignoring his admission of guilt, "every time this dad sees Matt, he just glares and clenches his jaw for a while. And then he goes to Jamal and says he wants Matt fired, he's not good around children, so on and so forth." Jamal is their boss, a short, worried man in his late twenties who seems perpetually exhausted by the logistics of camp, though by all accounts he's actually a pretty decent guy. "And," Georgia adds, "he always, *always* suggests that, quote, 'someone like Serena' might be better suited to 'taking care of my son.'"

Serena raises herself up on her elbows and tilts her sunglasses down to squint at us. "He thinks of camp like a day care," she says. "He doesn't even get why there are guy counselors. Plus, he likes watching me bend over to talk to the kids. One time he came over and put his hand on my ass, acting like he was asking me about the posters we were making. It's gross."

"Right," Georgia says, nodding at Serena, who resumes her usual position, black sunglasses firmly covering her eyes. "Jamal got mad at Matt the first time—I think you almost got fired, right?" Matt nods. "But then it kept happening, and now Jamal just tells the guy he'll take care of it and reminds Matt to stay away from the kid when the parents are around. It's this stupid vendetta."

I wince. "That sucks," I say.

Matt shrugs. "It does, but the kid's all right."

"Except that he literally never listens to me or Serena." Georgia sighs. "It's so frustrating."

"In fairness, I never listen to you or Serena either," Matt says. No one laughs.

Georgia picks up a new slice of pizza and nudges me. "Anyway," she says, "did your mom bother you about looking at the college book again?"

"Yeah. I actually read it for a while this time. Mostly for your comments."

"Wait," Matt interrupts. "*Best of the Nation's Colleges* or whatever? My dad gave me that book. It blows."

"Thank you, Matt, it does," I say, reaching over to ruffle his hair.

"Listen, the book might be stupid, but college is important," Georgia says impatiently. "You need it to get a good job."

"A bachelor's degree doesn't mean anything nowadays," Matt says, tossing aside the sentence in a dismissive tone that makes me guess he heard someone else say it first. "It's a waste of time and money. Especially if you're an artist."

"Just because you didn't get in—" Georgia starts, but Matt interrupts her with a laugh.

"I only applied to those schools because my parents made me," he says. There's a tiny edge of defensiveness in his voice, but he hides it pretty well. "I'm fucking delighted they can't make me go now. Because guess what I'm going to do come September? I'm gonna draw all the time, and I'm gonna get into one of those shows at the Campbell Gallery, and I'm actually going to spend my time cultivating my art career. Not wasting it in some pointless class."

"You know, you could draw now," Georgia says, exasperated.

"I do!" Matt says. "All the time. But I can't focus on it with this job. It's too draining."

"And your parents won't make you get a job after this?"

"My art *is* my job," Matt says, but he has started to look a little more uncertain. "I've already sold one piece. If I could just have the time to focus on it, I'd sell a lot more. They know that."

"What about art school? There's college for art."

"Sellouts."

"Okay, whatever," Georgia mutters. She turns onto her stomach and closes her eyes, her position an echo of Serena's. I feel suddenly guilty for agreeing with Matt about college. He's an asshole—and delusional. He's shown me pictures of his drawings on his phone, and they're not that great. Awkward, the shading too heavy, the proportions off. They're better than the paintings Georgia and her mom do at the Bev'n'Brush, but not by that much. Besides, we're different, I remind myself. I'm going to college someday. Just not now.

Jake texts me back, something about stocking a display of beer cans and trying to sneak one away. I respond, *haha oh yeah?* and set my phone on the ground. Its screen faces up and reflects the sun. It vibrates against the concrete. Jake has sent me another long text, and it trails off, a continuation of his beer story. He's moved on so easily from the frustration I felt last night—maybe he didn't even realize it was there.

When I look up, Matt is opening his mouth to speak again, and I know Georgia won't have it. I flash a frown. It must be enough because he rolls his eyes and scoots over to join Toby, Dave, and Devin, whose conversation about video games is loud and generic enough to ignore like white noise. I rub Georgia's shoulders, and she sighs contentedly.

"Fuck that guy," I say.

"Seriously," she says. "You have no desire to make your life better in any way, fine, but don't take it out on me." I press my fingertips into her shoulder blades.

"He's probably jealous of the flowers from this morning," I say. She laughs so suddenly that it shakes her entire body under my hands, and I smile.

I continue the back rub for long absentminded minutes until I look down and see that she has fallen asleep. Her light snores rustle the paper napkin trapped in front of her face.

"Georgia?"

"Huh?" she says with a tiny start, quickly relaxing back into the ground. She sighs. "Sorry, didn't sleep well last night."

"It's okay. Sometimes I almost fall asleep standing up at the register." I grab a half-slice of pizza from Georgia's mostly empty box. "Didn't you ever have a crush on a camp counselor like that kid does on you? Or a teacher's assistant, or something like that?"

Georgia shrugs, an awkward movement from her prone

position. "Nah. Not really. I've never had any really big crushes, actually. It seems so pointless."

"Love isn't pointless," I say. Out loud, it sounds a lot more awkward than I meant it.

She makes a sound halfway between a grunt and a laugh. "Well, sure. But two ten-year-olds giving each other Valentine's Day cards isn't love. That's..." She pauses. "Practice. For the future. And that's okay for other people, I guess, but for me, when the right thing comes along, I'll know." She rolls over and squints up at the sun.

I set down my empty Tupperware and lie beside her. The sky is the color of bleached blue jeans. The heat has seeped all the way through me now, leaving no trace of the air conditioning that bit at my skin all morning. Sweat runs down the middle of my chest. "I never felt that way," I say. "Every crush I had, I felt like it was real. I was wrong, I guess, but they were all important to me."

Georgia shades her face with her hand, so she can open her eyes with a full blast of incredulity. "So you were one of those girls who started planning a wedding with every kid who teased you on the playground?"

"No!" She isn't far off, but I won't admit that. "It's... I didn't necessarily think it was going to last with every one of them. Or that it was a serious forever thing. Most of them didn't even like me back. It's more that—"

"You figured out what your first name would sound like with their last names, didn't you?" she teases.

"Of course not." I scowl at her. But yes, I did. In my head, I have all the versions of my future self, stacked up next to the little boys whose last names I would have taken: Caroline Hart, Caroline Gardner, Caroline Quinn, Caroline Brankowski, since I was little. And now, with Jake, Caroline Peterson. I've had crushes since I was tiny, and, late at night, before falling asleep, I've gotten married to every single one.

"I just felt things, and I figured if I felt them, they were real," I try to conclude. Georgia doesn't respond for a moment. I sneak a peek at her through the side of my sunglasses. Her eyes are closed, her face tilted up to the sun.

"Emotions aren't always telling the truth," she says. I don't know how to respond to that. So I don't.

I tug up my shirt so the sun can get onto my stomach, and I check my phone. I ask Jake to tell me more, and he does. Georgia and I lie in silence while the buzz of my phone punctuates the languorous warmth of lunchtime, until Toby yells, "Time's up!" and everyone starts rising.

Georgia throws away the pizza boxes, jumping on tiptoe to shove them into the dumpster's dirty window, and then she turns around and gives me a hug.

"I'm sorry to invalidate your feelings," she says, so seriously that I can't help but laugh.

"It's okay," I say. "Five-year-old Caroline is pissed, but sixteen-year-old Caroline thinks we're good."

"Good," she says and smiles. Then she skips ahead to hold the door open for me and Serena, who is still pulling her T-shirt over her bikini. "Careful, Serena, soon my admirer might be after you."

"Fuck you," Serena says. She tucks her book under her arm as she walks away from us.

"See you later," Georgia says at the end of the hall. When I walk back into the gift shop, Jenny isn't there. It's empty and cold.

Later that evening, I'm gathering my things, folding the aluminum foil over my new chocolate bar (this one has a picture of a butterfly), when Toby drops by. "Caroline! Caroline, Caroline, Caroline," he says. He claps his hands and rubs them together, ambling toward the counter. "Ooh, chocolate," he says and takes a huge bite. I watch him swallow half an hour's pay.

"What can I do for you, Tobias?"

"Well, we here—the aquarium family—have not properly celebrated the Fourth of July together. So we are going bowling. And I would like you to join us, since you are at the very least a close cousin of the aquarium family—probably, maybe, a stepsister—at least a stepcousin, if nothing else—"

I throw a glitter pencil at his face. He dodges easily, grabs it off the ground, and puts it back in the container. "You should come. Jake's coming."

"Wait, seriously?"

"Check your phone."

Somehow I missed the text, but indeed, there it is: *hey toby says your all doing bowling tonight, I'm down.* I glance up again. Toby is finishing my chocolate bar, tossing the wrapper in the trash.

"You owe me eight dollars. That shit is expensive," I say to him.

"I'll buy you dinner tonight," he says. I raise an eyebrow. "Okay, I'll give Jake money to buy you dinner tonight," he amends. I shake my head.

"You owe *me* eight dollars."

Toby puts up his hands. "Whatever. Are you coming? We're leaving now."

I glance down as my phone buzzes, as if on command. A text from Jake.

meet you there?

yeah :)

Then I say to Toby, "Sure, just give me one second."

He moonwalks into the entryway, where all the other counselors are drifting out, having changed out of their ubiquitous shirts. Georgia is in the middle of an animated conversation with either Dave or Devin. Both average-looking, average-talking blonds; I think even their boss gets them confused.

I pick up my bag and knock on Jenny's door. No response, as usual. I poke my head in.

"Jenny?" I say. Her eyes flick up to me, and she mutes her computer. "Is it okay if I head out a little early?"

"Okay."

"You'll close up? Do you need any help?"

"I've done it before. Think I can do it again."

I close the door and exit the gift shop to the throng of people, which has now been entirely consumed by the spirited debate between Georgia and Dave/Devin. As if my arrival is the cue, the group starts moving out to the parking lot, where Toby opens the door to his car with a grand flourish.

"Let's go," he says, sweeping his hand toward the group. The guys pile in, some of them sitting on each other's laps, and Georgia follows. Between the floor and the bench seat, all of them fit. Serena sits alone in the front passenger seat, sunglasses on and texting, and it occurs to me that she and Toby might be sleeping together again.

I hesitate for a moment, my hand on the door. My parents were always big on car safety: *don't text and drive, don't drive drunk, everyone puts on their seat belt before you move the car, et cetera.* And most of the five—no, six counting me—people in this truck are breaking the seat-belt rule. The arrangement is definitely not legal.

But what the hell. I get in anyway, squeezing next to Georgia, and close the door. Maybe Jake can take me home.

"Toby," I say. I have to raise my voice to make myself heard over the arguing—something about if you could only have one of either cheese or oral sex for the rest of your life. "Where's the bowling alley?"

"Mooresville," he says cheerfully.

"Shit," I mutter as the car squeals out of the lot.

Serena pulls down the mirror to check her makeup, smudging color across her lips, and someone behind me yells, "But if I had to give up *cheddar cheese* forever? No fucking way!" I settle into Georgia's soft back, which is twisted to better position her for the discussion.

Mooresville is a solid forty-five minutes away, the next town over, known for its seediness. It's not Murder Central or anything, but it's the kind of place Mom always told me to avoid. I've never been there except to drive through. It apparently has a bowling alley, though, which our town does not, ever since Bonneville Lanes closed when I was twelve.

The alley in Mooresville is called StrikeBallz, and as we drive up, I see it is sandwiched between a liquor store and a dilapidated taxidermist's office. There's a grocery store and a few fast food restaurants across the street in a parking lot crowded with cars. But there are exactly zero vehicles in front of StrikeBallz. Except ours, which Toby now stops before yelling for everybody to get out.

We troop into the long, low building. The parking lot didn't lie: no one is bowling. One bleary-eyed, middle-aged man stands behind the counter. He glances toward us, expressionless, and then returns his gaze to a TV playing a baseball game with grainy sound.

Matt reaches the counter. "We're gonna need, let's see, two rounds for now, and shoes for everyone," he says, waving a hand to the group. "And…" He turns around. I can see his lips counting silently. "Eight Stellas. If we could just all split the bill evenly, that'd be great."

"Is Stella a kind of bowling ball?" I ask Georgia quietly.

"No, Caroline," she says, trying not to smile. "Stella is Stella Artois. Beer."

"But I don't have a fake," I whisper frantically. I'm immediately convinced this guy will call the police, we'll all be arrested, and I'll spend the evening cold and alone in a jail cell in Mooresville, where my mother told me I was never supposed to go. Fuck Toby and fuck Georgia and fuck Jake, who isn't even here yet, for convincing me to come on this stupid trip.

"Lemme see your IDs," the guy says wearily. My hand trembles on the strap of my purse, and I look around to see what to do. No one else seems concerned, despite the fact that none of us are of legal drinking age. They get out their wallets and pull out their drivers' licenses—I follow suit—but don't offer them up. And it turns out, it doesn't matter because the guy catches barely a glimpse at the laminated back of Matt's card before he turns away, ambles down to a refrigerator, and pulls out eight brown bottles.

"Bottle opener's over there," he says, jerking his head to the right. "Tell me your shoe sizes. For the beer and the shoes and the two rounds it's gonna be sixteen bucks apiece."

I text Jake as the others crowd forward to grab the bottles and wrestle off the caps. "Size ten," I hear Dave say as I type.

hey when're you coming?

I don't get a response, which is unsurprising since he's probably driving. I fiddle with my phone and stare at the floor.

Someone bumps me from the right. I look up and see Georgia's lopsided grin right before it disappears into her drink. She passes a bottle to me. We toast.

"You okay?" she says. "You look freaked out."

"This place is just kind of..." I gaze at the near-empty parking lot. The sun makes heat waves over the cement. "I mean, it's kind of scary, right?"

Georgia takes a long, thoughtful look around the building. "I don't think so," she says. "I used to. I was really skeptical the first time I came here with the counselors last year. But it's not actually that bad. Everything's just old and dirty."

"Oh. Okay," I say, a little awkwardly. I take a sip of the beer. It tastes rotten, but beer always does to me. "Wait," I add, a thought occurring to me. "You were fifteen last year. How did you work at the aquarium?"

174

"I didn't," she says. "Matt goes to my school. We were kind of in the same group of friends last year. He's a year older, so he worked here last summer, and I tagged along to a lot of his shit. I spent half of last summer at camp, but the other half, I was home, and my volunteering gig only took up twenty hours a week. We came here a bunch. Because as you know, there's basically nothing to do where we live. But this is only the second time I've been so far this year. First time was right before JAC kicked off."

"Huh." We shuffle forward as Serena plucks her size five shoes off the counter. The guy spots Georgia and his forehead wrinkles.

"Don't tell me. Seven?"

"Seven and a half. I grew."

"Weird for a twenty-two-year-old girl."

"I know. Bizarre, right?"

He glances at me as he drops a pair of dirty blue shoes onto the counter. "And your friend?"

"The same," I say.

We take our shoes and sit on sticky benches behind one of the lanes. The air is dank and gray, and only the fluorescents in the right half of the building are lit, leaving us in uneasy shadow. As we tie our shoes, I seriously consider calling a cab. But then Jake walks in, flooding the room with harsh outdoor light, and makes a beeline straight for me. And I start feeling like things might be okay.

"Jake!" Toby exclaims. "Bro. Get your shoes. Here you go." He passes Jake a Stella.

"Excellent," Jake says. He jogs to the bar to open it and takes a sip. "'Sorry I'm late," he says as he walks back over. "Got held up at the store. My bitch manager wanted me to stay late. I had to explain to her that wasn't gonna happen."

Georgia is sitting next to me, and it's impossible to avoid seeing her roll her eyes. I feel the now-familiar mix of guilt and defensiveness that rises whenever Jake says something she doesn't approve of. But before I can express it, Matt claps his hands.

"Okay!" he cries out. "It's time. Let's go. Everyone's signed up as the first four letters of their name. Except Toby is BALL and Dave is DICK."

Jake strolls over to me and wraps his warm arms around me from behind.

"Cay-roe," he croons into my ear. "Sweet as Karo syrup."

I snuggle back into him and smile. It's not really that big of an issue, to call someone a bitch, I try to convince myself. Especially when she is one. I've met his manager, a forty-year-old woman named Candy who is the very opposite of sweet. She once told me to leave the store because I was holding up his line. Which I might have been, but she didn't need to be an asshole about it.

Still, though, I'm pleasantly surprised when I turn a few minutes later to find Georgia looking relaxed. "So, Georgia, you're GEOR there?"

"I like to pretend it stands for George Washington," she says. "That's who my parents named me after. Father of our country."

"Wait," Jake says, sitting up straight. "Are you serious?"

"Nah, my parents went to Savannah for a business trip one weekend and fucked like bunnies, and then my mom got pregnant and decided to keep me, shockingly. Thus Georgia." Jake, having lost interest, looks down at his phone. "At the time it must have seemed very romantic," Georgia finishes. She downs the last quarter of her beer and slams it on the table, jumping up. "Let's fucking bowl!" she yells at Matt, echoing his enthusiasm.

He grins at her and passes her a flask he's produced from one of the several pockets in his cargo shorts, and she downs a long swig before passing it back to him. I stare a little longer than I should. I've tasted hard liquor before, but never drank it so casually.

"That would've been cool if she were named after George Washington," Jake says, tucking his phone in his pocket. He circles around to stare down the lane like it's his sworn enemy.

"Caroline, Tobias, y'all ready?" Matt asks.

"We're good," I say, raising my bottle.

"Excellent," Matt says. He is, of course, first up. He reels back, and I realize I have no idea what constitutes good bowling form.

I watch the lanes and the silhouettes of my friends against the lights. I try, at first, to figure out what the best technique is, but it's impossible—they all look the same. I can't focus on any of the shapes, so I zone out a little. I snap back awake when Jake comes toward me, grinning while the machine sets up the pins far behind him.

"Did you see that, babe? First strike!"

"That's so great!" I tip up my head. He plants a sloppy kiss on my lips. I can taste the beer, sour and wet, dampening the stubble around his mouth. He twirls around and yells in triumph.

"Your turn, Care-bear," he says.

Georgia passes me a ball, and I stagger clumsily under its weight. Everyone else makes them look so light. They could not have been this heavy when I was a kid.

"Oh, I forgot you're hella weak." She laughs, taking the ball from me with one hand and easily setting it back down beside the others. "Here's an eight-pound option. See, it's even pink. It's like it's made for you."

I give her a look. Her jokes feel meaner than usual.

All that said, though, the new bowling ball is easier to carry. I stand in front of the alley and swing back my arm, mimicking Jake's posture. He did the best, after all. I release it and the ball bounces in small stutters as it hits the ground. I don't think it's supposed to do that. But it eventually reaches a slow roll and gets to the end before it can careen into the alley, and I knock down two pins. Not great, but respectable.

Jake gives me a hug and teases me about how good a teacher

he can be, but then he has to get ready to trash-talk the next guy, and I return to my seat while Georgia steps up to the plate, already crowing her future victory. She swings her arm back and releases the ball, which rolls speedily halfway down the lane before falling into the gutter.

"Toby!" Jake hollers, laughing. "I think we can all agree that the proper method of bowling is my patented backswing, which thrusts the ball forward as a man should, not Georgia's weak-ass wrist flick. Can you back me up?"

Toby raises his beer. Georgia crosses her arms, but says nothing.

"Actions speak louder than words, my man," Jake says, gesturing toward Toby, then the lane. "Your turn."

Toby gets up, stretches, and jumps a little on his toes as if to warm himself up. Then he walks forward without a word, grabs a ball, and executes a straight, flawless strike. When he turns around to the cheers of the guys, some more tipsy than they'd probably admit, it's like he's taking the stage.

"It's a balance, my friends," he counsels. "You have to release it at the right time, but you also have to get some of that wrist action. Georgia knows what I'm talking about." He winks and the guys shriek in laughter. Georgia screws up her face trying not to laugh, but fails. Serena glances up from her phone and returns to texting.

"So," he says, turning to me. "Caroline, do you think you can walk the tightrope of bowling perfection?"

"I'll do my best," I say, finishing the last of my beer—only gagging a little bit—and strolling to the front of the lane. I knock down exactly zero pins and am told that under no circumstances did I get the swing right. Jake stands behind me and molds his body around mine, cradles my arm in his arm, and makes my motions for me, teaching me how to do it better.

Jake wins, in the end, yelling so loudly I have to throw myself at him and clap my hand over his mouth to keep from disturbing the dude behind the counter. I come in a shocking third after Toby, thanks to a few strikes near the end that I could not have predicted. It probably helps that with the exception of Jake and Toby, who are driving, everyone else has been drinking steadily since we got here. I count three more rounds of beer and I wasn't even keeping close track.

Georgia is dead last, which surprises me. She walked in with such bravado, I figured she was going to be great. Turns out, she really sucks. I approach her, planning on a little light teasing, and then I get a closer look: blood rushing to her cheeks and the thin veins in her eyes, unsteady on her feet. She is drunk. Real drunk.

"Oh, Georgia," I say under my breath. "It's time to go home. Come on, girl."

"I wanna play again," she says, slurring her words.

"Nope. Time to go."

Georgia starts crying.

"Jake," I call. He is with Toby, still replaying the best moments of the round, mimicking the swing of his winning strike. He'd love to play again, I bet, but it's eight and a weeknight, and Matt has admitted—to substantial teasing—that his parents expect him back home by nine. Jake turns at the sound of my voice.

"What is it, babe?"

"We gotta get Georgia home."

"Does it have to be now?"

"Yes," I say, panicking slightly, trying to figure out what to do. She won't be able to drive if we take her back to her car at work. We could take her home, but there'd be no way to get past her parents, especially because they'd have to drive her to work in the morning. And I can't even begin to imagine what her mother would say if she saw her like this.

Georgia falls into my arms, inexplicably weeping now. I turn the two of us in an awkward shuffle-dance, so I can look over her shoulder at Jake. He appears crestfallen. "Can you pull the car up to the front?" I ask.

"Yeah, okay," he says. He lingers for a final few words of triumph to Toby and walks out to the parking lot.

"Okay, Georgia," I say to her, pushing her away from my body. "We're gonna have a sleepover tonight at my house. Sound good?"

"I love your house," she sobs. "Your mom is so nice."

"Sure. One second."

I set her on a seat, where she curls up like a pill bug and continues to cry. I turn away from her and call home.

I fiddle with the hem of my shirt as the phone rings. My parents have been remarkably lenient about Georgia coming over this summer. No homework for her to interrupt, I guess. But Mom won't like the idea of having her stay on a work night.

"Hello?"

"Hey, Dad. How're you?"

"I'm good," he says. "What's up? You coming home soon?"

"I'm hanging out with Georgia, and…" I look over at her. She is morosely staring into space, tears still running down her cheeks. "She's having a rough night. I think she…had a fight with her boss or something, and she's really upset. Would it be okay if she stayed at our house tonight?"

"Well, I don't know, sweet pea, it is a work night."

"We work at the same place, Dad. And it's not like we're going to stay up talking all night. I think we're just gonna go straight to sleep."

"Right after the holiday, Caroline? She was here Thursday and Friday already. You two need to get back into the swing of things. We've been happy to have her over in the afternoons, but sleepovers are different."

"Dad, please, honestly, this is not a fun thing for me. She's just really unhappy and I want to help."

He sighs. "Did she get permission from her parents?"

"Yes," I lie.

"I'll ask your mother. If she's okay with it, I am too." I hear him cover the phone with his hand and call my mom's name. *Caroline wants Georgia to stay the night tonight,* he says as if from far away. Mom's muffled response, and his reply. *She says she's having a hard night. A fight with her boss. She says they're just gonna go to bed.* More of Mom's voice, annoyed but indistinct. *That's what I said. But yeah, Caroline says her parents say it's okay.* Silence. A few words from Mom. *I know it's a weeknight, but she's been responsible all summer. If a little absent. I know. I know.*

I chew my lip while their conversation continues. Finally, there's a rattling and Dad gets back on the phone.

"She can come over. But this is a one-time thing."

"I know. Thank you."

"You're welcome. Will you be home soon?"

"In like an hour, Dad. Thank you so much, I really appreciate it."

"Well, I just hope she's doing okay. Your mom and I like her quite a bit."

"Thanks, Dad. I love you. I gotta go."

"Love you too, sweet pea."

I hang up and hurry back to Georgia, kneeling next to her. Her phone is sticking out of her jeans like a broken bone poking from the skin. I pull it out of the pocket and press it into her hands.

"Georgia. Call your parents. Tell them you need to stay at my place tonight. Tell them, I don't know, say I'm having a panic attack or something." I sort of am. I've never seen Georgia like this. I glance toward the door. Jake's car is idling. It's still light out, for fuck's sake. Technically this is evening, but I think it qualifies as day-drinking.

"Fine," Georgia mutters. She sounds so out of it, and I know, in that moment, there is no way this is going to work. My heart starts to race. We're going to get caught, and I'm going to be grounded for the rest of the summer, and my last couple of months here are going to be miserable. Georgia absently taps her screen a couple times and holds the phone up to her ear.

"Yeah, Mom, it's Georgia."

My mouth falls open slightly. Her voice is perfectly clear and precise. I can tell she's focusing intently, her eyes trained on some point in the middle distance, bottom lip held under her teeth in concentration.

"Yeah, everything's fine, I was just wondering if it's okay for me to stay at Caroline's tonight. She had an awful day at work. Her boss is really mean to her. She just really wants me to stay and hang out."

A long silence.

"I mean, I got a 1550 on my last practice test." She coughs.

Silence.

"I was there this weekend anyway, one more night is no big deal."

Silence.

She is starting to slur her words, just a little. If she keeps talking, her mom will be all worried, and we'll have to figure out some way of getting her home, and shit, this is—

"Mom, please. You said if I kept the practice tests up." She takes a deep breath, and her voice is stronger when she starts speaking again. "I promise we'll go straight to bed. And I'll study before. Like always." A brief silence. "Yeah, if you can get off work early tomorrow, of course I'll come home." A longer silence. "Okay, thanks, Mom, seriously, thanks so much. Caroline says thanks too. You too. Yeah. Love you. See you tomorrow." She hangs up.

I lean back against the wall in relief. "Georgia," I say, "that wasn't as bad as it could've been, but seriously, you gotta get just a little bit better at lying to your parents."

Georgia smiles. It's not a very happy smile. She hands her phone back to me, and I slip it back into her pocket, as if I'm her intermediary to the world. I stand and take her hand to pull her up.

"I always come back from your family's place at exactly the same time every night. Y'all feed me vegetables, and they think my test scores are pretty high right now. They weren't happy, but they'll live. It's whatever. Let's go home."

She walks toward the door, her pace steady but her path wavering. I follow her. When I put my hand on the small of her back, like a boat I'm guiding into shore, she doesn't object.

She sits in the back and stares out the window while Jake and I talk in low tones. He tells me about his day. The rhythm of his voice, the cadence of his familiar problems—his boss, mean customers, a ludicrously high display of bran cereal—is soothing. This night had so much potential. Instead, it's become awkward and painful, like when you stretch a muscle wrong and it hurts.

As Jake's pulling into our neighborhood, he puts his hand on my leg.

"You look so sad, baby," he says. "Are y'all gonna be okay tonight?"

"Yeah." I chew on my lip. My parents shouldn't bother us. We'll make it upstairs without any comments. Probably. "I'm just..." I look back at Georgia. Surprisingly, she is not asleep. Her eyes are still open, blank, heavy-lidded, lips parted and chapped. "Maybe we can talk about it tomorrow."

"Whatever you want," he says and pulls up beside my house. I open the door. The sun has set almost completely behind a sheet of yellowish clouds, and the air tastes spoiled, like it's been left in the heat too long. I lean over to give him a quick peck, and he pulls me in for a longer, deeper kiss. It feels like something I need to get over with.

"See you tomorrow?" I say.

"Sounds good."

"Thanks for driving us home. Sorry about Georgia."

"It's okay. I love you." He so rarely says I love you first, and I start to wish I had taken a little more time with that kiss.

"I love you too."

I open the back door. Georgia's sagged against the seat, staring straight ahead. I pull her out, which takes some doing, but she willingly puts her arm around my shoulder and steps forward onto the curb. Jake makes a sympathetic face at me over her shoulder. I slam the door, and he drives away, leaving a cicada-filled silence in his wake.

Lightning bugs flicker around us as we walk up the sidewalk, Georgia dragging her feet. The damp underside of her shirt-sleeve rubs against my shoulder. We reach the door.

"I'm really sorry, Caroline," Georgia says before I can open it. Her voice is clear and quiet, and I wonder if she's sobered up. But there's no way to tell for sure, and besides, it doesn't matter.

"It's okay," I reply. I feel, still, a hard annoyance scratching at the back of my head, waiting for me to release it at her. So I expected my words to come out as a lie. They didn't, though. They too are vulnerable and soft, and she leans against me more heavily as she hears them.

I open the door and we go quickly down the hall and up the stairs. I hear Dad call my name from the den, but I get

Georgia up to my room—she climbs in bed and scoots over to her side immediately—before I come say hello. As I close the door behind me, her breath is coming in evenly spaced gasps. Small, tight inhale, huge exhale. I think she's asleep.

My parents are waiting for me at the bottom of the stairs. "Sorry," I say before they can start. "I just wanted to get Georgia into bed."

"Already? What's wrong?" Dad asks, his brow furrowed. "Where were you?"

"We went out to hang out with people after work, and…" I realize I was so busy getting her home that I'm not even sure what made her so upset. Alcohol is a depressant, sure, but it couldn't be that alone. "I honestly don't know. She seemed fine. I was talking to Jake, and then the next thing I know, she's freaking out crying."

"And she didn't want to go home?" My mother is equally concerned.

"I think she didn't want to deal with her parents asking her stuff. Or maybe she just wanted to stay with us. I don't know—she really likes you guys."

"Well, we like her," Mom murmurs. "I was worried about it being a work night, but if she's already asleep…but this can't be a pattern, Caroline."

"I know." I run my hand along the banister. "I'm sorry. I promise I'm just trying to be a good friend."

"You are a good friend," Dad says. He climbs up one stair to hug me.

"Do you want to watch TV with us?" Mom says. "We're just having some fruit salad."

"That would be great," I say, surprising myself. "That'd be really, really great."

I curl up in the easy chair, and my parents sit in their love seat, and we watch strong-but-vulnerable detectives solve murders and tough-but-fair lawyers prosecute the killers. My mom crochets. Dad idly glances over a ten-cent book of crosswords.

After a little while, I get a text from Georgia.

I threw up and I think I'm sober now. I'm so sorry. Where are you?

Downstairs, I respond. She doesn't text back. A minute later, I hear the shower come on upstairs. My parents glance that way, but don't do anything. I know her towel is still sitting out from this weekend for her to use. The water cuts off at the next commercial break, and by the time the show is back on, she appears wearing one of my oversized T-shirts and a pair of pajama pants. She sits next to me in the big easy chair, our hips squished together in the middle and tilted up on the sides. Her hair is wet and smells like flowers. My parents look over and ask her how she is.

"Good," she says. "Thank you for having me again. I'm really sorry for the short notice."

"It's okay," Mom says. "Always happy to have you."

And God bless them, they do not ask anything more, not even what her parents think about her being here instead of home.

We go upstairs when the episode is done and climb into our opposite sides of the bed. I text Jake for a while and listen to Georgia's unsteady breath. She's not asleep. I plug my phone into its charger, and the room is suddenly dark.

"Georgia?" I say, reaching out tentatively with my voice. She nestles deeper under the covers, but I can tell she's heard me.

"Did anything happen?" I say.

She makes a muffled noise of displeasure, and there's a rustle of fabric as she turns toward me. It's so dark I can barely see her, but I can smell the alcohol on her breath underneath the toothpaste.

"It's so stupid," she says, her voice low. "I'm really sorry."

"You don't have to apologize," I say, even though I'm glad she did. I reach out to touch her shoulder, end up grazing her arm. "Is everything okay?"

"It's fine," she whispers. "It's all fine. It's just…" She lets out an enormous sigh and turns onto her back. The glow-in-the-dark stars above us are pale, barely lit at all. "I had to take my SAT practice test this weekend, like I do every weekend, right? And I told my parents I'd do it on Saturday because if I had my practice test done by the time they got back that night, we could hang out together all day Sunday. Which was all fine.

"But I sat down to do it after I got back from your house, and I don't know if it was all the sugar, or the champagne, or just being tired, or what…" Her voice trails off for a minute, and I lie there, waiting, before she gives her head a little shake and continues. "Everything was off. None of the questions made sense. And when I reviewed it, I got a really bad score. Like, really bad. Way worse than the score I got in May, and that's the one I'm supposed to beat with this next test. Even worse than I did when I took it in seventh grade, and that's saying something. I mean, I was thirteen."

"You took the SAT in seventh grade?" I say, momentarily distracted.

"Yeah, it was this practice thing they offered at my school; it didn't mean anything. Anyway," she says, sighing a little. "I went back through, and I erased almost all my wrong answers and put in the right ones, and when my parents asked, I lied about it. I told them I got a really good score. So I could stay in the green zone and keep hanging out with you and everyone like I have all summer."

She takes a deep breath and releases it. I wait for the rest of the story before I realize that's it.

"So…you lied about an SAT practice test to your parents?"

"Yeah," she says. The word has an unbelievable heaviness.

"Not the actual SAT, but just a single practice SAT?"

"Well, yeah, of course it's not the real one yet."

"And because of this, you drank too much and started sobbing over nothing."

"Well, I was feeling really shitty and trying to forget about it. And tonight, yeah, I drank too much, but I didn't mean to. I was just having a good time." Her voice is a mixture of defensive and embarrassed. "But then Matt and Serena were talking about the SAT because she's taking it at the same time as me, and Matt was talking about how bad a score he got—almost bragging—and he said the number, and it was the score I got on Saturday. And I…" She pauses as if searching for the next phrase, and then gives up. I can feel her shrug through the mattress. "I freaked out. Because what if all my good scores are a fluke? And really after all this work, I'm gonna have an off day on the day I finally take it for real, and I'm gonna fail. And then I won't get into any colleges, and then—"

"Oh my God, Georgia, you have to stop," I say. I scoot closer to her and hug her, awkwardly, one arm squished underneath me. She laughs a little. "You already have a great SAT score. Right?"

"It's good, not great," she says, her voice muffled.

"Your good is other people's great. You're fine on the SAT. You have to know that, rationally." She nods with a tiny movement of her head. "And separately, you are the smartest person I know," I tell her as I pull away. "It's okay to lie to your parents every once in a while."

"Not about this," she says.

"Yes, about this. It's not fair that they would keep you from your whole life because of one bad score. Just don't consume a thousand grams of sugar and several glasses of champagne the night before your real test, and I think you'll be fine."

She laughs for real. "Maybe," she says. "Anyway. I really am sorry."

"It really is okay," I say. I look at the clock. It's late, later than when I usually go to bed. "We should get to sleep."

"Yeah," she says.

"Good night, Georgia."

"Good night, Caroline."

The room is quiet for several minutes, and I am drifting toward unconsciousness when she says, very quietly, "Hey, Caroline?"

"Yeah?"

"Thank you."

She presses the bottom of her foot against the bottom of mine. I press back, briefly, feeling the warmth of her body through this small surface, and then we both pull away and fall asleep.

10

Here's the thing about romance: sometimes, it's inconvenient.

"I wanna make it up to you," Jake says to me as we sit on his porch on Tuesday. He sets his jaw in an earnest square as he looks at me. His right hand is holding mine, warm and dry, and his left shakes in a jittery rhythm, ash falling from the cigarette onto the unfinished boards below.

"Make what up to me?" I say, because it could be anything. Our definitions of something worth making up for—well, they're different.

"Leaving this weekend. Going to the beach. I know you were…" He takes a long pause and a drag on the cigarette. The smoke is noxious and comforting, a soft bitterness in the air. "Lonely."

I stare at the kudzu through the screen window. He's wrong.

I spent the weekend surrounded by people: baking with Mom, laughing with Georgia, eating hamburgers with Dad. But he's also right, of course. I wanted him to be there with me, under the cheap cul-de-sac fireworks. I could press on the bruise he's beginning to feel. Or I could be sweet.

"I missed you," I say, trying for somewhere in the middle. "But I had a really nice weekend too. And, I mean, I get it. It's cool to hang out with your friends."

"Sucks you're so young," he says, rubbing my hand with his thumb as if consoling me for a great failure. "Coulda come with us otherwise."

"Yeah. I'll get older, though."

"For sure. So, you know how I normally have the early shift on Saturday morning?"

"Yeah."

"Right, well, Brittany needed to go to a birthday party or something on Monday, and I traded shifts with her, so I have off this Saturday. And I was thinking, maybe I can spend the whole day with you. Morning to night. We can ask your parents to extend your curfew an hour? Half an hour?"

I'm stumped. Jake rarely trades shifts—he likes routine—so I never expect him to tell me his schedule has changed. And in an unfortunate coincidence, Naima has to go out of town for yet another weekend, and Jenny asked me a couple weeks ago if I could cover her.

I said yes. I didn't feel like I could say no, having left her in the lurch on the Fourth, and I figured it's a little extra money—a fair amount of extra money, actually, since I'll be working overtime. But it also means that I need to be there for a full work day, from nine to six. Not a lot of time with Jake.

I tell him this as gently as possible. I'm already annoyed, and I can't tell whether I'm mad at him for trying to make up for something I just want to forget, or whether I'm experiencing a renewed hatred toward the generally incompetent administration of the aquarium. I pluck the cigarette from his fingers and bring it to my lips when I finish relaying the news. It tastes rancid. I love secondhand smoke, hate smoking.

"Huh," he says. I hand the cigarette back to him. He takes a smooth drag, exhales, the smoke clouding the air in front of us before it settles into the wood and my hair and the cotton of my dress. "Well, I guess that means I'll be getting pretty familiar with the gift shop."

"What do you mean?" I look at him, startled. He twists his torso in the chair to turn toward me and grinds out the cigarette.

"It can be take-your-boyfriend-to-work day. I'll just come and hang out. It'll be cool."

"I don't think that's allowed, though," I say.

"Who's gonna stop me?" He's right—if Jenny were there, she would cast him out of the store with a single look, but Wendell, Jenny's boss, will only stop by a couple times to make sure the place hasn't descended into chaos. And he probably won't even notice Jake is there.

"You're gonna be so bored, though."

"Naw, it'll be great. I'll squeeze your ass behind the counter. And I'll go on one of Toby's tours. Hey, maybe he'll let me lead a tour, that'd be cool. I don't know shit about marine life."

"Neither does he."

"Yeah, I know, that's why he gives such great tours."

"He doesn't always work on Saturdays. They bring in more…real adults on the weekends." Weekends are busier, I'm told, than weekdays. It's also harder to get away with bullshit on the tours, according to Toby. Jenny used to work the weekend shift in the summer, and she says you get the parents who work twelve-hour days during the week and don't know how to interact with their kids without structure.

Jake's phone buzzes, and he glances down. "Toby's working. I asked him earlier—he just texted me. We can have lunch together. It'll be cool."

"Well, okay, sure. That'll be good."

"How good?" Jake says, tilting his head toward mine.

"Amazing." Our foreheads meet, and the warmth of his skin comforts me. It tamps down an unease in my stomach, pushes it to the back of my spine, where it rests, an ache. As if I've run too many miles with bad form. Then Jake smooths his hands over my thighs and in between them, and the ache disappears completely.

That's how I find myself leaning against the back counter at 9:40 a.m. on a Saturday morning, Jake beside me on a stool he dragged in from Jenny's office. Toby half paces, half dances around the aisles, spilling tiny drops of coffee from his *Get wet! At the Bonneville Aquarium* thermos onto the fake-marble tile. He pokes the belly of a stuffed manatee, upright on the top of the pile. The manatee teeters and falls onto its side. Toby twirls away.

"Here's the thing about the end of the first season," Jake says to Toby, spreading his hands in front of him as if presenting a dissertation. "Greyson is just starting to really get interesting. Like, the evil chick redeems herself at the very end by not betraying his secret, and he could rescue her, but he *doesn't*. They build him up as this great guy, and then it turns out he has a dark side. And then for the network to end it like that? It's ridiculous."

"I firmly believe we haven't seen the last of Hilda," Toby says, doing a lazy moonwalk down the paper goods aisle. "Because he didn't rescue her, definitely, but he also didn't kill her. He left her on the outer planets."

"The show got canceled, dude."

"I don't think it's actually over. I think the network is only *saying* they cancelled it so people get more hyped up when they bring it back."

"I dunno, man, I really think *Universe Leap* is done. For good."

"I will not believe it. I need to know what happened with Hilda. Honestly, the only two things I'm looking forward to in

life are the Great Adventures trip this summer and *Universe Leap*
coming back."

"It's not gonna come back, dude. And when are you going
to Great Adventures?"

"Therein lies the genius of *Universe Leap*," I say. I've
only been half listening to the conversation. "It leaves us with
profound uncertainty."

"Nope," Jake shouts, pointing an accusatory finger at me.
"No making fun. You haven't even seen it yet. You refuse to
watch it."

"I don't refuse. I just haven't gotten around to it yet," I
protest. *Because it sounds incredibly fucking stupid*, I do not say.
I tried telling Jake this once, and he wouldn't talk to me for ten
minutes. But come on, a show about a space cowboy, his best
friend (a space vampire), and his ex-lover (Hilda, provenance
unclear) sounds so aggressively silly that I can't bring myself to
watch even a single episode. I've spent money to take Jake to
movies so he wouldn't make me watch *Universe Leap*. He has
the entire series—that is, the entire first and only season—on
DVD. It is the only set of DVDs he owns.

"I'm gonna get you one of these days," Jake says. "Maybe
tomorrow. Maybe after dinner tomorrow, we will watch the
first episode."

Toby sips his coffee as he inspects a bright green manatee
notebook. "You should try it, Caroline. It's great."

"Sure," I chirp, the required minimum of enthusiasm. I'm already trying to figure out what else we could do tomorrow to avoid sitting through an hour of angsty space vampires and exposition.

Toby stands up. "See," he begins, "what you have to understand about *Universe Leap* is—shitbuckets," and he grabs his travel mug from where it was balanced precariously on a stack of puffer fish picture books. "Duty calls."

For the last twenty-five minutes, ever since the first tour of the morning started, a small and excitable crowd has been gathering in the atrium. Saturday morning people seem to be generally happier than weekday visitors. The kids are chasing each other in massive circles while the parents stand in a smaller cluster holding their coffee and making aimless family small talk: school, camp, the price of new clothes. The children orbit the adults like comets, tiny and blazing. Sometimes one of them gets pulled in by the gravity of a parent and clings to a mother's bare calf, a father's khaki trouser leg.

Toby slurps down the last of his coffee and sets the empty cup on the ground beside the poster display. "I'll be back around lunchtime," he says over his shoulder to me and Jake. Then he strides out into the atrium, hands on his hips, huge grin on his face. The parents turn toward him and instinctively smile themselves. They know he's a guy they can trust to entertain and educate their kids. After all, he hasn't begun the tour yet.

He starts his spiel, which echoes, muted, through the glass

walls. I've heard it so many times I know the cadence of it, the moments where there'll be laughs, the smiling, barely audible response of the shyest kid in the group, whom Toby will specifically pick out to compliment.

"So, what do you actually do here?" Jake says, turning to me. "All you've done is stand here and draw for like an hour." I look down. Without realizing it, I've scribbled doodles all over the pad of aquarium stationery I keep next to the register in case someone calls. Tight black stars, spiraling tornados, little circles combining into clumps like bubbles coming up from deep water.

"Well, I answer the phones, if people call to ask when we're open or whatever," I say. "And obviously I sell stuff to people when they come in."

"Are these people gonna come in?" Jake tilts his head to the group of families spilling from the double doors, who are blinking and squinting against the light—the last tour leaving so Toby's group can enter. I see the first telltale sign: a boy jumping up and down impatiently, gesturing toward the gift shop with the wild motions of someone who hasn't yet figured out what movements go with what words.

"Yeah, probably," I say.

"You don't sound that excited," Jake teases me.

"It's not that exciting," I reply.

But the truth is, I do like it when big groups come in. People aren't friendly, but they're usually not too rude either. Every time I sell something, it feels like an important accomplishment. I don't get paid on commission or anything—I would make about ten dollars a week—but any act, however small, seems important. Someone comes to me with a request, and I fulfill it. I press some buttons and an item leaves the store. Concrete actions, concrete responses. Simple.

And indeed, this whole group is strolling slowly toward the store, one mom pointing at the display of tote bags I set up earlier this morning. Jake asks me if I need him to do anything. "Just chill," I say, and he leans back on the stool and pulls up a game on his phone.

After an hour and a half and three more tour groups, Jake is fidgeting like a child. I don't blame him.

One Saturday last semester, I hung out near the register at his job for half a shift. At first, it was interesting to see him work. He interacts with customers differently than he does with me. More formal, obviously, and more detached. I love the way his expressions jump from place to place when we're together, how he goes from surprised to excited to thoughtful in fractions of a second. At work, he was just cool. Slow, tired, too adult.

After a while, though, there was nothing more to see. I went to the coffee shop and watched TV on my phone on their WiFi until his shift was over. I spent four hours curled up ordering Frappuccinos until my teeth rattled with the buzz. When he snuggled me later in his bed, my eyes still felt like they were going to jump out of my head.

I wonder if he's seeing me as I saw him. But I don't think I'm that boring. I enjoy talking to people; it feels purposeful. Granted, my job has way more breaks than his does. Grocery stores in the suburbs—you never get a second off.

When Toby comes out with his most recent tour group, shaking hands with the dads and discreetly receiving phone numbers from the single moms, Jake hops up. "I'm gonna go on the next tour," he says. "It starts soon, right?"

"Yeah, like five minutes."

"Great," he says. "I'll see you at lunch?"

"Sounds good," I say, and he thrusts his phone back in his pocket and lopes out into the lobby. Adjusting his pants next to the gathering group of families, he looks very out of place. But then a little boy points at his untied shoe, and as he squats down to talk to the kid, he looks right at home. He'll be a really good dad someday. I look down at my belly. A few months ago, the idea of having a baby with him made me feel warm and excited. Now I feel vaguely ill, and I cannot place exactly why.

The sick sensation lingers through lunch, which is sandwiches, Jake's choice. Without the JAC counselors, the concrete slab behind the building feels big and empty, even though there are normally only six or seven people out there.

I feel ill through the rest of work too. Through a customer

grumbling loudly when I come back two minutes late according to the sign on the front door. Through Jake jiggling his legs while I sell stuffed animals and puzzles. Through Toby ducking into the store between shifts to tell us about the kid who got overexcited and kept slamming himself into the glass to try to "let the fishes loose."

It's still there when I get Georgia's midafternoon text showing me her mom posing with a Bev'n'Brush creation in progress: a cactus in a desert scene, the spines as thick and long as toothbrushes. Georgia's mom's mouth is open in faux surprise at the quality of the painting, her hands gesturing to the canvas like a game show hostess. *What a fuckin goof,* Georgia's text says, and that makes me smile, at least.

The feeling stays all the way through the end of work, when the clock finally hits 5:30 p.m., and I ring up a pad of sticky notes for a middle-aged couple, the last customers of the day. Jake jumps up as soon as the couple exits the atrium.

"Come on, come on, come on," he says, bouncing on his heels. "I have so much shit planned for tonight."

"I have to close first," I say. I'm unreasonably irritated with him. It's just because I've been on my feet all day, and he's been doing nothing. Less than nothing. Fucking around on his phone, the charge cord getting in my way after 2:00 p.m. when it died from too many rounds of Lawnmower. Jake moans about mowing the lawn when it's his turn every other month, but he can attack killer grass and evil bugs in Lawnmower all day, apparently.

I breathe deep in, deep out because it's not his fault that I had to work today. When I turn around from closing the cash register, he has the sweetest smile on his face, cocky yet vulnerable, as if he's waiting for me to come to him.

And I do. He opens his arms and legs, and I walk right in. When he closes his limbs around me, it's like the sun on my face after a long winter. We stay like that for a few long moments before I pull away and say, "Okay, seriously, I have to close."

He says, "Okay, go fast."

I finish the closing checklist, leave it on Jenny's desk, and turn off the lights and lock the doors. We walk across the atrium hand in hand. The air hits me in the face like a tsunami when we take the first step outside. It's a stagnant slush of wet heat that fills my mouth and nostrils.

I grew up around this heat. I'm used to the South and how it feels. When my cousins visited from California as kids, they'd always have to go inside from overheating. Their faces got red as hot peppers and their foreheads crinkled up in confusion, and I was left alone in the yard, no one else to play house with in the elaborate rooms we had carved into the mulch. I would yell for them to come back out and curse the weather for stealing them away.

Sometimes, that heat can be a comfort. The second blanket your mother pulls over you when you're sick, even though you're already a little too warm—a feeling of heavy, soft security, like you're safe because you can't move.

This is not that kind of heat. It is the same in touch and texture, but it feels ominous. Like when the sky gets that sickly yellow before a tornado. This sweltering warmth has that same low hum of prediction.

It presses on us from all sides, and Jake is just holding my hand and combing his fingers through his hair and squint-smiling out into the parking lot. I wonder why he doesn't sense it too and think of asking him. But no. When he hears abstract questions like that, he wants to dig really deep into them, analyze them. Or he laughs and rubs my neck and doesn't respond. There's no in between.

He opens his truck door for me and offers a hand to help me in. The car smells like smoke and french fries and this low-key cologne he wears that I love. He put it on once as a joke at a department store, and I couldn't keep my hands off him. The next day, he went back and spent his whole paycheck on every bottle they had in stock.

He gets in on the other side and starts the engine, radio blaring to life in the middle of an ad for a research study on pregnant women. He presses the off button quickly and looks me right in the eyes with this big shy smile.

"So where are we going?" I say, both pleased and unnerved by this sudden onset of earnestness.

He leans over and kisses me. "Not gonna tell you 'til we get there," he says as he pulls out of the parking space. When he reaches the edge of the aquarium lot, he turns left. Which is weird, because town is to the right. Left is a few sad shopping centers, a wide swath of run-down suburbs, a retirement community, and past that, nothing but fields and forest.

We drive in silence for miles. Jake's hand rests on my thigh, and he draws circles with his thumb. I rest one hand on top of his and the other out the window, the air slipping past my skin like water and that sticky heat collecting in sweat at the nape of my neck. The shopping centers pass. The suburbs pass. We have to pause at the light near the retirement community; there's a bus stop on the side of the road. Five elderly folks, hunched and gray, are sitting in wheelchairs in the dirt near the bus sign, not talking to each other.

After we're ten minutes into the country, I ask Jake again where we're going. He shushes me peacefully. Fidgety all day, but now that we're in motion, he's feeling good again. I glance at the speedometer; at eighty-five, the country roads are blasting by, but they're all so much the same that I can't tell the difference between fast and slow.

"Where are we going?" I try again. Jake laughs.

"Do you really want me to tell you? It's gonna be such a great surprise."

"I guess not," I say. My stomach flutters. I used to think I hated surprises, but that was only because my parents did them really poorly. Jake always pulls it off.

"It's gonna be worth it," he says, looking over at me with that big smile and squeezing my shoulder. "I promise. It's gonna be so good."

Ten minutes later, we pull off onto a skinny dirt road speckled with potholes. Grass grows in a long strip in the middle. The truck rattles and rumbles its way down the line for one, two, three, four minutes before the track opens into a clearing filled with tall grass and wildflowers. In the middle is a house.

My mouth drops open. "Jake, what?"

His smile gets even wider, and he wraps his arms around me, snuggles my shoulder against his chest. "You like it?"

"This place is gorgeous. God." A strong breeze blows away that sense of unease in the air. A butterfly alights on top of a tall, rotting stalk of sunflowers and flies away again. "Where are we?"

"Joe's cousin's..." He rolls his eyes upward. "...cousin's cabin. Chick named Janice. Yeah, that's it. So like a third cousin or whatever."

"Does Joe's cousin's cousin know we're here?"

He smirks. "Joe knows. I think the first cousin knows. Don't know about the girl who actually owns the place, but hey, we're not gonna mess it up. It's just for tonight. Have to get you back before curfew, unfortunately."

House, I should say, is a generous word for the structure

in front of us. *Shack* would be a little mean, but not incorrect. *Cabin* is probably most accurate. As we exit the truck, I can see some small gaps in between the planks, windows that look like they either stay open or closed but don't give you the option to choose which. The roof slopes into a small overhang, but there's no porch, just lush green vines and weeds growing right up to the walls. The door is orange, once bright, now chipped and fading to the color of an overripe peach. Even though it's run-down, it really is beautiful—like something enchanted out of an old children's book.

"Can we go in?" I say, still overwhelmed by the fact that this place exists—just forty minutes from home—and we're here. I thought the suburbs went on forever.

"Yeah, yeah, absolutely," Jake says, hurrying toward the front door. He pulls me lightly by the hand as I jog behind him. "Joe said the key would be…" He pulls out his phone and scrolls through some texts. "In the birdhouse."

He cranes his neck to look around, and I point down the right side of the cabin, where a battered wooden structure painted the same orange as the door is hanging from the overhang by a piece of twine. He reaches up to shake the birdhouse on its side—thankfully, it appears that no bird has lived there for some time—and out falls a tiny brass key. It looks like something you'd use to open a chest of drawers from the nineteenth century.

He holds it up as if he's found a treasure, grinning big and goofy, and unlocks the door. It creaks as he pushes it open for me. I step inside.

The place is dark and the air is stagnant, swirling with flights of dust, but everything seems otherwise clean. Two doors rest in the wall opposite us, both slightly open, revealing a bathroom and a closet. A futon and a few armchairs sit on one side of the cabin flanking a large wood fireplace. On the other side are a sink and a ring of countertops and cabinets. A camp stove is curled like a cat in the corner, and two large coolers sweat beside it.

"So this place has…"

"Everything we need for the evening," Jake says, putting his hands on his hips in satisfaction.

"I mean, in terms of water, heat, air conditioning?"

"Water, yes, definitely. AC, unfortunately no. They use the fireplace for heat, but we won't be needing that today, will we?" He flips a light switch that is literally covered by a spider web. It does nothing. "I think there was electricity at some point, but it appears that it is no longer connected. Just means we'll use candles! Very romantic."

"And!" He squeezes me around the waist and then strides a few steps over to the coolers. He stands next to them like a game show presenter offering the grand prize. "Open it."

"These are yours?" I ask as I come over.

"The coolers are mine; what's in them is for you. Well, for

us." He beams as I lift the lid of the top cooler. Inside, nestled among bags of ice, is a preposterous amount of food and drink. Crisp lettuce, bright red strawberries, pasta salad, avocados, beer, lemonade. All my favorites. A veritable summer feast.

"Jake, look at all this!" I exclaim, shocked. Jake's the hot dog guy. He has never cooked anything more than pasta with me. I didn't even know he knew I liked avocados.

"So, you like it?" he says, almost shyly. And I realize this is the first time in a long time, maybe ever, that he's taken a risk on making me happy. Usually we're safe in our routine.

"I love it," I say, and I pull him close to kiss him.

The food rests patiently in its icy nest while we have sex on the floor. There's an old, green rug that somebody's white dog used to lie on. I see the hairs in minute detail when I turn my head to the left. My back scrapes against the fibers and I wrap my legs around him, and there is no one in the world to hear us, and the crickets are getting loud, and it feels better than sex ever has before, full and hot and complete. I haven't felt this good about sex since we first started having it.

Afterward, I curl up in an armchair wearing a sundress I found in Jake's car. It's my skimpiest, left there by accident after I changed back into aquarium clothes one night he drove me home. He chops up vegetables for a salad and heats up the chicken on the camp stove and doesn't even ask me to help. I turn on the playlist my mom made me at the beginning of junior year, songs, she said, that every sixteen-year-old girl ought to know. A lot of old stuff.

Dinner is ridiculously good. I ask him if he practiced on the chicken, and he looks down and smiles and says, "Yeah, it took a few nights, and a lot of meat went in the trash."

I tell him it was worth it. My phone croons Frank Sinatra and the air in the cabin turns blue as the light slowly dies outside.

Jake lights the candles with his little silver lighter, and suddenly everything is gold. It is magic: as if fireflies came in and fell asleep still all lit up. I put my plate on the floor and snuggle against him. I am full and contented. I do a quick time calculation in my head—the sun just set, so it's no later than nine, we have time—and relax into his chest. His hand glides up and down my arm and across my chest, lingers on my breasts, continues down and around and around.

"So," he says after a few minutes of silence, "I have something to tell you."

"Oh?" I twist up to look at him, but from this angle, his head is distorted, eyes hidden behind solid cheekbones. I can see the stubble growing in under his chin. He must have shaved this morning.

"Yeah." His chest rises and falls in a deep breath underneath me. "I think I've told you how my dad has been living in Florida for a little while, with LeeAnn."

"Sure." LeeAnn is Jake's dad's former mistress, now long-term girlfriend. Their relationship status changed eight years ago, when Jake was ten, the night his mom packed her husband's clothes in three duffel bags and told him to send her an address for divorce papers. "Orlando, right? But you've never actually visited."

"Right, yeah. I was gonna go down there this spring, but it's a really long drive and I didn't have the gas money, and my mom, of course, wouldn't lend it to me and it just…" His hand pauses in its journey down my arm, then continues. "I never got to it. But that's no big deal now, because he's moving. Moved, actually, a couple weeks ago."

"Anywhere close to here?" That sick sensation is starting to creep its way back into my stomach, through the humid darkening air and underneath my dress. I don't know why. Something about his tone, the measured movement of his thumb on my skin.

"Well, it's, uh…" He wiggles his arm around my neck to scratch his chin. "Kentucky. Out in the country. LeeAnn's family had a goat farm out there, and apparently it used to be a lot of fun. There's this big old house they're gonna fix up. And a barn. Huge barn. The kind with a loft up top and a window that looks out over all the fields and everything. Small town close by, supposed to be real cute."

The sickness deepens. I am on the edge of knowing why, but I can't quite reach the reason. My breathing gets shallower. I wait.

"And, well, we're only a month and a half away from

leaving, and I know we've talked about going a lot of different places, but we haven't made a decision yet. I'm just thinking about how hard it would be to live out on our own. Of course, we'll do that someday," he adds quickly. "But I think right now, it might be good to, you know, be somewhere that can support us a little more."

There is a long, long silence as the words sink in. I am waiting for him to continue before I realize that he's going to make me draw the inevitable conclusion myself.

"So you're saying we should go live with your dad and LeeAnn," I finally respond. A part of me is startled at how normal my voice sounds. The rest of me feels flat and red.

"Well…yeah." He clears his throat, scratches his chin again. I adjust against his chest in a way that makes it more uncomfortable, but I don't want to move again. I can hear his heartbeat thumping against my ear, fast and erratic. I swear his skin moves up and down in tiny beats. Ten seconds pass, twenty, thirty. "What do you think?" he asks at last.

I guess that's the question.

I don't know. I know that in all my wild imaginings, I never thought of us living in a field, far away from a city. I know that I have no desire to be anywhere with old ladies who will refuse to sell us condoms at the Walmart because we're not married.

I know that I always imagined us alone. The two of us and the truck and the stars. The infinite possibilities of every new day. Not LeeAnn and Patrick, checking on us in the morning, guilting us into helping with the chores, eating dinner with us at night. Not that.

I know Jake is in love with me, and I know he wants to leave this place with me. I don't know why he wants to go somewhere that sounds like it would become even more of a trap.

And I don't know how to say any of that, or at least how to say it well. So instead, I say, "Have you talked to your dad about it?"

"Well," Jake says, clearing his throat again, shifting underneath me. "He called me a few days ago, to let me know that he'd moved. And I kind of mentioned it." I am silent, so he continues. "I didn't want to tell him about all our plans because I know that's kinda between me and you. But I mentioned us visiting, maybe for a while."

"So it would only be for a while."

"Yeah, yeah, definitely, not a permanent thing." His voice quickens like he's excited, but there's no reason for him to be. No reason at all.

"How long is a while?"

He sighs. "Oh, I don't know, Caroline, maybe a month or two, maybe—"

"And we'd stay in Kentucky after we left? Near the farm?"

"Well, assuming we got jobs, we could move out, get a place of our own—"

"Jake," I interrupt, almost without meaning to. I twist as I sit up too fast and tweak my back. "Stop."

This is the beginning of a longer sentence, one where I tell him there's no part of me that wants to be in the rural South, no part that wants to live with a man who cheated and is therefore not to be trusted, no part that wants to be in debt to another set of parents. It's an introduction to the word *insulted*, as in: *I am insulted that you would think this is good enough for me.*

But instead, I catch his eye, and the look he gives me is so painfully earnest that the words about to come out of my mouth, messy and angry, stick in my cheeks and under my tongue, and I am quiet. All that comes out is a sigh.

The way his face drops at that, how those heartfelt eyes turn down and his hands fall away from me—I'm glad I didn't say anything, because he looks so terribly sad. The anger is still resting in that sick cramping place in my stomach, but I'm thinking now I won't ever have to release it, that it will just bubble away in my sleep, because he understood what I was thinking.

"You don't want to do it," he says.

"No," I say back. Quietly.

He drops his head. I disentangle my body from his, push away to the other side of the couch so we're facing each other. He doesn't try to stop me. It's dark now, and from a little farther away, his expression is unreadable. The light of the candle dances onto his skin and off it. He's lit orange for a moment; he is devastated. The light's gone, back; he's pissed. Gone again, back again; he's at peace.

It feels as if we're sitting like that for a long time. Holding the weight between us like a wool blanket we're waiting to fold in half, but neither of us wants to be the one to step forward and kneel, gather the folded crease. The crickets and frogs whisper and gossip, and some howling thing cries out in the distance. We are utterly alone together.

Finally Jake tilts his head up and says, "Will you think about it?"

I can pretty much guarantee that it's all I'll think about for the foreseeable future, and I won't change my mind. But I say yes. Of the two words available to me in this moment, it's the one I know how to deal with most easily. How do you say no to a question like that?

He breathes out, eased perhaps a little, and reaches for me. I crawl into his arms, let my face fall into the crook of his shoulder.

"I love you," he says. I can feel the vibration of it in his chest. The words echo around like they're bouncing off water and stone.

"I love you too," I say, and I expect to feel the syllables bouncing inside me as well, like they used to, starry and joyful in my throat. But all can I hear are the hymns from the crickets. And all I can feel is Jake's heartbeat beneath his skin—steady, slight, and slow.

11

I don't sleep that night, or Sunday.

I guess that's an exaggeration. I nod off a couple times while I'm standing behind the counter on Sunday. I nap during my lunch break, a short hour curled up in Jenny's office with her back pillow tucked under my head. I doze on the couch after work while Mom makes mac and cheese and talks to my aunt Nancy on the phone.

But at night, I do not sleep. I stare at my phone, or at the old clock with the big green numbers on my bedside table. My eyes adjust to the dark. I can see every detail of the dream catcher twisting in the window, the slats on the closet door, the spines of my childhood books peeking out of the bookcase. I can see the lines of the postcards on my corkboard. None of the postcards show Kentucky. When I go to the bathroom, the light is blinding, and I squint while I wash my hands.

Will you think about it? he asks over and over again in the half-sleep state that leaves me tossing and turning. My *yes* weighs me down so I can't move my legs, my arms. I am stuck.

On Sunday night, I drag my heavy limbs out of bed and try going down to the porch. I even take a sleeping bag this time, like my mom suggested when she found me earlier this summer. But it's not a good night for porch camping. The stars aren't out. Clouds wash across the sky fast and dark, leaving sporadic glimpses of the moon.

It starts raining. One of those summer storms that leaves the air impossibly humid in the morning. I duck my head inside the sleeping back and hear rather than feel the raindrops hitting the waterproof coating. I stay in there until it gets too stuffy. When I come out, the rain hits my face in thick panels, and I'm soaked before I get inside.

All of which is to say that when I get in the shower before work on Monday morning, I am exhausted. My hair is still cold from the rain, and a mossy scent comes off it as I lather the shampoo. My skin feels too sensitive and my stomach tight, which makes sense because I haven't eaten since Saturday night. I turn up the water until it's so hot it makes my whole body turn red, and for the first moment since he said it, I forget *will you think about it?* I stand there for as long as I can before I jump out of the water stream, hissing and muttering expletives, and the sentence slides back inside me, easy as breath.

Will you think about it?

Will you think about it?

I've been thinking about it.

Work is a slow blur. When Georgia ducks in to say hey, dripping chlorine from her long ponytail, I lie and say Jenny's making me do extra admin stuff so I can't make it to lunch. Her office door is closed, so I think I'm getting away with it, but she comes out after Georgia leaves and raises an eyebrow. I don't say anything, and neither does she.

Except at noon, she beckons me into her office, says, "You look exhausted," and pulls the back pillow from her chair, offering it up to me. For the second day in a row, I spend my lunch hour sleeping on her floor. This time, her sitcoms are my lullaby.

I wake up to my phone alarm, feeling even sicker than before. My eyes are cottony and dry, and my stomach is a cavern. I start to get up and groan. Jenny turns to look at me skeptically.

"Did you have lunch?" she asks. Her laptop is playing commercials. She doesn't turn the volume down.

"I was asleep," I say, which I realize, a good three seconds later, is a stupid answer.

Jenny rolls her eyes. "Did you have dinner last night?"

I don't say anything. The right answer is yes but the real answer is no.

"But your parents feed you, right?"

"Yeah, of course," I respond, defensive.

"That's what I thought, but you never know." She scoots her swivel chair over to a filing cabinet in the corner. She pulls on a drawer—the screeching sound taps on the headache I've had for the last thirty-six hours—and removes a jar of peanut butter, a plastic knife, and a bag of tortillas. She puts a tortilla on a napkin, spreads peanut butter on it, folds it in half, and turns to me.

"Eat," she says, scooting the napkin toward me. "You'll feel better."

"I'm not hungry."

"Bullshit."

I look at the napkin, and the pain in my stomach sharpens itself into hunger. I've been this hungry before. The weekend my mom looked at me in the dressing room during school shopping last year and asked the saleslady to get the next size up. The Thursday and Friday after one of my then-friends raised her eyebrows at the cookie I was eating with lunch. But I haven't thought about food like that nearly as much this summer.

"I don't know what's going on, but you should eat something. Last chance. I love peanut butter. I'll take it if you don't."

Mom and Dad used to make me these on nights when neither of them wanted to cook. Dad called them PBQs—peanut butter quesadillas. He warmed them up in the microwave.

I take the tortilla, and Jenny turns back to her laptop, tipping her feet up on her desk. I eat it in exactly twenty small, precise bites. It tastes better than lunch with the counselors, better than family pizza night. I almost start crying.

Jenny glances at me. "Want another?"

I nod.

She scoots over to the filing cabinet again and takes out two tortillas, spreads peanut butter thickly between them. The peanut butter coats the inside of my mouth, rich and sticky.

"Listen," she says, turning to me and hiking one ankle up over the other knee, so she resembles a pretzel in denim. "I'm not your friend. I don't need to be. Nor do I want to be. I was sixteen once, and I don't need to relive that experience ever again." She looks at me almost pityingly.

"But you do have friends, right? I know you have at least the one, that counselor girl, because she's always in here distracting the customers every goddamn free moment. So, you know..." Jenny waves her hands in an exasperated sum-up motion. "Talk to her. You don't have to be miserable."

My mouth is filled with peanut butter and I don't know what to say, so I just nod. She sits and looks at me and waits for me to swallow my bite, like she's expecting something.

"I will," I say, the words awkward around my sticky tongue.

"Good." She turns back to her laptop and continues watching. I sit there with the unfinished PBQ. It appears we're done talking, but I can't be sure. She looks at me. "Lunch is over. Get back out there."

I eat the last few bites of peanut butter leaning against the back wall in the shop. I unwrap an almond chocolate bar and eat one square, hide the rest in a drawer. My belly feels tight and full around the food.

I stand there and stare out the thin sliver of window in the wall across the room while a preteen girl and her mom browse quietly. My headache ebbs into a soft pain behind my eyes. I sell the girl a notebook covered in cartoon manatees.

Outside it starts pouring, one continuous flow, like water from a pitcher.

It's been a dry summer. All the water in the air, nothing on the ground. *Good to get some rain,* my mother will say.

I've had two visions running through my head for the last two days. They are twins, connected.

The first is of me and Jake waking up at the same time in his dad's barn in Kentucky. The air is warm but not too humid, the sky a pale blue that I know will brighten into cobalt. Outside, a dog barks and a chicken clucks, and inside, a cat prowls around the edges of our mattress on the floor. We're naked and Jake snuggles closer to me, murmuring his dreams wordlessly into my ear. I'm thinking about the day, how we're going to get up in half an hour and go in the house for breakfast, fresh eggs and bacon that we'll cook ourselves while his dad and LeeAnn are out feeding the animals, and then go into town, where he works at the general store and I work at the pharmacy. Nothing has ever been so perfect.

The second looks the same at the beginning. We're lying together naked on a mattress in the barn. But in this one, Jake's arm across my chest feels like dead weight I can't shake off. I'm fully awake, staring out the window. He's still asleep, content. He talks in his sleep. He murmurs his dreams wordlessly into my ear and the sickness in my stomach is there, getting worse and worse. I hear his dad and LeeAnn having their first fight of the day as they go out to feed the chickens. The air is already stifling, and it's not even seven in the morning. Breakfast is dry toast with LeeAnn while she makes snippy conversation about when we're going to leave. We don't go into town because we don't have jobs. Jake helps out his dad, and I stay inside, shades drawn, trying to get reception on my phone.

The visions start in the morning in that loft, and as they go further into the day, they get more and more vague, until it's evening and I can't picture what's happening. What do you do, evenings in Kentucky? Watch TV? Watch Jake play video games? Smoke on the back porch? The same things I do now.

What's left by the evening in my imagination is just a feeling. It's in my chest. In the first vision, it's a good feeling. Amazing, really. Like walking outside in the spring after a week of rain and inhaling everything fresh and cool and new. It's how I felt when Jake looked at me in the grocery store that first time.

In the second vision, it's a tightness. The wind knocked out of me. A summer day so hot that when I go for a run, even a mile, I end it gasping. Accidentally taking a breath underwater. My cousin smothering me with a pillow when we played at a family reunion as children. Tight, and burning, and scary.

I'm tired of the visions. I thought I was *thinking about it* like he asked, but these looping reels aren't productive, and I am spent. My whole body hurts. I remember my mom telling me that when her grandfather lived with them when she was little, he used to complain about aching in his joints every time it was about to rain. Maybe I've inherited his pain. Or maybe it's just not sleeping or eating for two days. That could be it too.

I watch a lot of people come into the store, walk around, and leave. I don't ask if I can help them with anything, and Jenny doesn't come out to tell me I should, not like she would anyway. I sell a stuffed penguin to a woman pushing a stroller. A starfish necklace to one of a group of twelve-year-old girls, their mothers in the lobby gossiping and passing around a tin of breath mints.

The JAC kids run in and out of the activity room and the aquarium, the counselors shepherding them and texting behind their backs. I look down when they go by. I don't want Georgia to talk to me.

She does come in, though, at the very end of the day, as I'm gathering my things to leave.

"Oh my God what fucking bullshit of a Monday," she starts,

out of breath. "First, Zack shit in the pool, which, sure, he's *six*, you would think he'd have better control of his basic faculties but whatever, we all clear the fuck out. But we don't have anything else planned, so we do *drawing time*, only we ran out of the coloring pages, and the ones you sell here are preposterously overpriced—no offense—so we just hand them printer paper from the office and all these crayons, and this is what we do for an hour and a half. They were bouncing off the walls by the end of it. And so were we! And then—"

She stops, finally, and studies me. I feel too conscious of my body. For once, I didn't even think about how I looked when I walked out the door today, but I can imagine now: sallow skin, frizzy hair, the bags under my eyes big and purple. Not great.

"Are you okay?"

I look at the ground. I feel like an egg about to break. I'm afraid I'll fall down crying right here behind the counter if I meet her eyes, that if I say anything, everything will come out. And then, she'll draw back in judgment when I tell her. About the plan, the secret, the going away.

But when I open my mouth to push out some half-convincing "fine," my lips won't form the word. I am too tired in too many ways to lie to her now, when it would be so obvious, and I'm ashamed that it takes so little—just one difficult conversation and two crappy days—to break me down. But I've been keeping this from her for a long time. So I breathe in deep and try again.

"Not so good" comes out in a childish tone.

Georgia mutters, "Aw shit," and ducks her head to see the line of minivans piling up outside. She says, "Okay, hang tight. Everything's gonna be fine, okay? I just have to go out and talk to this one parent, and then I'll be right back."

Mentally, emotionally, I give myself up to her. I took care of her that night at the bowling alley. Now, I can tell her the truth, and she'll take care of me. I gather up my things as she talks to the little kid and his mom, and when they drive away, I come outside to meet her.

12

It happens at Buona Tavola, which is just three strip malls down the street from the aquarium. It turns out that some nights when I hang out with Jake, she's been coming here after work, eating dinner alone and lingering over tiramisu, to spend less time at home. "This place is a godsend," she says as we sit. "Before it opened, I used to go to the sandwich shop, and they would get mad at me for sitting around so long. You can only take so many minutes to eat a sandwich, you know? But this place isn't so successful yet, and they actually enjoy having me here. I sit in one of the window booths so it doesn't seem so empty."

I am grateful to have her talk at me, even if I have nothing to say in response. She orders for me—eggplant parmesan. Then she looks me straight in the eye—I look down—and says, "Do you wanna eat first, or...?"

I nod. While the waiter goes back into the kitchen, she talks to me, tells me about her day and its tiny disasters. There is no one else in the restaurant. The light slants in, still hot and full, and strikes the edge of our table. The air conditioning is turned up so high I'm shivering. I pull a sweater out of my bag, drape it over my knees, hug my arms tightly against my chest.

When dinner comes, we eat for a while in silence. I'm so glad Jenny gave me lunch. I'm still starving, but if I had eaten all this on an empty stomach, I would have vomited immediately. As is, it feels good. My head clears more, figuratively and literally, with every bite. After I put down my fork and take in a big long breath—half the food still on the table—Georgia puts down her fork too and says, "Okay, what's up?"

I tell her. I am not sure where to begin, and there are a few false starts. I stumble. She listens. She does me the great service of not looking right into my eyes, but down at the edge of the table, or out at the parking lot, which is good, because I can't look her in the eyes either, not even a little.

In pieces, I tell her everything. Mostly stuff we've talked about before, on the back deck with her SAT book or in my bed at night, in whispers, so my parents won't wake up. How Jake and I met, how we dated through the school year, how awful my friends were about him. How close we grew so quickly. How we wanted to be together more than anything.

Then I tell her what she doesn't know. Our deciding to leave together back in April. That all those postcards on my walls aren't really just places I want to go, they're places I want to move to, with him. September 1. I even tell her about the dreams I've had, flashes of our future life together that come in like lightning and make no sense.

Last, of course, I tell her about Saturday, the field and the cabin and the dinner and then the conversation about the barn in Kentucky. The way we lay there for so long after talking and drove home without speaking, no music or anything. How I didn't start crying until I had locked the front door and all Mom said was "Are you hurt? Did he hurt you?" and I said "No no no," even though he had, because I knew what she meant, and he hadn't done that. And how she sat with me in bed until I cried enough that I could doze, if not really sleep. How her brow furrowed, and she held me, and I let her, and the words she used to tell Dad to leave when he tried to come in to help. How, on top of everything, the guilt about my plan to leave them crept into my mind like a cat, and how I shooed it away, no room to give it the attention it deserved.

I say it all the way through as if I'm talking about the plot of a book. I am too overwhelmed to put all of this in slow motion, to examine it, dissect it. And what I feel in my whole body is something that has no words, that is too big for words, and if there are words, I don't know the right ones.

I'm no good at that, anyway. Naming things, understanding them. Georgia is.

I finish talking, ending with work and Jenny's lunch today, and I look down at the cold food, and I hope she doesn't get up and leave. She could. I think she might. Because we both know I should have told her a long time ago.

I'm waiting for the scrape of her chair against the floor and the ring of the bell over the door. But I don't hear it. Instead, there's just a long, quiet sigh. Her hand enters my field of vision. Reaching across the table, palm up.

"Caroline."

I look up at her. She doesn't seem angry. Not too angry, anyway. There's a lot in her expression, disappointment, sadness, but mostly pity. I put my hand in hers. It's small and soft and familiar.

"Are you mad at me?" I ask. I sound so stupid.

She sighs again. "I'm not mad at you, but I kind of can't believe you were going to do this."

I jerk upright. She's talking about it in the past tense, as if these were past plans. But I'm just bringing her up to speed.

"I mean," she continues, "I figured you were planning something with him. You always get so secretive when you're talking about the future. But I thought it was going to be, like, a courthouse wedding, or moving in with him. I didn't think you were actually going to leave town."

I don't know what I expected, but it wasn't this.

"I guess it's good that he came up with a plan that is so, you know, upsetting, because it'll make it way easier to just forget about—"

"Wait, no, Georgia, I'm still going."

Georgia stops mid-sentence. "What?"

"What...wait, what do you mean?" I say, caught off guard.

"He wants to move to the middle of nowhere, this has made you feel sick all weekend, you haven't eaten, you haven't slept, so obviously the only rational answer is that you're not going with him."

"Well," I stammer, "I mean, you know, it's not all settled yet. He wanted me to think about it, but I still want to go with him, just...not there."

Georgia stares at me. I am beginning to feel very uncomfortable.

"So you're going to convince him to go somewhere else with you."

"I...yeah, I guess so."

"Even though he undoubtedly has all kinds of psychological issues from his dad leaving his mom for some slut, and this is the first chance he's had since he was a little kid to spend time with his father. You're just going to convince him to...do something else? Because he loves you more than his dad."

"It's not a matter of—it's not about loving me *more*—he doesn't have *issues*. Of course you'd be upset if your dad left—"

"Yeah, I fucking would. And I'd want to go live with him on a farm, like a *real man*, and I'd want to drag my hot little girlfriend along with me, but that doesn't mean it's the best choice for *you*, Caroline. You have to think about you."

I stare at her, but she's staring back, expectant. Like she's daring me to argue. *Hot little girlfriend?*

"I, um…" I start and stop. "So you're not mad about me leaving with him, generally. You just don't think I should go with him to Kentucky?"

She props her head in one hand, the other hand poking at the tines of her fork. "I mean, listen. I don't think it would be smart to run away with him or whatever. For one thing, it would be unbelievably hurtful to your parents, who are great. But more importantly, I think even *if* you guys stayed together, you would be, you know, who the fuck knows where, with no high school degree, no chance of going to college—"

"Jake didn't go to college."

"Jake works in a grocery store. Does he want to do that forever? And he could still go to college because he'd only be one or two years late to start, and there's a decent state school right here. But he won't because he has no aspirations."

"That's not fair. You can have aspirations without going to college."

"Okay, sure, whatever, he has aspirations I'm not aware of." She presses the tines of the fork into her arm, making tiny white dots in her tan that disappear when she pulls the fork away. "So yeah, no, I think it'd be stupid to run away with him. And I think it would be even more stupid to run away to a farm in Kentucky where not only would you be basically trapped were your relationship to fail, but where you probably wouldn't even have the freedom of getting a job to fill your days. I mean, you don't own your own car.

"But mostly, Caroline?"

She puts the fork down and places both her hands outstretched on the table, reaching out to me. She looks right at me, and I try to look her in the eyes, but I can't. I focus on the bridge of her nose, the soft pale place where her sunglasses have interrupted her tan.

"Mostly, it doesn't matter what I think. It matters what you think. And the idea of doing this has seriously fucked you up. I don't know whether it's this whole Kentucky deal specifically or whether it's been building up for a while, but it's made you sick, literally. I mean, you look awful, no offense. Anything that made me feel that bad… It's like the definition of listening to your gut. You shouldn't do it."

I feel like I'm going to cry. I didn't expect to ever hear anyone else talk about my plans with Jake, much less in this way—so negatively. She's speaking aloud so many things I have thought myself, and more I haven't thought about at all. I want to defend myself, but I have no idea what to say. There is nothing to say. *I love him completely* is the only defense, and for her, I don't think it would be enough.

I do start crying, but it's like even my tear ducts are tired. They can't produce the same force or volume I have demanded of them this weekend, so it's just pathetic little rivulets. I don't put my hands in Georgia's. I pull twenty dollars out of my purse and put it on the table.

"I want to go home now," I say, and my voice is very small. There's a long pause. Georgia pulls her hands back into her lap.

"Okay," she says, and she leaves my money on the table and goes up to the register and pays for the meal. We go to her car, and all the way home we don't say anything at all.

The next few days pass in a fog, slowly and quickly at the same time. I eat lunch in Jenny's office and watch TV with her. I go home to my parents and eat Mom's rice-chicken-vegetable meals. She and Dad say they're happy to have me home when I'd usually be at Jake's, and they ask me if everything's okay. I tell them it is. I can tell they don't believe me, but they don't press it. We do puzzles and watch television together after supper.

I avoid talking to Jake, which is hard, and to Georgia, which is easy, because she's still mad. When Jake texts, I don't respond. When he calls, I lie and tell him I'm sick. I don't think he believes me, but I don't have the energy to say anything else, and neither of us wants to have this conversation over the phone. I leave work fifteen minutes early every day, hopping in the car as soon as my dad pulls up, so Jake can't surprise me after his shift. On Wednesday, he comes in looking for me, and I see him before he sees me. I hide in Jenny's office, and she covers for me, tells him I'm home with a cold.

On Thursday, I spend my lunch break in the aquarium's jellyfish room. I sit in a corner between the glass and the wall to the next room. When I lean my head against the glass and squint my eyes, it feels almost as if I'm inside the tank. For an hour, while my phone lights up with Jake's texts, I watch the jellies propel themselves through the water. The skinny threads inside their translucent bodies pulse and shimmer. They move with no purpose and no destination. When I go back to the store, it's like waking up from a fever dream.

By Friday, the fog has cleared enough that I know I have to do something. I have also returned to myself enough to feel the slightest bit guilty that I have taken up Jenny's food and space this entire week without giving her anything in return. I'm not sure if she wants to talk to me, but I should at least try to get to know her. That afternoon, sitting in her office and eating a salad—having finally gotten my shit together enough to remember the food my mom packs for me—I look at her eating her sandwich and wonder what to say.

She glances away from the laptop. "What?" she says. "Stop looking at me. It's creepy."

"Sorry," I say.

We eat in silence until the next commercial break.

"Why were you so upset after the Fourth of July weekend?" I ask. Immediately, I regret it. I could have asked her so many more innocuous questions. What her favorite TV show is, how long she's been working here, whether she has any hobbies. But this was the first thing that came to mind.

She rolls her eyes. "Seriously?" she asks. I shrug. "I was mad because I had to work while all my best friends went to the beach, like we do every year for the past eight years. Because *you*"—she points a carrot stick at me—"had to have the weekend off, I missed my annual vacation."

I shrink into my seat. "Sorry," I say again. There are a few minutes of silence in which I try to figure out a way to make this better, just in case I have to eat lunch in her office every day for the rest of the summer.

"I don't know if this makes it better," I say tentatively, "but my mom made me take the time off. We have a big family party. But it always really sucks." I remember the light of the sparklers and the warmth in my belly, Georgia's hair frizzy and wild against the night sky, and I feel the slippery, sinking guilt of our fight alongside the lesser and lighter guilt of this lie. But I plow ahead. "My boyfriend and his friends went to the beach too. That's what I wanted to do."

She raises her eyebrows.

"So we both missed our beach trips," I conclude weakly.

"Well, you missed a weekend with your boyfriend who you see every day. I missed a reunion with my four closest friends from college who I see once a year. But sure, we both had equally shitty weekends." She sighs and seems to deflate slightly. I am pretty sure at this point I've ruined any chance of a good relationship with my boss, but then she starts talking again.

"No, it's fine. It really is. I've been mad at you for taking off that weekend since you started here. But it turns out where my friends were, it rained the whole time, and Brittany got food poisoning, and Allison couldn't drink because she's still breastfeeding her son. Apparently it was the worst Fourth ever. And anyway, it would've been sort of weird and shitty to hear about everything happening in their lives while I'm still stuck working here."

"Is that bad?" I ask, feeling foolish yet again, but not knowing the answer to the question.

"Yes. No," she says, more uncertain than I'm used to seeing her. Then, she amends, "Well, it's bad, but it's unavoidable."

I look at her, not sure about the right question to ask. She exhales heavily.

"After college," she explains, "I moved to Atlanta with these same friends. I worked as an accountant for this big law firm for a while. Then my mom got sick. My dad passed away a long time ago, and between me and my brother, one of us had to come back here. It ended up being me." She says it simply, without malice or sadness. "The doctors said she had six months. After a few months of me hanging around all day, she told me to get a job. Something I could leave in the middle of the day if she really needed me, something I could quit easily after she died, so I could get back to my life. But that was two years ago. She's not better, but she's not worse either." She shrugs. "So I'm still here. Lucky in some ways. Unlucky in others."

Silence hangs between us for a minute, not wholly uncomfortable.

"I'm sorry," I say. "I'm really sorry."

"It is what it is," she says. "I look forward to the beach because it's the one time I get away from..." She waves her hands abstractly. "All of this. But because I stayed this year, we saved money on a nurse for my mom. And besides, next year, I'll definitely force whatever poor shmuck is in your position to work that weekend, so I only missed the one."

She casts a sideways glance at me. "I did eat your chocolate bar, though," she says.

"I knew it," I say under my breath.

She laughs, and I laugh, and the characters in the TV show start laughing at some silly joke, and for a moment the tiny office seems like a bright little haven.

Twenty minutes later, as I'm going back to work, she stops me on the way out the door.

"Look," she says. "I don't know what's going on in your life, and you don't have to tell me because I told you about my mom. But I'm pretty sure there's no excuse to be moping around like you've been. Tomorrow, you eat lunch with your friends."

"They're not really my—"

"Bullshit," she cuts me off smoothly. "Go spend the hour with them. I like you just fine, but if you try to come in here, I'll lock the door on you."

"Yes, ma'am."

"And say a goddamn hello to the customers. Ask them if you can help with anything. I'm pretty sure your sad face has been scaring them off this week. We understand each other?"

"Yes, ma'am."

"Great. Get outta here."

As I turn the sign in the window back to OPEN and remove the cutesy clock ("Back under the sea at 2:00!"), her door slams behind me, and my phone buzzes in my pocket. It's Jake: *can I see you, pls? I really wanna talk.*

Jenny is right. It's time. *That sounds good*, I type back. **Pick me up at 6?**

He responds instantly. *for sure*, he says. *I missed you.*

The rest of the day is easier than any single hour of the past week. I've made my choice. I am calm. I feel a flicker of panic when I see Georgia crossing the atrium alone, carrying some papers to the office from the activity room. She usually drops by the store to talk when she's on these errands, to procrastinate a little before facing Jamal's unsmiling face. But today, like all week, she doesn't even turn my way.

It is easier this way—better. We'll make up soon. Or we won't. But it doesn't matter much either way, because I'll be gone in a little over a month.

Maybe the sickness came from doubting myself. We've planned for so many weeks that it's not a choice at all at this point. I made the promise a long time ago.

Jake is nervous when he picks me up. I can tell by the way he rubs the back of his hand on the stubble on his chin, how he plucks at his shirt. But he's trying to be normal. He says some stuff about his day, and it sounds forced, but it's better than silence. I missed hearing his voice. The scratch in it. When I put my hand on his leg, it's such an enormous relief to feel the warmth of his body that I have to resist the urge to kiss him right there, while he's driving.

He asks me about my day and doesn't even mention that we haven't talked all week, so I tell him about today, with some editing. A woman came in with the chubbiest baby I've ever seen, and I tell him about that. He laughs and automatically, a joke about our future baby comes up from my throat. I swallow it. I don't want to ruin the moment, unnatural though it is.

He takes me to his house. None of his roommates are there, but we still go out to the porch. That's when we stop talking.

He lights a cigarette, fumbles with the lighter. Everything seems loud in the absence of his voice. The click of the flame, his even inward breath on the cigarette, the shush of my legs uncrossing and re-crossing while I wait. As one minute passes, then two, then three, and he lights another cigarette, I realize I will have to be the first to speak.

"I…" My voice cracks and I clear my throat. "I want to go to Kentucky with you."

He turns toward me, and that moment, the moment when our eyes connect, is the happiest I've ever seen him. I think it's the happiest I've ever seen anyone.

"Really?"

"Really."

"Oh, my God, Caroline, oh my God, I don't…shit, really?"

"Really," I say, and I start laughing, because he is so happy. He puts his head in his hands, and then he turns his whole body toward me to give me a huge messy hug across our chairs, and he is grabbing at me, so I climb over to him and sit in his lap and kiss him for a good long time.

When we pull back, I say, "Just, I want to make sure…" Fear comes into his eyes, and I quickly continue. "You know, that this is temporary. While we get on our feet. We can still live somewhere else later. Move around. After a few months or something. Right?"

He relaxes and laughs. "Absolutely. After a few months, whenever. Whatever works." He takes my face in his hands and says to me, "We are going to have such an amazing life together."

I lean back in to kiss him and let those words sit where they fell on the sweat-dampened skin of my chest, willing them to stay there forever like a tattoo, trying, so hard, to believe him.

13

Summer days feel so long. The heat is waiting for me when I walk out the door with my dad in the morning, and it's there at night when I come home. The sunlight is there too, even and white until it finally fades to orange and falls into darkness when I'm not looking.

You would think with the days so long, the nights would feel shorter. But they have a weight and depth to them that isn't there the rest of the year. So hot and humid that when I open my window, the room doesn't get cooler. It just equals out to the rest of the world: a warm, wet blue.

The city finally fixed the streetlights in my neighborhood. I had gotten used to sleeping in darkness, startling when headlights slipped by. Now it is hard to sleep. I keep waking up thinking my blankets are a maze, and pulling my body out to go to the bathroom—or downstairs to watch TV, or outside on the porch—is the hardest thing in the world.

It's still July. Home doesn't want to let me go. It's keeping me here and awake.

The night Jake and I talked, after he took me home, I couldn't sleep. I turned on the lights in my room and looked at my bulletin board. I let myself skip from picture to picture, future story to story, accepting one by one that they were no longer options.

I had no postcards of rural Kentucky. It hadn't even been on my radar. The closest was one from Nashville, a cheesy picture of downtown. I pinned it in the center and squinted as if by doing so, I could see past the buildings and into the country that lay beyond.

But I kept coming back to one picture, pinned on the bottom like an afterthought. Georgia had found a disposable camera back at the beginning of camp, put it in the lost and found, and asked all the kids if it was theirs—but none of them wanted it. Whoever brought it had probably forgotten, and after all, who uses film cameras anymore? A nostalgic parent, a child who didn't understand how you could take a picture and not immediately see it. After a while, Georgia took it and started keeping it in her purse or pocket, taking pictures at random times.

Most of the photographs are pretty bad, with no sense of color or composition, and this one is no exception. It's a selfie of her and me, a crooked scene with her on the right. We're lying on the cement one day at lunch. Our heads are touching slightly, and our hair is loose, tangled together. She's got a huge grin, mouth open as if she's about to say something exciting, and she's looking right at the camera. I'm smiling next to her, calmer, eyes closed.

It's blurry and oversaturated and not the best angle for either of us, but we look so happy. Best friends on a summer afternoon.

Jake and I spent that weekend together after we talked, and all Monday morning, Jake and I text about Kentucky. He sends me a picture his dad sent him, of this gorgeous field with a forest in the distance, and of the barn, which is smaller than I imagined and more of a shed, but the choice is made. In between, I think about lunch.

Jenny won't let me stay in the store, and I haven't brought a lunch, having snoozed through my mom's offer to make me a salad and failed to grab anything myself. My choices are to sit alone outside on the curb and eat nothing, texting with Jake whenever he gets a free moment, which would be okay. Or I could walk a mile to the deli down the street and pay eight dollars for a shitty sandwich, which would also be fine.

But both choices sound exhausting. I am exhausted with exhaustion. It would be so easy to go out to the back patio and slowly eat a slice of pizza, making it last for a half hour, and lie down next to Georgia.

Fighting with her, though, would be the most exhausting thing of all. And as she jogs through the atrium practically carrying a groggy latecomer four-year-old, she glances at me only once.

So it's the curb. I walk outside and sit near the slowly wilting flowers and pick apart a leaf while I wait for Jake to text me back. I am fully prepared to spend the entire lunchtime sitting there. But after about five minutes, a shadow falls over me, and I look up, squinting into the sun until the shape moves and blocks the light. It comes into focus.

"Are you fucking kidding me?" Jenny says. "You're the biggest mope. Go eat with your friends. This is the saddest thing I've ever seen."

"I think Georgia's mad at me," I say, the words sounding childish as soon as they come out. I shred the leaf between my fingernails.

"Well, work it out. That's what adults do. Come on, get up, go." She nudges me with her foot, and I look at my phone. Jake still hasn't texted me back.

"Yes, ma'am," I say, and she shakes her head as she reaches out a hand to help me up. I take it, and she pulls me upright, surprisingly strong.

She watches me as I walk back into the atrium, the air conditioning hitting me like a sudden gust of wind. I glance back at her, still standing there squinting into the sun, as I walk through the door to the back hallway. The hallway seems longer than ever, silent but for the air conditioning buzz.

When I come out, the sun is blinding, and the air smells like pizza grease and cement. Toby turns at the sound of the door and grins.

"Hey, it's Caroline! The triumphal return! She's been gone for weeks!"

"Barely a single week," I say, breaking into a smile despite myself.

A whoop arises from the gathered group, lounging in various states of undress on the ground. Toby gets up and claps me on the back. Matt throws a balled-up napkin at me, missing by a mile. Even Serena looks up from her book. She tilts her head down to look at me over her sunglasses, nods and smiles briefly, and returns to form. Everyone's happy to see me.

Except Georgia. She doesn't even look at me. She's hunched over the SAT book, sitting cross-legged with her hair in a messy topknot. As the others fire a loose barrage of questions at me—mostly asking where I was and suggesting that Jenny might have tied me up in her office as punishment for some imagined infraction—she continues to stare down at the book.

She's not really studying. When she's focused, she scratches her pencil against the back of her neck and furrows her brow. Sometimes at the end of a really long SAT session, her neck is practically silver from pencil lead. I can't stand it. I think about lead poisoning, even though she's told me over and over that pencil lead isn't the same as the dangerous stuff.

There's no lead on the back of her neck. She's not even holding her pencil.

I stand around and listen to Toby and Matt joke for a while, and eventually, their shallow river of words passes over me and Jenny and on to Melinda, the administrative assistant who we never see, except—as they tell me—she's intensely pregnant, and they've started a pool to bet on when she's gonna have her kid.

They talk and they talk and they talk, and Georgia stares at the cement through the hundreds of thin pages. I am not sure how to approach her at first, but after a few minutes, I walk over and sit next to her. I can see her eyes barely flick toward me and return to her book. It feels like everyone should be quiet for this dramatic moment, but no one looks at us; no one cares.

I put my hand on her knee, and she tilts her head toward me, eyes still pointing down. Her skin is warm and soft from the sun, coated in a thin dark layer of fuzz. She doesn't shave as much as I'd think she would for someone whose legs are bare all the time.

"I'm sorry," I say.

I'm not sure what I'm apologizing for—keeping the secret for so long, or not coming to talk to her before, or compromising with Jake when she thought I shouldn't. Not that I've told her yet.

"I'm going to Kentucky," I say. There's a long pause.

"I know," she says. "I just…I think it's a mistake. I'm not judging you. But I really, really don't think you should go."

I take a deep breath, feeling off balance. I open my mouth to argue, but there's no point. Instead, I say, "I know."

"Okay," she says.

"Okay."

We sit there like that for a long time, my hand on her leg, her chin tucked into her chest, strands of hair clinging to the sweat on her cheeks.

"I'm really sorry, Georgia," I say again.

She puts her hand on top of mine and says, "Me too."

I don't know what she's sorry for either: blowing up at me at the restaurant, or not coming to talk to me before, or believing what she does about my life and my boyfriend. But I turn my hand over, and we fold our fingers together. She pushes aside her SAT book and lies down, pulling me with her, and just like that we're back as we were in the picture: heads touching at the side, eyes closed, squinting into the sun, together.

Plans are starting to come together. The process of deciding specifics gives a new dimension to my conversations with Jake. This week, on the nights I spend with him, we sit on the porch for hours talking details. How much money we have, how long the drive is, what kinds of jobs there are in the small town near the farm.

Jake and his dad talk on the phone every day now, though from what he tells me, I gather the conversations are still short. He's started calling it "our farm."

Despite all that, I can't get a clear picture of what our lives will be. I can't fit the pieces into a whole. He says his dad talks about the horses on the farm next door. I say, does our farm have horses? Jake says it might. He says his dad talks about the sunset over the fields. I ask what kind of crops there are, if it's a functional farm or simply a big plot of land. Jake doesn't hear me. He's talking about the path his dad is building down to the river, how he wakes up in the morning and hacks at trees, and how he wants Jake to help.

The mosquitoes get in through holes in the porch screen as Jake talks, and I listen. I ask questions, and he kisses me and doesn't answer. I rub aloe on my bites. When the mosquitos come back, they get caught in the aloe and I hit them, leaving a red mark on my sticky greenish legs.

We don't have sex as much as usual. On Tuesday, I climb on top of him while he's talking and straddle him in the flimsy plastic chair. Sometimes, when I can't listen to the thirteenth recounting of a conversation with his dad, I look at his body, let my eyes linger on him for a long time, all up and down, and good God, he is so hot. The lean line of his chest down to his legs and the muscles in his calves. Looking at him makes me remember why we're leaving.

"I want you," I whisper. I kiss his neck.

He gently pushes me back, hands on my shoulders. "Baby, we have so much to go over, there's no time. Dad says there's a coffee shop and a hardware store hiring. I feel like I'd be a good fit at the hardware store, right? I mean, I've spent tons of time pushing carts around at the grocery store, it can't be that different." I must look disappointed, because he laughs and says, "Okay, down, girl, we'll do it. But later, not now."

I dismount, my limbs awkward, while he gestures like an orchestra conductor about the pros and cons of this job versus that one. When we do have sex at ten, his roommates are home, and I can hear them laughing at some stupid action movie through the walls. My heart isn't in it. It's quick and hurts a little and I don't even pretend to come.

Driving me home, Jake turns on the radio, and it's my favorite song. He turns it up and rubs my leg, smiles, tells me he loves me.

It feels like a fist stretched out, offering a gift as a surprise, but inside the hand there's nothing. Or less than nothing. Something worthless, like a slip of paper from a fortune cookie.

Everything is becoming more real. Jake knows how many days are left now; he texts it to me every morning with a smile and a heart. When I said yes, it made something shift inside him, and so it shifted inside us.

It's more than us who are different. Georgia knows too, and though I was worried about telling her, it turns out to be an immeasurable relief. She comes over to my house on Wednesday, like usual. Except unlike usual, I just talk. I don't think she says six words from when she picks me up at the aquarium until dinner. I talk and talk and talk, first out on the porch and then inside when it gets too hot, checking over my shoulder every few minutes in case Mom got home from her tennis date too early.

I thought I told her everything before, but there is so much still to tell. Months and months of planning and conversations, and all the times I wouldn't go to the movies with her unless my parents would give me ten dollars for a ticket. The reason I don't like the SAT books, and why I haven't talked about college at the dinner table.

We sit on my bed as the sun melts into the horizon. She hugs her legs while I tell her about all the places I wanted to go and why. She takes the postcards as I hand them to her and inspects them closely, then pins them back on the board. By the end, she has organized them into a neat grid. Pictures of my family and my old friends from school and Georgia are on the right and left, postcards from other places and pictures of Jake are at the top and bottom. In the middle, there's a hole.

"What goes there?" I ask, even though I know the answer.

"Kentucky," she says. She looks down at her feet. "If you're still sure."

Mom calls us down to dinner.

Meat loaf, broccoli, pasta. Mom beat her tennis partner so bad that the woman wanted to play another couple matches to make it best of five, then best of seven, which is why dinner is late. Dad has a new coworker who keeps messing up his code. From Georgia, we hear about the latest installment of the ongoing saga of her young admirer. Today, he gave her a cookie from his lunch. My parents love these stories. I manage a weak contribution about a ten-year-old girl who, after almost an hour of browsing, chose the most terrifying thing in the store—the stuffed octopus.

Then my mom, slyly, in between bites of broccoli says, "You know, we're almost at September, and all the books say that's when you should really start your college applications."

I roll my eyes, but my stomach drops.

"Just one Common App essay, Caroline," Mom pleads. I shrug and shove more food into my mouth. She sighs and turns. "Georgia? Are you sure you can't convince her?"

Georgia looks at me a beat too long, and for a moment I'm terrified that I have underestimated her anger, that she's not over it or sorry at all, and that I'm screwed.

She combs her fingers through her hair and says, "Sorry, Ms. Weaver. Not gonna happen."

Mom sighs and regroups. "Well, Georgia, honey, have you narrowed it down any further?"

Georgia nods. "I'm thinking I don't really need to apply to *all* the Ivies, so if I limit those to only four or five, I'm down to like sixteen total. Obviously there's Stanford too, and I've been having trouble choosing my safeties, but I think…"

Mom props her head in her hand, distracted, bringing a forkful of pasta slowly to her mouth. Dad pats me on the shoulder in an awkward attempt to comfort me, I suppose, for not having made up my mind about this, apparently the most important decision of my life. And it is comforting, but not for the reasons he thinks.

Georgia sits there, talking, feeding my mom all the beautifully laid-out future plans she wants. I am lucky she's not a vengeful girl, because God, she really could have fucked me over.

The next day at work, I use Jenny's computer and the twitchy office printer to print out one of the photos of Kentucky that Jake sent me. It's the prettiest one, featuring the fields with the sun starting to set behind the trees in the distance. It's hard to visualize where the house and the barn are. The one picture of the barn is from far away, and it looks less than idyllic.

So I print the one of the fields, and I cut it out with a sticky pair of scissors in the cramped administrative office. Melinda looks at me with vague suspicion as she trundles in to get a box of highlighters. I feel somehow guilty, as if she knows what I'm planning and could tell someone. Like she can see into the picture to discover where it came from. She leaves, though, and I glue the printed paper onto an index card and go back out to lunch.

That night, sitting in my room with Georgia while she watches TV on my laptop, I pin the picture in the middle of the corkboard, right in the space Georgia left for it yesterday. I look down, but she's absorbed in her show.

"How does it look?" I ask her, kneeling on the bed and craning my neck back to see her reaction.

She looks up, but doesn't answer immediately. Her face moves in small, incomprehensible ways. "Why didn't you put up the one of the barn?" she asks after several long moments.

"It wasn't as nice a picture, I guess."

"I thought it was nice."

I sigh and look at the picture in the middle. On the printer paper, its pale matte surface looks dull next to the glossy landscapes of the postcards and prints all around it. I wish I'd gone to the drugstore to print it, like I did the others, but I wanted to get it up there as fast as possible. "The barn just looked so *small*. And…falling apart."

She gives me a look, and I moan and fall into my pillow. "Jake says he's gonna fix it up," I say into the stuffing. "The sunset was prettier. That's all."

I feel Georgia flop onto the bed with me and nestle into my side. I turn my head to the wall, away from her.

"Listen," she says, "I won't mention it again if you don't want me to. I promise I'll never say anything about it ever again, seriously. And I know my personal…" She pauses. "…ideas about this whole situation probably make me prejudiced. But it's not about what I think. You don't seem happy. You don't seem like you actually want to go."

"I really do want to go," I say. "I'm really excited about it." But even I can hear I'm not convincing. It sounds hollow and sickly and thin. All the emotion behind those words is somewhere else, outside in the night, belonging to some other girl.

Georgia doesn't say anything. The weight of her in the bed is a comfort and a pressure, both.

I roll over to face her. My face is so close to hers that I can only focus on one part of it at a time: Right eye. Left eye. Nose. Lips. Like a modernist painting, I try to look at her fully and I get cross-eyed. And like when my history teacher called on me to ask me the meaning of the painting, I don't know what to say.

"I'll stop talking about it," she whispers. Her breath blows warm across my chin.

"It's complicated," I say. Again, God, the words feel weak coming out, not nearly enough to cover everything I want to say. "I have to go. I promised."

"People break promises," she says. So quiet, so warm.

"Not this one," I say, and because I cannot stand to hear what she might say in return, I turn away again. The bottom row of pictures line up with my eyes. Texas. Massachusetts. California. Orange desert, red brick, blue ocean. The colors blur together in a messy watercolor. I don't want to cry right now.

Georgia wraps her arm around my waist and snuggles into me. Her bare prickly legs tuck into mine, and the curves and lines of her body follow the curves and lines of my body, and even though she is at least three inches shorter than me, she feels protective—almost as protective as Jake does. Unlike Jake, though, she doesn't grab at my boobs or nudge a hard-on into my ass or whisper into my ear, all things that are nice sometimes, but that he does all the time when we're in this position.

She just lies there and holds me, and she doesn't say anything.

I focus on breathing in and out. When my breath gets even and my eyes dry up, still she stays and still she says nothing.

I'm waiting for her to respond, because I know how she feels. A part of me wants her to say again that I can break this promise, I can break any promise, I don't have to go, but she is good enough to stay quiet.

She stays quiet long enough that I think I fall asleep, and when my mother cracks open the door and says, "Georgia, it's ten, time to go," she turns off the lights when she gets up. I think I remember reaching for her after she's gone, trying to find her and finding only her body's imprint in the mattress, making a noise halfway between a whine and a cry. But I don't know for sure. I was long unconscious by then.

AUGUST

On August first, Georgia stops by the store in between errands at 9:15, just after I've arrived. We haven't even opened yet, but I unlock the door for her. She jogs in place while she stands in front of me, hand up.

"High five," she says, out of breath.

I give her one. "And, uh...why?"

"Do I really need a reason?" She winks at me.

"No one pissed in the pool this morning?"

"Better." She starts jogging backward, ponytail swinging behind her. "Birthday month, baby!" She grins extra big and then turns, dashing out the door.

I honestly haven't even thought about my birthday. The

month of August is significant because it is the last month I'll spend here, not because I'm turning seventeen.

But even in a normal August, I wouldn't be as excited as Georgia is. Birthdays have never been big in my house. We have cake and ice cream, my parents give me a couple gifts, and maybe we go to a movie, but that's about it. It comes with having a summer birthday, I guess. August 20 is right before we go back to school, so my friends are usually busy—on last-hurrah summer vacations with their parents or spending time with camp friends who will soon return to their normal lives.

Besides, the beginning of the year is when friend groups break up and new groups form. Having a big party right before that happens, when everyone knows it's coming… Ever since I was in middle school, it seemed awkward. It's easier not to bother.

Georgia's birthday is a week before mine, August 13, and she's told me this before, but I keep forgetting. It matters to her, though, and I have to remember that. We had a conversation about it in June. She asked me what I usually did for my birthday. I told her nothing much. She was shocked.

"Birthdays are the most important," she said, as if it were a fact. "My parents don't give a single fuck about Christmas or Easter or the Fourth or even Thanksgiving, really, but birthdays they go all out."

"That's weird. Especially since your parents are not, like…"

"The most affectionate?" she finished. She rolled her eyes. "True. But..."

"They do love you, obviously," I said quickly. "They just expect a lot out of you."

"Right," she said, "exactly. And they always frame birthdays as this celebration of everything I've achieved in a year, which is pretty great." She was smiling bigger and bigger as she talked. "Anyway, I can't fucking wait. It's gonna be great. And listen, I'm sorry, but as your friend, I'm going to make your birthday a time to remember."

I laughed. "Well, shit, I guess I'll do the same for you."

"That's what I like to hear."

Needless to say, I haven't come up with anything. With all my thoughts occupied by leaving with Jake, I forgot about her birthday as thoroughly as I forgot about mine. I spend the rest of the morning wondering how big she means when she says birthdays are big, and subsequently, how much I have to plan. I don't know any of her friends from school. She mentions them sometimes, but only in passing, and I know she's said most of them will be out of town on her birthday. Normally, I'd think her house was off-limits since it was so awkward the last time I came over, but if her parents are really into birthdays, maybe...

It's a welcome distraction from the minutiae of Kentucky. Jake debates those details endlessly, and they pile on top of me like snowflakes, each one light on its own, gathering into a drift so heavy it's hard to escape. There are too many to keep track of. So it's kind of nice to wonder what kind of cake Georgia likes best and consider a guest list. A birthday party can only have so many specifics.

I spend that morning doodling pictures of cakes and pondering what I should get Georgia as a gift. It will be the first gift I've given her in the course of our friendship, and somehow it feels critical to get the right thing. Between the cold of the AC in the store and wanting to talk to her about birthdays, I am counting down the minutes until lunch.

At 12:50, with no customers having come in for at least an hour, I glance at Jenny's closed door and decide it's a day to cut out early. I practically run down the hallway leading to the patio.

I'm about to push the door open when I hear a female voice outside yell, "For fuck's sake, Toby!" I pause, my hand on the push-bar. It takes me a moment to recognize the voice because I've heard it so few times. For a moment, I think it's one of Toby's exes come to visit. But I do know this voice. It's Serena.

I should leave. But the others will be here soon, and would it be better for one of them to walk in on this argument? So, I should go outside. But God, I don't want to get in the middle of a fight, sitting there awkwardly until everyone else arrives. I stay where I am, trying to decide, and also, to my own shame, leaning closer to the crack in the door.

"Serena," I hear Toby say, "calm down, you're being completely unreasonable. I'm sorry if you're upset, but—"

"But what?" Serena shrieks. "But fucking what, asshole? You tell me you want to get back together, and then I see you out with some other girl? Practically fucking her?"

"I would not say we were—"

"Fine! Kissing! Whatever!"

"Technically, I never said I wanted to be exclusive, so—"

"Are you fucking kidding me?" If anything, it seems like Serena is only getting angrier. I know I should back away, but the worst, most gossipy part of me wants to hear the end. I knew that Serena and Toby had dated, but since they always seemed to tolerate each other easily, I'd assumed it was pretty casual. Apparently, I'd been wrong.

"Why are you even still here?" Serena says, her voice low now and furious. I have to strain to hear her. "You're almost twenty years old. You've been working here since graduation. You're not doing anything with your life. All your friends are in high school. It's pitiful. It's fucking creepy."

Silence from Toby for a moment.

"You know I didn't get into—" he starts.

"Oh, seriously?" Serena interrupts, the volume rising again. "So your first choice rejected you. Big deal. You got into other colleges. You could've gone to one of those places. Or you could've taken a year off and applied again. But instead, you just fucking stayed here. At your high school job. You have the power to overcome that inertia, you know. You choose not to."

Silence from Toby.

"You know what?" Serena continues, "The first time I brought you home, Helen told me she thought you were weird and she didn't like you. I thought she was jealous of how much time I was spending with you. But she was right. And she's nine! My nine-year-old sister is more trustworthy than you."

More silence.

"Nothing? Okay. I'm done."

I hear footsteps marching toward the door and finally break out of the trance I've fallen into. I duck into the bathroom a few yards down the hall, the door closing just as I hear the door to the patio opening. I set my lunch on the counter and start washing my hands, hoping Serena won't come in.

But she does, of course, her omnipresent sunglasses pushed back on her head and face splotchy and red from crying. She turns away quickly as she sees me and goes into a stall.

I turn off the sink and dry my hands. "Are you okay?" I ask into the silent bathroom.

"Fine" comes her response from the stall. I stand there for a moment longer, but I don't know her well enough to help, so I step outside. Just then, like the sun coming out after a rainy day, I see Georgia and the rest of the counselors making their way down the hall, laughing.

"Caroline!" Georgia yells. "One of the kids finger-painted Matt's face! His whole face!"

Matt walks behind her, grumbling, and though he's tried to wash it off, there is a distinct blue and green streak down the middle of his forehead, nose, and cheeks.

"That kid's on my shit list," he says. "I thought I could teach them something about art. But no. This is what I get for trying to spread my talents."

"It's a gift," Georgia says, elbowing him. She grabs my hand, swinging it as she pushes open the door. "God, I'm so hungry."

I look around quickly for Toby, but he's not there. The usual stack of pizza boxes sit in the middle of the patio, unopened and waiting.

"Huh," Georgia says, her brow furrowed. "I wonder what happened to Toby. He was getting the pizzas today."

"Don't ask," I murmur.

"Wait, what?"

"I'll tell you later," I say to her.

Dave, Devin, and Matt don't even seem to notice his absence, so focused are they on defending the paint job and making fun of it, respectively. Serena slips through the door, her sunglasses hiding her eyes, but her cheeks slightly redder and puffier than normal. She takes off her T-shirt and lies on the ground with her book, like she always does, but this time, she faces away from the group.

Georgia nudges me. "What's up?" she whispers.

"I almost walked in on Toby and Serena having a huge fight," I say to her in a low voice. "She was yelling at him about cheating on her. And about the fact that he's almost two decades old and all his friends are in high school."

Georgia blinks. "Shit," she says. "Wow. I mean, she's not wrong. But at the same time..."

"He's Toby," I finish.

"Exactly. He's Toby. He's just around, all the time. But I told you he was a cheater, remember. I'm not surprised about that at all. I'm just surprised she puts up with him. That she even has any time to put up with him."

"What do you mean?"

"Well, her parents have been divorced for ages now, and her dad married this woman who was way, way younger than him, and they had twins, and Serena takes care of them all the time. Her stepmom works weird hours, so she's basically responsible for them after school. Or camp, I guess, in the summer. They don't go here, though—they're too old."

As we're talking, Toby walks back from around the corner of the building, his stride as brisk and cheerful as it's ever been. I try hard not to stare. I can see Serena looking up, but she doesn't leave, simply turns back to her book and brushes her long hair over the side of her face. Toby doesn't even glance at her as he sits next to Matt, Dave, and Devin.

"How do you know all this?" I ask Georgia. I had no idea.

"Well, her dad works with my dad, which is how I know the stuff about the divorce and also why he can't take care of his own kids like a responsible adult. And plus, Serena and I are the only two girls at JAC, so we talk a fair amount. She's pretty private, but you can't help but learn a little about someone when you talk to them every day."

Georgia lies down, apparently thinking over the new information, and I follow her lead. I never thought of Serena as a person with any depth at all. I am so lost in thought that I don't catch any of the chatter among the guys, so I am startled when Toby yells, "Shut the fuck up, y'all." Georgia and I raise our heads.

"Friends," he says. "The boys and I have been discussing something. Georgia, Serena, I believe you've been privy to the earlier portions of this discussion. It is in regards to the end-of-summer Great Adventures trip, and as I believe everyone understands, it is utterly unprecedented." He's looking around the group like a prosecutor at a jury. Serena is still facing away from him, but she's turned her head to listen. "Great Adventures has always been of an egalitarian nature. For the people, by the people, et cetera. And what we're proposing is to make it a birthday party, a joint birthday party."

"Yes!" Georgia yells, sitting straight up. "I told you this was a great idea months ago!"

"And I do not think," he continues, raising his voice, "that we would commit to this, this crack in the great wall of tradition, were it not to honor two of the most high-quality ladies in the area. Georgia and Caroline, after great pains and hours of deliberation, we offer you this rare opportunity: the chance to celebrate your birthday, with us, as the guests of honor at the end-of-summer Great Adventures trip."

"Yes, yes, yes," Georgia says, bouncing up and down on her heels.

"What are we talking about again?" I ask.

"Go with it, Caroline." He extends a hand to each of us. "Do you accept?"

"Uh, sure," I say. I put my hand in his. It's large and damp.

"Obviously," Georgia says. She's way more enthusiastic, grinning ear to ear and bouncing in place. Only a few minutes ago, we were talking about what a shithead Toby was, and she appears to have forgotten all about it. But I get it. His excitement and charisma are infectious.

"We have a deal," Toby announces. He raises our hands as if we're two prizefighters who have somehow both won the match. "Caroline. Georgia. Great Adventures. August 30. The greatest, grandest, most historically significant end-of-summer aquarium party I will have ever organized or experienced."

The group cheers—except for Serena, who totally ignores us and turns back to her book. Georgia cheers loudest of all, throwing an arm around me and squeezing. "I am so fucking excited," she says to no one in particular, and Matt nods.

"Gonna be excellent," he says. "It was fuckin' great last year, and we didn't even have anything to celebrate except not having to work anymore."

They keep talking like that, going over the rides at the park, the carpooling situation, and the history of the event—which I forgot existed, although now that I'm thinking of it, I have heard them mention it.

I'm torn. As I listen, Georgia chiming in with questions and requests—who's driving, if they'll be able to smuggle in booze, a nonnegotiable demand for soft-serve ice-cream cones dipped in chocolate—it does sound pretty great. The last time I went to an amusement park with friends, I was eleven. It was also for a friend's birthday party. I remember it was a Saturday in May, and even though I was too scared to go on the roller coasters, I still had the time of my life, getting dizzy on the Tilt-a-Whirl and eating mountains of junk food. I didn't stop talking about it for the rest of the summer. I loved it so much that I begged my parents to take me back for my birthday, and they did. Except of course, none of my friends could come, so it was just me and them. It was still fun, but a little awkward.

This will be much better. With real friends. It's hard not to smile as Georgia giggles and crows in delight at each new promise.

"There's no reason we can't have cake in the car on the

way down," Toby says, and Georgia launches herself at him in a clumsy hug. Serena starts to turn, then sighs. I try to imagine her on a roller coaster: sitting there totally expressionless while she's whirled up and down and every which way.

But the only reason this isn't absolutely 100 percent perfect is that August 30 is two days before I leave, and I was kind of planning to spend some time with my parents, seeing as I won't be anywhere near them for the foreseeable future. I've been avoiding thinking about how pissed they'll be when I leave—or even how to tell them I'm going—and whenever I do let my mind wander to them, the guilt pulls on me hard like a riptide. Jake and I haven't talked about Christmas and Thanksgiving. I don't know if he's planning on us coming back or not. Even if he is, September to the end of November is a really long time. Plus, setting my parents aside, I'm sure there will be all kinds of things to hammer out with Jake in that last weekend. It'd be nice to do that with him in peace, so we aren't so rushed on Sunday.

But I can't bail now. It's clear that what I thought was a minor social gathering is actually a big fucking deal. And most of me really is excited about it, this last hurrah of summer.

So I try to set aside the uneasy, scared part of myself, as I have been doing so much these past few weeks. I launch into the conversation, wrapping an arm around Georgia, oohing and ahhing at the answers to her unending questions. After a few minutes, the uneasiness is almost gone entirely, so far off to the sides I can barely see it in my peripheral vision.

Later, as Georgia is driving me home, she puts her hand on my knee. Her palm is warm and dry, slightly cracked from the chlorine.

"I just want you to know," she says, "that I recognize it's a big deal for you to come to this birthday party, with it being only two days before school starts." That's how she's been referring to it: *school starting*. It's technically accurate, but it feels like a euphemism, as if she is talking around my impending absence to pretend it won't exist.

"But," she continues, "it really matters to me, and there's no one I'd rather spend my birthday with than you, because you've kind of become my best friend, and I'm just really excited and happy to have you there. And..." She looks at me. "I hope you are too."

The light turns green, and she removes her hand from my leg to turn left into my neighborhood.

"Honestly, it's not that big a deal," I say, and as I say it, I start to believe it. "I actually can't wait. It's gonna be great. I mean, I know birthdays are important to you, but I haven't had friends at my birthday since elementary school, so it's a pretty big deal for me too."

She flashes a glance at me before looking back to the road. "Really?"

"Really. Seriously, Georgia, I'm excited."

She smiles a little and turns the radio up. It's one of those songs that always played at the pool when I was a kid. I associate it with cold water and hot plastic chairs and soft-serve ice cream from the truck that came by on Saturdays. A song about teenagers from a time when I wanted to be a teenager so badly, because it seemed like the most perfect and glamorous age, the freedom and knowledge of adulthood with the glory and style of youth. In this moment, that dream is real, and I am sixteen and beautiful and perfect, the universe spread out before me on this slim suburban road.

Georgia's birthday is a Wednesday. I'm hanging out with Jake the night before when she texts me:

sooo my mom told me dinner tom is gonna be earlier than i expected gonna miss the thing tom night

:(

"Aw, shit," I mutter while I text her: **noooo! can't you push it back?**

"What is it, babe?" Jake looks up from his laptop screen, which is filled with Kentucky rental houses. Georgia texts me back: *nooo, they had a reservation at buona tavola, not like you'd even need a reservation, but then my dad's business partner got us into this french place that's so so great but it's like an hour away so I'm leaving right after work.*

"We were gonna do this whole birthday thing for Georgia at work tomorrow night," I tell him while I text Toby to let him know it's off. "Toby got his boss to let him keep the building open for an extra few hours for a team meeting. I was gonna go get streamers and cake and stuff right after work. But now I guess we'll have to have cake during lunch, so…" I look up. "Would you mind taking me to the store?"

"You were never this excited about my birthday," Jake says. His eyes have dropped back down to his keyboard, and I can't tell if he's serious or not.

"Babe, last year you and your mom were on vacation, and I had a ton of papers due, so it was kind of hard to have a party," I say, a little cautious. He doesn't respond, so I try to do better. "But this year we're gonna be in Kentucky! And it'll be so great! You have no idea the kind of stuff I'm planning for you."

"No, you're not. It's whatever."

"I am, Jake. I promise," I say, and it's not a complete lie. I was certainly planning to do *something* for his birthday. I'm thinking about it now. That has to count as a mark in the truth column.

"Seriously?" He looks up again, so hopeful and handsome, and I take a step forward and kiss him right there.

"Seriously," I say, looking into his eyes.

He looks down again.

"It just seems like you're doing all kinds of shit for Georgia that you would never do for me."

"Oh my God, Jake, no," I plead. This is not an argument I want to have right now. It's not an argument I want to have, ever. "You are my boyfriend. You come first, you know that."

"You've only known her for like two months."

"Two and a half, and—no, I mean, listen, we're friends, but I'm only doing this because it's such a huge deal to her. We're only gonna be hanging out for a couple more weeks. I don't want to spoil it."

"But..." He pauses while he struggles to find the words. I wait, my stomach clenched tight. "Why does it matter? If we're leaving and you're not gonna see her, like, ever again?"

All of a sudden, I am furious. It's as if someone planted anger in the ground below me, and it grew up through the foundation and the carpet and my feet and into my bones. It overwhelms me. My vision narrows to a sharp point.

My thoughts are a tornado, and I can't pluck out what has me angriest. It could be the implication that Georgia would never visit us or that I'd never come back to visit her, the idea that we wouldn't continue to talk every day. Or maybe it's the idea that I shouldn't care about my life here, my whole almost-seventeen-year-long life here, just because we're about to live somewhere else. Or it could be the simple fact of Jake's unbeliev-able, unspeakable selfishness in this moment.

Then I breathe in and the fury recedes, and the tightness inside me barely even makes it into my voice when I say—like the sweet, rational girlfriend I am—"Well, you wouldn't want to have drama with your roommates, right? Even now?"

He shrugs. "I guess not." He closes his computer and grabs his keys. "I'm planning something for *your* birthday, for sure. Although given that I have to work all weekend, and it's in the middle of the week, it's not gonna be a blowout or anything. I figure we can do something big once we're moved in together, and you don't have a curfew and shit."

"Yeah, totally, I would love that," I say as the anger drains out of me. It leaves me feeling deflated, and the idea of a belated birthday party is no help. But he's not wrong. My birthday is a Wednesday, and he's picking up extra shifts to get the most out of that last paycheck before we leave. I appreciate the hard work. Plus, there's the trip that next weekend with the counselors. I feel a flicker of resentment toward Georgia, for making me care about something as foolish as a birthday and sowing this discontent in my relationship. But I can't really pretend that it's her fault.

"And listen," he says. We walk outside, and he opens the car door for me. "We're obviously gonna be with Dad for a while, but it looks like there are a lot of great rental options around there. I guess there aren't a lot of apartment complexes, but there are definitely some cool houses. So maybe next year, we can celebrate your birthday in a house of our own."

"I thought we were moving on after a few months."

"Well, sure, that's definitely still a possibility, but I just figure, if we settle in and really like it there, why not move into our own place in the same area?"

He smiles, so delighted, and leans over to kiss me. As his lips touch mine, I fight an instinct to pull away, try to convince myself to be happy. A house of our own—how great would that be? But next year seems forever away.

It's golden hour, and the sun blinds me as he drives. I close my eyes while he talks. His voice takes on the same lulling tones I used to hear when I would listen to him and his roommates playing video games, talking about their armor and their strategy and their victories. I used to fall asleep to it. Now I can't fall asleep because all of it involves me. I have to help make the decisions, or at least pretend to, so he doesn't feel alone.

"So, what kinda cake are you getting?" he says as we walk into the grocery store, finally talking about something other than house rentals and farming duties. "I liked that cake you made that one time last winter. That was so good. You should do that again."

"I don't have time," I say as I inspect the various brightly colored options in the case. Behind the counter, a girl roughly my age texts and glances up at me every once in a while. "Besides, that was from a mix. Georgia doesn't like box cakes. She likes ice-cream cakes and really nice chocolate cakes."

"Well, shit," Jake says. He picks up, inspects, and eats a sample of luncheon meat. "I thought you were a really good baker."

I choose a quadruple-chocolate cake swathed in frosting an inch thick. It's not as nice as she would like, but it's probably the best I can get without driving half an hour to the organic grocery store one town over, where I couldn't afford to shop anyway.

The girl doesn't talk to me while she gets it out of the case. Jake wanders off and comes back with six cheese cubes and a free cookie, limit one per child of any age. I decline his offer to share the cheese. He does carry the cake on the way out to the car, which is nice.

The cake goes in the fridge when we get home. It's almost nine, the sun settled low on the horizon, a thin orange line against the black and blue. Jake wanders down the hall to the bathroom without turning on the light; the whole house is thick with shadow.

"Where are your roommates?" I call down.

"No idea," he yells back, his voice muffled by the bathroom door. "Hold on a sec." I hold on. "Oh, they texted me, they're at a movie."

The toilet flushes and the door opens. He walks toward me with a mischievous grin.

"Means we've got the house to ourselves."

"In a few weeks, we'll always have the house to ourselves," I reply, trying to smile even though the words make me feel like I'm on unsteady ground.

"Well, the barn."

"Right."

"And then the house once we find a place."

"Right, no, yeah."

He walks toward me until he's so close I have to back up into the cabinets. He puts his hands on either side of me, presses into me at the hips. He kisses my neck. He's hard, but all I can think about is the fact that the toilet flushed right before the door opened. He didn't wash his hands. One of those hands pulls at the left strap of my tank top, and I turn away. Inch away, because I'm pinned against the sink.

"Babe, not now," I whisper.

"Why not?" He switches to the other side, and I let him pull the strap down my arm, let him lift my arm up and drop it again, strapless. I feel like a doll, hinged at the joints.

"I don't feel like it."

"I bet I can make you feel like it." He returns to the left strap and gently tugs it down. His fingers glide over me in famil-iar patterns. Their familiarity does not make them welcome. Instead, they are a song I've played too many times, a song I loved so much I set it as my wake-up alarm, and now I hate every chord in the chorus.

"Babe, no."

"Mm-hmm."

Jake kisses my collarbone, lifting up my arm to kiss the skin all the way down, and I do not respond. He stops at my elbow and meets my eyes. In the dark kitchen, the light is blurry and thin, and it is hard for me to see him. I focus on the whites of his eyes, not the dark pupils, not my own reflection in those wide black circles.

"Do you really want to stop?"

There's still lust in his voice, but it's softened by boyish fear. I look into his eyes and I love him, and I am so sad. I don't want to deal with his insecurity right now. I don't want him to have to feel that complicated emotion, and I don't want to feel it radiating out from him, and I don't want the hassle of his jaw set and silent on the way home.

So, I take his arm in mine, and I kiss my way up the strong thin muscles starting at the wrist, making my way to his shoulders where I nudge at the fabric of his T-shirt with my nose, and he peels it off.

"I don't want you to stop," I say into his mouth before I kiss him. The words feel like lifting something heavy. A strain in my back.

"Thank God," he whispers, and he picks me up in his arms and lays me down on the couch, strips off my shirt, pulls off my shorts, kisses me all over, everywhere, and the kisses feel like rain falling on me when I'm already cold. I make the sounds that I usually make and it's okay.

He takes so long, though. Maybe it's because he's stressed about the house or because I resisted at first, but he doesn't stop for minutes and minutes. My throat starts to get hoarse. It starts to hurt a little and then a little more.

"Uh, Jake?" I say.

"Yeah," he groans. "God, baby, you feel so great."

"You feel amazing too," I say, giving up.

I lie there on the couch for a while as he keeps going and going and going, and I'm so tired. It doesn't hurt bad enough for me to make him stop, but it hurts. I want it to be over. Finally, he picks up the pace and his breath quickens. As he comes, he kisses me, and no part of me wants to kiss him, so much so that when his lips touch mine, I actually cry out a little, the sound coming out of me without my consent.

But he thinks that means I've come too, so he doesn't say anything. He just laughs in pleasure and relief as he slumps, spent, a heavy weight on top of me.

17

Georgia likes the cake the next day at lunch. She shrieks with glee when Toby carries it out from its hiding place in the shared refrigerator. We couldn't find any forks, so we eat it with our fingers. Someone brings chips and cheese dip from a Mexican place, and that's our meal. Grease and frosting are everywhere.

It's been a shitty morning. When I came in, ten minutes late, I hurt between my thighs and felt vaguely dizzy. My legs were wobbly and tired, as if I'd been doing squats. Jenny took one look at me when she left her office the first time, rolled her eyes, and tossed me an Advil. "Girl, you gotta get your shit together, seriously," she said. "You're young, you can be happy. It's allowed."

"Okay, Jenny, sounds good," I said, and she shook her head and left to go to the bathroom. The Advil helped. She gave me another when I asked. I drank a ton of water and rallied to serve a ridiculous barrage of kids—another camp, visiting the aquarium for a field trip—and since then, it's been okay.

Georgia is happy, at least. We all sing over the cake to her, and she doesn't even do the thing people do where they pretend to be ashamed and say no, stop, don't sing. She giggles in delight and throws out her arms to take it all in. To my surprise, a lot of people have little gifts for her, some of which I sold to them over the past few weeks: a turtle plush, a cheap necklace with a porpoise on it, a chocolate bar.

I have a gift for her, of course, but it's not here. I got her a blue flowered bathrobe, supersoft on the inside. She always borrows my bathrobe when she's at my house and talks about how great it is, and it's not even that nice. It's a few years old and it's been through the wash too many times. This one is softer. My mom and I went to the mall after dinner a few days ago, and she helped me pick it out, though I bought it with my own money—some of those precious savings for Kentucky.

A part of me is sad that Georgia hasn't asked if I'm okay today. But I guess that means I've been hiding it pretty well. As I should—it's her birthday, and the better part of me knows this day should be about her. And besides, what would I say if she did ask? Had some bad sex, I feel shitty today? I wish I could have gotten you a nicer cake? My problems always sound stupid when I imagine saying them out loud.

Even though I'm preoccupied, the hour passes more quickly than any hour has passed for the last few weeks. I give Georgia a tight hug before we all go back inside. She lifts me off the ground and twirls me around, and I laugh in surprise and delight. The last time someone did that, it was my dad and I was twelve and had just placed third in the spelling bee.

"I have your present at home. I promise it's good," I say when she pulls back. Her messenger bag is full of other people's gifts, and I feel a need to justify my friendship to her.

"I believe it," she says with a wide smile. She leans in and smooches me on the cheek, a big wet kiss, and then opens the door to the air conditioning and the dim fluorescent lights. We start to go inside.

"Wait, wait," I say. Georgia holds the door for me. Toby is still gathering up the trash. "Do you have any more of those chips?"

"Yeah, tons," he says, holding up two greasy paper bags.

"I'm gonna give 'em to Jenny," I say. He hands them over to me.

"Y'all getting to be friends, then?" he teases.

"Maybe," I say. Georgia whines that her arm is getting tired, and I relieve her. Back in the gift shop, I toss Jenny the chips without saying anything. She doesn't acknowledge me beyond catching them, but I hear crunching before she starts her show, and a sort of satisfied yawn.

I spend the evening with my parents, since Georgia is at her family birthday dinner and Jake is working a later shift. Mom had a big fight with Vivian about catering companies for their next volunteer event, and they almost never fight. Dad dealt with a difficult client, and since he usually doesn't deal with clients at all, he seemed pretty depressed when he got home.

So, we eat dinner at Buona Tavola—my recommendation—and go see a movie together. It's one of those animated kids' movies, the kind I used to go see with them as a child, except it's been getting really good reviews and all the commercials say, "kids *and* parents will love this film" so whatever, we go. Mom gets sour gummy worms and we share.

Nestled between them in the movie theater, I feel like a baby. It's exactly the type of feeling I've been resisting all summer, and longer. For as long as I can remember. I want to be independent. I will be independent. But right now, watching a 3-D giraffe leap from a burning building into a hot air balloon, it feels good to be a kid again.

I start crying near the end when it looks like the giraffe might float up into the sky and be lost forever. It's the place in the movie where you're supposed to cry, but I cry a lot, tears streaming silently from my eyes. I lean into Dad's shoulder and watch the end of the movie through the blur. He doesn't say anything. Just puts his arm around me. We sit like that through the credits, and when my eyes are dry and the lights come on, we leave and go home together.

18

If I were Georgia, I would say that my birthday passes without incident. But since I'm not Georgia, and I'm used to minimal festivities, this year is the biggest birthday celebration I've ever experienced—and we haven't even gone to Great Adventures yet.

Jake takes me to a fancy steakhouse the night before, this meal being his gift to me as we save money for September. We share a piece of strawberry cheesecake and barely even talk about Kentucky. I tell him I want to stay in this moment; he abides by that wish. We talk about our days, and my parents, and work, and the funny things we've seen on TV lately.

The day of, Georgia and the others at work surprise me at lunch with an enormous fruit tart and a bunch of baguettes and cheddar from the organic grocery store. "Because we figured you're always complaining about the grease, so we might as well get you some cheese and bread that pretends to be healthy," Georgia says with a pronounced eye roll as she hugs me. At the end of lunch, after everyone else has gone inside, she gives me a small box containing a pair of blue glass earrings that look like the ocean. I put them on immediately.

That night, my parents and I go out to dinner too—so many different kinds of celebratory food—and the waiter brings me tiramisu with a candle in it, and my parents sing happy birthday. They don't ask about college.

At the end of that night, I wish it could be my birthday all the time. No one would make me talk or think about any of the things I want to ignore. We could keep everything light and easy and good.

They give me a blue sundress wrapped in gold paper when we get home. I go into the bathroom to try it on, and my parents applaud when I come out to show them. Dad is very proud; he was the one who found the dress, not Mom. I don't know where they got it or how much it cost, and they won't tell me, but it is beautiful. It is soft cotton, just stiff enough to stand up against a little summer sweat, but light enough not to be hot. It even makes me look like I have boobs. I almost text Jake a picture, but I want him to see it in person.

Instead, I text the picture to Georgia in bed that night, my belly full and the covers pulled up warm over my chest, and she replies fast.

hot damn

you look fucking incredible

nice earrings btw

:) :) :)

i see why you like having big birthdays

the last couple days have been sort of amazing

right tho???

bdays are the best

speaking of...

She texts me a selfie—she's wrapped in the robe I got her for her birthday and sporting an enormous, goofy grin.

omg!

it's the softest thing I've ever touched

THANK YOU

you're welcome!!!

god I'm so excited about Great Adventures

next weekend will be SO GOOD

It's all we talk about at lunch. Not just me and Georgia, but the whole group. It's partially because of how exciting the trip is, but it's also because we have a silent collective agreement not to talk about what will come after. Neither Serena nor Georgia are excited for the summer to end, so no one is talking about the upcoming semester—though, of course, I'd have to fake joining those conversations, anyway. Dave and Devin are leaving for college at the beginning of September, and they are excited, I'm sure, but I can tell they're nervous too. They change the subject when I ask about it. Matt doesn't talk about what's coming next for him either, because as far as I can tell, it's nothing in particular. I know that I can't talk about what I'll be doing, so I don't even try. Honestly, I don't want to.

Then there's Toby, who is staying at the aquarium. The summer rush ends shortly after the camp does, and all of us are leaving. He'll be eating lunch by himself.

Or maybe with the other tour guides, I guess, but they're a pretty sour lot. They don't like him because he's young and happy, and also maybe because he lies to the visitors. Some of them take the job really seriously. One time, he told me, he got yelled at for fifteen minutes straight about the reproductive habits of sea turtles—he'd told a group they made babies by removing their shells and rubbing their butts together. Starting September, those tour guides will have to be his friends again.

For a few days, the Great Adventures trip even manages to take over my conversations with Jake. We carry on two different one-sided talks at the same time. He tells me about an opening at a grocery store near his dad's town, and I talk about our carpooling arrangements for the party. He says he's found a townhouse he likes, and I describe how Georgia's trying to convince Matt to come on the roller coasters, but he's surprisingly too scared of heights to do so.

Not that Jake's coming on the trip, mind you. When I

asked the group whether he could join us, everyone got quiet. After a long pause, Toby shrugged and said, "Sure, boyfriends and girlfriends welcome." But if you don't count the girl Toby cheated on Serena with, which I don't, only Dave and I have significant others, and Dave's girlfriend is already at a college pre-orientation program. No one seemed happy about Jake coming, really, and I understand why. It's a party for us, to celebrate us as friends.

But it's not fair for me to do something like that without at least inviting Jake, so I ask him anyway. Fortunately, he has a shift that is nonnegotiable—taking over for several older folks who need to do back-to-school stuff with their kids.

He does get pissed at me after a couple days, though. "Caroline, you're talking about something that I have no interest in. I mean, I know it's interesting to you, but I don't get to go, so it kind of sucks. I'm talking about our future. Don't you want to discuss that at all?"

He's right. It just feels, recently, as if he's much more invested in the move than I am. That it's something he is doing, and something that is happening to me.

We're both doing it, though, and it's happening to both of us together. So when he asks, I give him my best I'm-sorry face and say, "Yes, love, I want to talk about it." And we go over it all again.

It's getting to the point where we've figured out all we can before we actually get to Kentucky. But he's always coming up with another detail: what snacks we'll bring in the car, what he wants to name the chickens, where his dad goes to church, what their favorite barbeque restaurants are.

I swear if he applied this level of micromanaging to the majority of his life, he'd be running the world. I've never seen him get this interested in anything.

"Dad thinks I'm really gonna like his girlfriend," he tells me, and I picture the three of them in a family picture, Jake between his dad and LeeAnn, me holding the camera. "There's a bar where Dad always goes to play pool, and he's gonna teach me how to do it," he says, and I imagine the two of them standing in the smoky room, hands blue with chalk dust. "He's planning to cut down his own Christmas tree this year, from the land," he murmurs as we lie in bed after sex. Father and child together in my head, hands brown with dirt, the scent of pine.

I have never seen a picture of Jake and his dad alone together. There are no pictures of his parents in his house or his wallet, and the few times I've been to his mother's house, it's all her side of the family: glitzy gold frames stocked with cousins, aunts, friends, and, of course, Jake and his older brother. The only image of his dad I've ever seen is in a wide family portrait of his mom's family, taken at Easter over a decade ago. Jake is a freckled, beaming boy in the front row. His dad is in the back, hands tucked into his pockets, jaw jutting out in an animal grin.

When I looked at that picture, I knew who he was without having to ask. There's a date in the corner, the mark of a cheap film camera. It was taken the year before he left. Jake would have been nine.

But never them together. No proud poses at soccer tournaments, no parent-night exhibits at school, no Christmas morning snapshots. I asked Jake about it once. He shrugged and said his mom must have put them away, and that was the last I heard. That night, I tacked up an old picture of me and my dad on my corkboard, a snapshot of the two of us from the father-daughter camping group we went to when I was little. Dad kissed me on my forehead when he saw.

One evening, when Jake has been talking about his dad for half an hour straight, I get frustrated. "I thought this was about *us*," I say.

"It is," he says, impatient, defensive. "Caroline, you know it is."

In that moment, I see him doubly: the boy in the front, smiling big and joyful, and the man in the back, teeth bared and bright. Both of them stare back at me, and in his eyes, there is such a fierce and terrified hope that it makes me afraid, and I have to turn away.

19

The next week feels remarkably normal, with moments of surrealism that flit in and out like fireflies. I go to work and back to Jake's house to hang out on the porch, and one afternoon he takes me to the bank, and I withdraw most of my savings. The cash sits folded in the innermost pocket of my purse, waiting for Kentucky. I eat pizza at lunch and Georgia takes me home, and while she flips through magazines and the ever-present college book, I squint at my laptop, looking at the Kentucky town's official website in private browsing mode.

It is blindingly, screamingly hot. Over a hundred degrees every day, the heat index almost a hundred and ten on Monday. News anchors say we're breaking records. I shower in the morning, after work, and before bed. On Tuesday, Jake gives up on the porch and blasts the air conditioning inside, saying he'll be gone before the electric bill arrives. At my house, Georgia stays outside with me. Her hair is stringy with sweat, even more so than it's been all summer, and her skin smells like Dove deodorant.

I expected the last day of work to be full of tearful goodbyes, but since we're all hanging out the next day at Great Adventures, it's a lot less climactic than I thought it would be. In fact, it turns out that our last lunch together was actually Thursday, because on Friday, the camp is having an end-of-summer "gala" lunch with the kids' parents. Georgia runs a plate of food across the lobby to me before the parents arrive, and it occurs to me this is one of the last times I'll see her face peering around the door frame. I try to squash that thought as quickly as it comes. I spend my final lunch hour in Jenny's office, watching sitcoms with her in silence.

At the end of the day, Jenny trundles out of her office. I am starting to close, going through the familiar motions. She stands there and watches me straighten poster displays.

"Well," she says finally.

"Yup," I say.

"You weren't the worst employee I've ever had."

"I appreciate that, Jenny," I say, genuinely touched. I open the drawer of the desk and pull out the gift I got for her. "I got you something." It's a little glass bottle, stopped with a piece of cork, filled with artificially white sand and little porcelain starfish and sand dollars. We sell them here, but I tied a piece of ribbon around it to make it feel a little more special. "I made you miss your beach trip, so I figured I should bring the beach to you."

She smiles slightly as I hand her the bottle, and I keep cleaning. She stands there for a moment longer.

"Everything's gonna be okay with you," she says. I don't know whether it's a question or a statement, and I don't know exactly how to respond.

But she's still standing there. "Yes," I say. "It will be."

"Good," she says. She walks back into her office, closing the door behind her. I leave the counter sparkling clean.

That night, I take two Benadryl to fall asleep at 8:00 p.m. I want to be rested for the next day. Even with the medication, I toss and turn for forty-five minutes, texting Jake meaningless shit. I fall asleep hard and fast and wake up before my alarm at 4:00 a.m. My purse is packed already. The whole house is quiet. When I brush my teeth, the bathroom lights feel harsh, and I'm grateful to step back into the dim hallway.

Outside, the morning is warm and soft and dark. Crickets and frogs sing to each other. I sit on the front steps and wait for Georgia to come pick me up.

No one is driving at this time. The last night I was awake this late, or this early, was right after Jake asked me to think about Kentucky, and all I remember is that the blankets in my bed felt like straitjackets. This morning, the air is silky and wet, the streets are utterly empty, and my best friend is on her way to me.

I get a text from Georgia: *five min!* I respond, **stop texting and driving**, and put my phone down beside my feet. It buzzes, *ok ok*, vibrating against the rubber edge of my cheap flip-flops. Apparently the park has water spouts that come up out of nowhere sometimes, so Georgia said not to ruin a pair of nice shoes. I'm okay with it. I still wanna look cute, but given that Jake's not coming, I guess it doesn't matter as much.

Nine minutes after I get her text, her headlights appear around the corner, an arc of yellow as the light hits the trees. It blinds me briefly as she pulls up to our house and idles, waiting. She rolls down her window.

"It's time!" she whisper-yells. It feels like we have to whisper, even though normal talking voices wouldn't wake anyone up. Everything is too quiet for us to speak. I cup one hand around my eyes as I get up, letting my pupils adjust away from nighttime.

I get in the car and roll down my own window. Georgia looks over and says, "Happy birthday, Caroline."

I smile back at her. "Happy birthday, Georgia."

She turns up the radio as we drive out of my neighborhood on the way to the aquarium. There are fewer commercials at four in the morning, and the ones that are there are weirder.

"Find the love of your life with the power of a genuine psychic," intones a woman over a faux Bollywood soundtrack.

"I feel like I'd be good at that job," Georgia says thoughtfully. I start giggling, which makes her laugh, which makes me laugh more. Nothing's that funny, but it's too early, and I'm too happy to be rational.

Serena, Matt, Dave, and Devin are waiting in the aquarium parking lot when we arrive. Matt looks like his usual self, bored and shaggy, but this is the first time I've ever seen Serena without her sunglasses. Her eyes are a pale, watery blue. She climbs into the car toting a purse the size of a duffel bag. Matt jumps in after her, tossing a backpack on the floor, a tray of cupcakes balanced on his lap.

"Y'all ready for this?" he yells, scooting up to put his hands on the back of my and Georgia's seats. "Let me tell you. Gonna be epic."

"You brought cake!" exclaims Georgia.

"As promised. Want one now?" He stretches practically his entire torso into the front seat to hand us both a cupcake. I set mine in the cup holder, but Georgia eats the icing off hers with a single bite, delighted.

"Happy birthday," Serena says from the back seat. I turn back to look at her; she's pulled out a baseball cap and is snuggling into the door as if to nap, but she's smiling.

"Yeah, happy birthday, ladies," Matt says.

"Put on your seat belt," I tell him. He sits back with a groan. As Matt is buckling, Toby's car swings in, and the rest of the guys climb onboard. His window rolls down and his arm reaches out, long and gangly, and points forward like an explorer.

The drive is just over three hours. If it were up to Georgia, we would go straight through without stopping, getting to the park half an hour before it opens, the first in line. She's told me this is her style—no-nonsense, get where you're going—and I said I was okay with it. Really, though, I would much rather have a nice, leisurely drive. Stop for a meal, take a break to get a drink at the gas station, and so on. But I'm not going to say that, because she's driving, and also because I want zero drama.

Fortunately, Matt and I appear to be of the same mind, because at six he declares we should get breakfast. He and Georgia spend about half an hour arguing about it—she says that cake *is* breakfast, and he wants a bacon-and-egg biscuit—before Serena wakes up and says unceremoniously, "I gotta pee."

And I say, kind of because it's true and kind of because I want scrambled eggs, "Me too, a little."

Georgia throws up her hands in defeat, a dangerous move since we're doing eighty-two on the highway. She says, "Whatever, okay. I'll text Toby, we'll stop."

"*I'll* text Toby," I say, quickly grabbing her phone from her.

We stop at a fast food restaurant. "You know," Toby says to the man at the register, gesturing at me and Georgia. "It's these two ladies' birthdays, so if you could do anything special for them…" The man smiles and shakes his head, but he gives each of us a kids' meal toy with our meal. Georgia cheers. The toys are little planes, and she flies hers around from person to person as we wait for our food. I spin the tiny propeller on mine and dive-bomb Matt, who shrieks in faux-horror.

We all crowd around a single table, though the only other people in the restaurant are a group of elderly ladies eating sausage biscuits. The sun is beginning to color the sky with pink and blue. I lean my head on Georgia's shoulder. At this table with all my friends, laughing and together, I feel peaceful in a way I haven't in a long time. I am exactly where I am supposed to be.

"Isn't this better than not stopping?" I ask.

"I refuse to answer on the grounds that it may incriminate me," she says, pouring half a cup of maple syrup on a pancake.

We stop once more after that because someone in Toby's car *really needs* a soda, and we get to the park just as it's opening. We are not the first in line, but we're close. When we get inside, Serena insists we get a locker to put our stuff in, which the guys moan about, but actually proves to be helpful. I hadn't even thought about where I would put my purse when we went on rides. Shows you how much I know about amusement parks.

It's 8:15 and the park is starting to come to life, the sun low in the sky but strong, and as we wander down an empty path, Georgia spins around, arms outstretched.

"I love this place," she says. She walks backward, hooking her thumbs into the belt on her too-tight shorts. She tells me, "My parents used to take me and my friends here every summer for my birthday."

"I never knew that," I say. We're naturally splitting into our separate groups now, Dave and Devin having some kind of animated discussion about roller coasters, Toby and Matt scampering ahead of everyone and talking about music, Serena behind us on her phone. And Georgia and me. I take a step forward, she takes a step backward, moving together.

"Yeah," she says. "I didn't, you know, want to intimidate you with my deep knowledge of this park." I can't tell if she's joking or not. "But seriously, over there"—she points to a food stand whose owner is rolling up the metal grate—"that's where you're gonna get the best funnel cake in the game. And up ahead and around the corner twenty minutes is a gift shop where they always put the new people, so you can usually scam them into letting you buy stuff for cheap."

"As a gift shop associate, I'm offended you'd even suggest taking advantage of my brethren," I say.

"Oh my God, how thoughtless of me."

"Where are we actually going right now?" Serena asks, catching up with us.

"Oh," Georgia says confidently, and then she calls out, "Toby! We're going to the Pluto, right?"

He turns around and gives her a thumbs-up. She turns back to me.

"We're going to our first roller coaster of the day. It's a little one."

"Shouldn't we go to the biggest one first, to beat the line?"

She shrugs. "I guess, but then you don't have anything to look forward to. This way, you build up the thrills. Always better to start small. At least that's what I think, and Toby says since we're the birthday girls, we get to pick the rides. I picked for you," she adds as an afterthought, and I smile and shake my head.

When we reach the roller coaster, we're the third group in line. Matt waits on a bench and eats a hot dog, having informed us that he is "not a roller coaster guy, y'all, too fuckin' scary. I'm not gonna lose a limb on some poorly inspected death trap."

I am not necessarily a roller coaster girl. In fact, I have never been on one, so I'm slightly concerned about this situation. But everyone is so excited—and making so much fun of Matt—there's no way I'm chickening out.

As the ride ends and the first group starts getting out of their car, Georgia pulls me aside and whispers, "Are you sure you want to go? You can fake sick if you want. I'll tell everyone you have a headache."

"What?" I say, trying to feign surprise. "No, I can't wait."

Georgia rolls her eyes. "Okay," she says. "Seriously, are you sure?"

"I'm sure," I say. The dead-eyed twenty-something running the roller coaster opens the gates, and the group starts to file in. I look back at Matt, who waves at me, smirking. My stomach lurches.

"I'll hold your hand," Georgia says.

It's not terrible at first. I'm sitting between Georgia and Serena, Toby and the other guys in front of us. I'm holding on to Georgia's hand so tight that both our knuckles are stark white. I am about to ask what I should expect, but just as I open my mouth, the ride jolts forward.

It goes up and up and up. I can hear myself saying, "Oh shit, oh shit," and I can hear Georgia next to me saying, "Oh fuck, yeah," and then after all that climbing, we're at the top. We are there for maybe half a second, but the moment imprints itself in my head. This bright, blurry vision of the whole world spread out in front of us: the park, the forest, the highway, billboards and water towers. Apart from being on airplanes, I have never been this high up.

Then we fall. I pretty much lose it. We fall, and we curve, and we climb and fall again, and repeat. Beside me, Georgia and Serena are screaming their heads off, and in the middle of this whirlwind a thought comes into my head—that this is the most I've ever liked Serena—and then it leaves my head, to make room for what's really taking up space: sheer fucking terror.

Turns out, I wasn't lying to myself: I'm really not a roller coaster girl. I don't know how long the ride lasted, but when it ends, I am frozen. Georgia and the others have already jumped out, giddy with adrenaline, when Toby notices I'm not moving.

"You okay?" he says, inspecting me.

I shake my head.

"Okay, come on, we gotta go. You're gonna be fine," he says. He gently unlatches my fingers from the safety bar and picks me up—just like that—scoops me into his arms and carries me back down the path away from the ride.

Most of me is still terrified, but a part of me is reveling in the feeling of being in someone else's arms. There is nothing untoward about this—it isn't cheating, it isn't anything. But it feels like something. It's been a long time since I've been this close to any other guy, and it's not so wonderful in and of itself, but it's different, and different feels good. Then Toby readjusts me, I feel like I'm falling for a moment, I freak out, and the thought is gone.

Toby lags behind the others a little bit, for which I am grateful. They are so, so happy. Georgia is bouncing around, giggling and shrieking, nudging her shoulder against Serena, who has the widest smile I've ever seen on her and is even laughing a little.

I'm still pretty shaky when he sets me down on the bench. Matt sits there placidly. I tremble for about a minute before he holds out a half-eaten plate of funnel cake.

"Not your thing, huh?" he says.

I shake my head.

"Me neither. Funnel cake?"

"It's nine in the morning. And you've already had cupcakes." I thought I was too traumatized to speak, but I guess the audacity of having that much sugar this early has overcome my fear.

"A nutritious third breakfast," Matt says and sets the plate in my lap. I eat. It's great.

As I'm taking my fifth bite, Georgia turns toward me, and I can see her finally notice that I have not had a great time. Her face falls, and she looks like a miserable puppy.

"Oh no, you didn't like it, did you?"

"It was okay," I say, but I'm not convincing. She shakes her head.

"I'm so sorry. I thought you would love it. I loved it."

"I know, you were so happy!"

"I still am, but I'm not happy you're not happy. Are you gonna be okay?"

"Yeah," I say, and actually, sitting on this bench, I can understand some portion of the thrill she's feeling. I hated the ride, but there is a comfort in the fact of now being safe after I thought I was going to die. I do feel more ready for the day now, having had the funnel cake and gotten the roller coaster thing over with. Ready for twelve more hours of time with friends.

And maybe some time getting to know Matt better while we sit on the sidelines together. "I am never doing that again,"

I tell Georgia, but I say it with a smile, and she laughs and puts her arm around me.

"I'll never make you," she says.

The next few hours are a whirlwind, sometimes literally. Everyone else will go on any ride, so we snake our way through the park, stopping every three minutes for something new. Toby buys Georgia a lemonade taller than her face, insisting on paying for her food as a birthday treat, and half an hour later, we have to run around for ten minutes to find a bathroom. We go on the Tilt-A-Whirl; we can't walk straight when we get off. Georgia and I fall against each other, giggling, the sweat of one another's arms soaking into our tank tops as we wander on.

Matt wins a tiny stuffed teddy bear and gives it to Serena, who carries it under her arm like a tote bag. I sit next to him while everyone goes on one of those drop towers, and he buys an order of fried Oreos for us to split, promising they'll be incredible.

"These are disgusting," I say after taking my first bite.

"Bizarre how you can be so right about roller coasters and so wrong about snacks," he says, blissfully chewing.

"Everyone else was excited about this trip *because* of the roller coasters," I say. "I assumed they would be fun." He shakes his head.

"Not me. I know better. I'm here because it's the last time we're all gonna hang out together, and I love you guys."

"I love you too," I say, oddly touched. "But Georgia said

you were friends before this job. Don't you think you'll still be friends after?"

He laughs a little. "Please. She'll be back in high school and I'll be...living with my parents, not doing anything. She's not gonna want to hang out with me. Neither is Serena. Neither are you," he adds pointedly. "And Dave and Devin are both going to college. I guess Toby and I will still be friends." He screws up his face as if considering the idea, then shrugs and takes another bite of Oreo.

"I would be your friend," I tell him. It's true—if I were staying, I would be. Matt can be a real asshole sometimes, but I like him a lot.

"Yeah, right."

"No, really," I protest. "And wait, I thought you were going to focus on your art." I've never seen Matt this uncertain before, and in the middle of the color and sound of the amusement park, it feels out of place.

"I say that, but I don't know what I'm going to do." He sighs. "Honestly, Caroline, I'm a fuckup. I don't have a plan. I've just gotta figure it out." We sit there for a long moment, watching the roller coaster curve and twist in the air. "But," he says conclusively, slapping my back, "it's been a great summer. Hasn't it?"

"Yes, it has," I say.

A few minutes later, Georgia and the others run toward us,

laughing and out of breath. Serena's hair is tousled, and Toby looks as if he's been struck by lightning.

"A bird nearly hit me!" he yells as they get close. "I was nearly murdered by a bird! A goddamn hawk!"

"It was definitely a pigeon," says Georgia.

"It's for the best y'all didn't go on that one," Toby says, putting his hands on his knees to catch his breath. "It was the highest one yet."

"We had a grand old time here," Matt says, stretching out his legs. "What's next?"

We pass a fire-breathing performance, a cinnamon roll cart, and a booth where Dave tries and fails to win a bright yellow baseball cap with the Great Adventures logo. Georgia and Devin debate the merits of soft pretzels versus kettle corn; Devin ends up buying both, and they pass them back and forth as we walk, argument settled in favor of the kettle corn. Farther into the park, there's a mini-water park—water coming out of towers and play structures built to look like a magical forest for kids. We get soaked. After this summer, the smell of chlorine is comforting to me, a balm.

We walk for so long without passing anything I recognize that I begin to wonder if this place just goes on forever, before I realize we actually *have* passed these places before. This pizza stand looks different in afternoon light than it did in the morning; that roller coaster seems new when the line of people is five hundred deep rather than twenty.

When Serena says she has to return to the locker to get more cash, I say I'll go with her. Jake has been in the back of my head all day. He probably wants to know how the day's going, figure out last plans for leaving. I get a headache every time I think about it, but I know I should be there for him. I told him I'd be checking my phone every once in a while, and it's been too long.

Serena and I walk mostly in silence. I don't think she likes me very much. Then again, I don't think she likes anyone. I try anyway.

"You going back to school Monday too?" I ask.

"Yeah," she says. Another thirty seconds of flat nothing.

"Do you go to the same school as Georgia, or…?"

"Yeah."

"Have any classes together?"

"A few last year. I don't know about this year."

"Cool." We walk quietly for another minute before I speak up again. "For ages I thought you were already in college."

"I'm glad I project an air of sophistication," she says, laughing a little. "I am older than you, if it makes you feel better."

"Yeah?"

"Yeah. I turned eighteen in March. I got held back in first grade. Poor hand-eye coordination."

We reach the locker, and she opens it, digging past the paperbacks and makeup in her bag to reach her phone. Her fingers are a blur as she texts. I pull out my phone from the squished mess of my purse, expecting a barrage of texts from Jake.

There's nothing. No texts. No missed calls. Nothing. I even turn the phone off and back on again, draining precious battery life, in case it was some kind of software glitch.

I shouldn't be surprised, I guess. I told him I'd be busy all day today. I just thought that he'd want to be talking to me two days before we run away together.

Serena hits send on a final text, puts her phone back in her bag, and tucks a twenty-dollar bill into her bra.

"Who were you texting?" I ask.

"My sisters," she says. "They want to play a prank on my stepmom. I was advising them of the strongest hair dye available in your standard drugstore." She tilts her sunglasses down at me and says, "Ready?"

I look at my phone again and nod. "Sure." I put it back into the locker and try not to inspect my thoughts on Jake too closely. I want to ask Serena about the prank, but she doesn't even look at me once while we walk back, and I don't want to intrude. I stay quiet.

The group promised to meet us at the end of the Raging Dragon roller coaster, but when we get there, they've only just made it to the front of the line. Serena and I join Matt at a picnic table, and the next time the coaster starts, I try to spot Georgia in the cars. Once, I think I can see her black hair, but I lose sight almost immediately. The track spirals and winds through the sky, leaping and falling and rising again. From here, I can see the beauty in it. I'm still glad I'm not with them on the track.

They join us at the table after. I split a soft-serve ice cream cone with Georgia, meaning she eats a soft-serve ice-cream cone and I take obligatory licks when she tells me to. It seems as good a place as any to reconvene before the evening comes on. It's a little after seven, golden hour, the sunlight buttery and the shadows deep. We've managed to stick together so far, but now we're breaking up into factions.

"Let's go to the hunting rifle game," Dave says.

"I have no interest in that," Georgia says.

"I wanna go to the gift shop," Serena says. "I told my little sisters I'd get them presents."

"I kinda needed something at the gift shop too," says Matt quickly.

"I'm down for hunting games," Toby says. "Given that I'm the only one of y'all who's actually hunted, I'm pretty sure you'll regret that choice, but your funeral."

"What do you wanna do, Caroline?" Georgia asks, turning to me.

"I don't really need to go to the gift shop, and I have no idea how to shoot a gun. So that doesn't sound great. But otherwise, I'm down for whatever you want," I say, and then add, "except roller coasters."

Georgia laughs and leans her head against my shoulder,

smearing soft-serve on my tank top as she takes another bite. "Let's go to the swings," she says. "You'll love those. You're not afraid of heights, right?"

"No, I just don't like how the roller coaster jerks you all around."

"Yeah, no, you'll love it. The swings aren't as exciting, but they're still really great. They were my favorite when I was a kid. And I think your tolerance of rides is about the same as mine was when I was eight, so…"

I make a face at her. Toby claps his hands together.

"Sounds like we're heading our separate ways. Let's meet back at the main gift shop at, say, nine thirty?" he proposes. "Park closes at ten."

"Kill fake deer!" one of the guys starts to chant, and they get up and go down the path to the right, Toby at the front. Serena rises and starts ambling to the left, and Matt hastily throws away his soda cup and follows her. Georgia and I are left alone at the table, Georgia munching on the last of her soft-serve cone.

"I know I said we were going to the swings," she says, "but I need some real dinner before that. And I know you do too, but you'd never say it. Right?"

"Right," I sigh. "But I am so fucking sick of pizza."

"Hot dogs it is, then."

We have to walk around for a while to find a hot dog stand, and we eat them at an identical picnic bench next to an awkward couple a few years younger than us. I can see their parents hovering a few tables over, trying to keep an eye on them and also give them some privacy. The girl is wearing a padded bra. The boy has braces. I look at the couple and look at my hot dog and think of Jake, and it's like Georgia's reading my mind.

"How are you feeling about Monday?" she says between bites. My stomach turns over. "I won't judge you, I swear," she adds. She looks down. "I know I haven't always been so great about that."

Maybe it's her admission of judgment in the past, and her promise that she won't do that right now. Maybe it's the long hours of walking in the sun. Maybe I'm just tired. But I don't try to push away that nausea like I usually do. I set down my hot dog on the greasy paper plate and reach my hands out across the table.

"I'm so scared," I tell her.

It feels good to say it out loud. I have never said it, not to anyone, not to Jake and not to Georgia, and not even to myself alone at night. Putting it into the world makes me feel everything more acutely—the growing sunburn on my shoulders, the rough wood under my wrists—while I wait for her answer.

She takes my hands and intertwines her fingers with mine. Her eyes hold so much pity that I have to look away, down at our fingernails, her chipped blue polish and my broken French manicure.

"You know it's still your choice," she says. "You decide, not him. You don't have to go."

"I do," I say, and I am so close to crying. "I want to." Even to me, my voice sounds unconvincing.

I keep trying to convince myself, but I can't.

I'm so ashamed by my failure that I try to unlace my hands from Georgia's, but she doesn't let me. She holds tighter and looks at me so hard that I have to look back up at her.

"I'm here for you, whatever you do," she says and finally releases my fingers. I look down and take a deep breath, eat the last bite of my hot dog. Georgia throws away our trash and comes around behind me to give me an awkward hug, wrapping her arms around my back.

"I'm sorry for making you sad," she says quietly.

"Not your fault," I sniff.

"It is, sort of."

"Sort of, but…"

"We can talk about it later," she says. She bites her lip, both of us, I'm sure, counting the hours until Monday morning. There's not much *later* left. "Tonight after we drop off Serena and Matt. Or tomorrow. Yeah?"

"Yeah." I wipe away the tears and take one more breath. "Yeah. It's cool. Swings, right?"

"Swings!" she says, pulling me up, smiling. "Time to be happy. At least for the rest of the night, okay? You gotta give yourself that."

"Okay," I say. Georgia takes my hand and leads me down the path toward the swings, and her touch makes it a little easier. The sky is such a beautiful blue, fading into purple at the edges, and the crowd is joyful and the rides are loud, and all of that makes it easier too.

We spend maybe twenty minutes looking for the swings, Georgia pulling me around corners, muttering, "I thought it was this way," and then turning to try a new direction. When we finally get there, the sun is resting low in the sky and I'm out of breath. The ride is at the end of a long side street that starts with some boring shops and games and gets even less interesting as it continues. The last few stands are shuttered.

But then there are the swings, which rise out of nowhere as we turn a corner. I didn't know at first what Georgia was talking about when she said swings, but I recognize them now: chairs like baby playground swings sized for adults, attached via very long chains to an enormous circular brim at the top of the ride. The ride looks more like an old-school carousel than the bright neon machinery in the rest of the park—all fake gold filigree and deep red and navy blue.

It is also completely empty. Maybe the closed stores have scared away the kids, or maybe it's just difficult to find, but the swings are dangling unused and there's no one in line. The only person in sight is a grizzled woman who looks about three steps away from death.

"Y'all in line?" she croaks in our direction.

Georgia and I look at each other. I shrug. "Sure," Georgia says. We step up to the platform and strap into two seats right next to each other. The woman comes by and checks that we're safe. Then she trundles back to her post and hits a couple buttons, and the swings jolt to life.

They start slow, lifting us a few yards off the ground and spinning gently. Then they speed up and raise higher, as if the machine is standing up straight from a crouch, and we start to go faster, and we swing out wide. Suddenly we are so high up I can see everything. I can see the sunset in the west with the roller coasters silhouetted against it, the lights of the park spread out below me, and all those people, people everywhere, swarming together and breaking apart like flocks of birds. I am flying.

I don't mean to start laughing, but I do, a huge, gasping, surprised laugh. The wind streams my hair out behind me and dries hours of accumulated sweat, cooling my skin to goose bumps. It's so strong it forces tears out of my eyes.

I turn my head to my right, and Georgia looks the same as I feel: laughing, delighted, hair a ribbon of black against the purple air. Our eyes meet. She reaches out her hand toward mine, and I reach out mine in return, tilting my chair to reach. Even then, only the tips of our fingers connect, a featherlight electric touch, and then the forces spinning us pull us away from each other again as we arc high out into the sky.

Then, all of a sudden, there's another jolt and the momentum slows. The pillar in the center of the ride begins to lower. It takes a minute, maybe, to get back to the ground, and when my toes touch the aluminum floor, I let out a breath.

"That was incredible," I say to Georgia.

"Right?" she says, grinning from ear to ear. "I knew you'd love it."

"Y'all wanna go again?" the old woman calls from her seat in the center. I glance around. There is no one else in line. The whole area is empty.

"Want to?" I ask Georgia.

"Nothing better to do," she says.

"Yes, please," I shout to the woman. She turns to her controls and it all begins again.

I don't know how long we're on the swings, how long a single ride is, or how many times we repeat. After the third time, the operator doesn't even ask us whether we want to go again. Twice, a few kids come and join us for one ride, then leave again after it's done. We are giddy. I lose my hair tie to the wind, and one strap of Georgia's tank top falls down her arm, revealing a blue bra strap and pale tan lines. I feel like one of the magical creatures I used to read about in fantasy books, invincible and almighty.

The sky around us is made of brilliant colors, and for a little while, I don't register that everything's getting darker, just that those colors are changing. But then, we finish a ride and don't immediately start back up again. I look around for kids waiting in line; I can't see any. It's only then, in looking, that I realize the sky is black. The air is dark and the lights of the ride, previously just a complement to the sunlight, are the only things illuminating us.

"That was the last one," says the old woman, coming over and fumbling with our belts to unbuckle us.

"Wait, why?" says Georgia.

"Park closes at ten. Rides stop at nine. That's the deal." She walks away.

"Well, whatever. Caroline, you ready?" She looks at me.

I'm still sitting in my seat. My whole body feels like it's vibrating. My hands are shaky. My skin is cold but my blood is warm, and my heart is beating too fast.

"Caroline?"

I took physics last year. I wasn't very good at it, for the most part—as soon as the teacher started using variables and writing equations, I got lost. But I did understand some of the theories. I learned that when you stop something that has been going very fast, the momentum doesn't just disappear. It has to go somewhere. And if the thing that stops it is immovable, the force has to reverberate back onto the thing that was stopped. If you run straight into a wall, you fall backward, but it's not really you falling. It's your own strength and speed coming back to push you in the opposite direction.

I get up from my chair, slowly, wobbling on my feet. I nearly fall, reach out for Georgia to catch myself. She grabs hold of my shoulder and turns me toward her.

"Caroline, are you okay?"

There, under the black sky and the golden lights, I let my forehead tip forward onto hers. I close my eyes. I wait for the words to rise in my throat.

"Don't go," she murmurs. "Please."

Her hand stretched out to pull me up. The sole of her foot pressed against mine in the dark of early morning. Sun-warmed cement and the scent of chlorine; the fireworks like a hailstorm of light above us. Her smiles across the aquarium's atrium, my parents' dinner table, the books she's always studying. The two of us laughing in her car, our hands trailing out the window as if through water. All those endless perfect moments in the sun.

"I'm staying," I whisper to her.

Those two words have been living inside me for so long that I feel naked without them. I kept them hidden deeply so I could not bring them out into the light where they might hurt me. I thought they would put an end to everything I wanted, everything I had planned for.

But I haven't wanted to leave for a long time now. Maybe I never did.

Now, as I slide my head onto Georgia's shoulder and feel her arms wrap around me, holding me tight, I am not afraid. In this moment, the world black and bright around us, I feel like I never stopped flying.

WINTER

I shiver as I walk from my car to the aquarium entrance. In the dim January light, the building looks more squat and gray than ever. The golden glow of the gift shop, which I never noticed from the outside when I worked there, is the only color around. Walking inside, the heat hits me so fast I start sweating under my coat. This place was never good at temperature control.

It's been a few weeks since I was last here. After a two-week stretch in October in which we didn't see each other due to schoolwork and family stuff, Georgia became concerned that we'd stop being friends. So we made a pact to meet here on the second Saturday of every month. It turned out to not be necessary. We talk every day. And we see each other a lot, just like I knew we would—sometimes hanging out with Serena and Matt, and every once in a while with Toby, but mostly just the two of us together.

Still, though, I'm glad this is the place she wanted to go, rather than Buona Tavola or my parents' house. I always come early and say hi to Jenny if she's around, chat with Toby a little, walk through the aquarium. Today, the woman at the front desk tells me the next tour will be starting in twenty minutes, but I know the schedule.

"I'm just gonna wander, if that's okay," I say.

She nods. She's used to this.

I walk through the rooms with the fish, past the two lonely turtles and the empty tank they've been cleaning for months. In the jellyfish room, I sit, lean my head against the wall, and wait for Georgia.

I have come here a lot since Jake and I broke up. More than the once a month Georgia required. Some weeks so often that Jenny asked if I was hoping for my old job back, which I wasn't. It's only a half-mile walk from a bus stop on the route home from school. Sometimes I visit Jenny, bring her a smoothie and talk about school and the store, or just sit and watch TV in her office. When it was still warm, I'd do my homework on the back patio sometimes, the silence strange in comparison to our summer lunches. Now, I just come to this room, to be alone in the wide chill blue.

Jake didn't take it well when I told him I wasn't going to

Kentucky. He yelled and threw his suitcase across the room. He said he didn't understand why I had changed my mind so suddenly. He said no when I asked him to stay. He called me names I hope he regrets.

But the worst part was when he fell back onto the bed and started crying. I had never seen him cry before, and it broke me down. I started crying too, both of us sitting there sobbing. He kept asking me why, and I couldn't answer. The fact is, there were hundreds of answers, spread throughout the summer—things he had said and done that I was only just starting to see for the hurt they'd caused, like bruises rising on my skin. But I couldn't articulate any of them. The best I could do, finally, was to say, "It just doesn't feel right." Even to me, it was a truth that sounded weak.

I crawled up into bed with him and held him close, told him I loved him. Then I got up and left, thankful I'd had the foresight to borrow my dad's car instead of asking Jake to come pick me up. I drove a mile away before I stopped and pulled over and cried for what seemed like forever, until I couldn't breathe, couldn't see.

It was over by noon on Sunday. I spent the rest of the day in bed. When Mom came to check on me, I said, "I broke up with Jake."

"Oh, baby," she said, but I shrugged her away when she tried to rub my back. She sat back and hesitated before saying, "Did anything happen? In particular, I mean?"

I almost told her everything. The whole story, from April

onward. But then I imagined her reaction, and the horrifying truth of what I had almost done came crashing down with renewed force. I thought about her and Dad walking into my bedroom and finding a note, Dad picking up the phone, Mom shaking. I thought about being with Jake and two unfamiliar adults in the middle of nowhere. How I would have wanted to talk to my mother. I sat up and hugged her fiercely.

"I'm sorry," I sobbed.

She stroked my hair and said, "Sweet pea, you have nothing to be sorry for."

I did, of course. But as I played out the first few days of that alternate future in my mind, I couldn't bear to tell her. I was too ashamed. Instead, I let her hold me and murmur comforting words, and I promised myself I would tell her later—when I was older. When I could explain myself. Because I could not explain myself to anyone right now.

Georgia texted me too, several times, asking first, *did you do it??*, and then, *are you ok?*, and then, *I'm really, really sorry, Caroline*. She offered to come over. Only when she texted me, *okay I'm getting in my car, I'll be there in ten*, did I respond, **no no, it's okay, I'm fine, I just want some time alone.**

Finally, as the sky was getting dark, Mom knocked on my door with a plate of food.

"I know you don't want to, sweetie," she said gently, "but we probably ought to get you ready for school tomorrow."

I rolled over, nauseated.

"Senior year! It's pretty exciting."

When I didn't respond, she continued. "I bought you some new notebooks and binders, but we can go to the store after school tomorrow if you need more. Now, what were you thinking for an outfit? Let's get more light in here so we can see properly. Goodness, it's getting dark earlier and earlier these days."

She went over to the closet and pulled out the blue dress she and Dad got me for my birthday, and I realized I never got to show it to Jake. It was the dress I was going to wear the next day, for our long, long drive. "How about this?" she asked. I shook my head. A wave of cold shivered through my body, followed by overwhelming heat, as if I had a fever. "You're right, probably too nice for the first day." She put it back in the closet. "Maybe separates. What do you think?"

I didn't answer.

"Caroline," she said, putting one hand on her hip. "Work with me here."

I pulled the covers up to my chin, and my eye caught on a white T-shirt with the aquarium logo, crumpled on the floor. They made promotional shirts to sell in the gift shop, except the printing company got the words wrong, so they say *Get wet! At the Boneville Aquarium.* We were allowed to take the reject shirts for free. We made "Boneville" jokes for weeks.

"That one," I croaked, pointing. Mom picked it up and wrinkled her nose.

"Really? This one?"

I nodded.

"Well, okay, Caroline, it's up to you."

School was almost as bad as I'd expected, except it turns out my old friends didn't hate me. When I told them I broke up with Jake, they didn't crow in delight. Chandler gave me a hug, and Erin spent the whole lunch hour asking questions.

All the attention felt awkward, and I tried to deflect questions back to them. Erin told us about her friends at camp, and I could sense the wistfulness in her voice when she talked about their late nights around a fire. Chandler had met a guy in Rhode Island, where she went to stay with her mom every summer, but he'd ended things when she left. Both of them seemed kinder than they used to, and I wondered whether they had grown up or I had been wrong.

I texted Georgia a lot. The first day, she woke me up before my alarm with a text that read: *I KNOW YOU'RE NOT EXCITED ABOUT SENIOR YEAR BUT IT SEEMS LIKE YOU DON'T WANT TO TALK ABOUT JAKE SO WOOOO SENIOR YEAR WHAT IS YOUR CLASS SCHEDULE.* We texted at lunch and after school and made plans to get dinner at Buona Tavola on Friday. That first night, while I was doing my homework, she texted me twelve hearts in a row, and when

I asked, **what was that for?,** she said, *I'm just really, really glad you're still here and I hope you are too.* Looking down at my math worksheets, I hesitated for a moment and then typed back, *I am.*

I tried texting and calling Jake on Tuesday to see if he had made it, to no response. I tried the next day too, and the next, and the next, and then a few weeks later, and then again a week after that. He never responded, not even once, and he blocked me on all his social media accounts.

I gave up on talking to him. Instead, I talked about him. All through the fall, my and Georgia's conversations kept coming back around to Jake. Unlike in the summer, though, we mostly talked about his flaws.

It wasn't intentional at first. I didn't bear him any ill will. But Georgia did. One day in mid-September, we were at my house, and I was taking down everything on my bulletin board, placing each item carefully in a shoebox to make room for a new set of pictures. More than half of the photos were of me and Jake. Most of the rest were pictures of the places I'd hoped to go with him.

"I'm glad you're taking these down," Georgia said as she highlighted something in her history book. "He was never good enough for you."

"Well..." I started, and Georgia cut me off with a look.

"Just look at what was up on this board," she said. "You had all these dreams. Of all these amazing places you wanted to be.

And he used your dreams to get to his dad. He is…" She paused to choose her words. "Unbelievably selfish."

I opened my mouth to protest, then closed it again. She was right. And I didn't have to defend him anymore.

It kept coming up. One weekend, Georgia and I were eating pizza with Serena and Matt, and I mentioned something I had done with Jake earlier in the summer.

"Oh my God," Serena said, "he was the worst."

"What did he do to you?" I asked, a little alarmed.

"Nothing to me," Serena said, "but that one time we hung out at bowling, he was so obnoxious. And didn't he make you invite him to the Great Adventures trip?" She shook her head.

"That fuckin' sucked," Matt added. "That trip was for us."

"It just seemed like he was never okay with you having your own friends," Serena said.

"The lady is correct," Georgia said definitively.

"Y'all are being a little harsh," I said. They dropped it, but I knew they weren't wrong. I just wished I had known it earlier.

After these conversations, I always found myself wanting to talk to him. Sometimes I wanted to yell at him, or ask him questions, or make him explain himself; sometimes, I just wanted to know how he was doing. If he was happier without me.

Finally, at Georgia's urging, I went to visit Toby at the aquarium and asked him if he'd heard anything. He seemed uncomfortable. "Jake said he didn't want to talk to you, and I don't know if I'm supposed to tell you what's going on with him, or what." Eventually, though, he showed me the picture: Jake and his dad, broad smiles across both their faces, standing in a field and half-silhouetted by the setting sun. I felt all the residual doubts of the last few months well up inside me and fall away, a structure finally crumbling. "Thanks," I told Toby and left.

Now, I am back here, waiting for Georgia. Meeting at the aquarium is just a formality today. We're going back to her house to get ready for dinner—we're going out with her family to celebrate. A few weeks ago, she got the letter telling her that she got into Stanford early action. She'll be going to California in August. Her parents have been a lot more relaxed since then. For the first time ever, they lowered the standards of the green zone to include an A– rather than only an A.

I have not gotten any college acceptance letters. I didn't apply anywhere early decision. At my mom's insistence and Georgia's gentle coercion, I did submit a few applications— some to in-state schools, including the one nearby, and some to farther-flung colleges that my parents and Georgia deemed the right balance of cost, quality, and likelihood to accept me. They are scattered all over the place, one in the northeast, one in the southwest, and one, yes, in California, just a few hours away from Stanford.

I don't expect any letters until April. When Georgia got hers, I printed out a picture of the campus and put it on my bulletin board. It hasn't been there long, but already it draws my eye, how bright the sun is, how green the trees. And equally it hides something I cannot think about: Georgia standing in that sun and me still here, so far away.

I have no idea if I'll get into a college, or whether I'll go if I do. I don't like the idea of more school or starting out life as an adult with thousands of dollars of debt. But after months of conversations, Georgia has convinced me that a bachelor's degree might be worth it. After I get acceptance or rejection letters, I'll have a little time to decide where I want to be and what I want to do, and it is both a relief and a terror that whatever I choose, I'll be alone.

It is a relief, too, to know that Georgia and I will both be working here next summer. We applied early to be JAC counselors. When I asked Georgia if she shouldn't be doing an internship or something more serious, she shrugged.

"Maybe," she said. "But there's not a whole lot that's interesting here, so I'd probably have to find a job and a cousin to host me somewhere else, and I think my parents are gonna miss me more than they let on. I'd kind of like to stay at home for one last summer. And there's nothing more prestigious than working at Bonneville's number one aquatic learning center."

We both know this isn't true. But I don't try to argue.

Around me, the jellyfish drift in aimless groups. I press my hand against the glass, sticky and warm.

The doors beside me push open, and a tour group shuffles into the room.

"...my personal favorite room," Toby proclaims. "Jellyfish are remarkably adaptable creatures. If the water around them gets rougher, they actually grow more of these long tendrils so they can propel themselves through the water rather than get tossed around in the waves. They also—shit, Caroline, didn't see you there, don't just lurk like that—"

"It's not like I'm hiding," I say. The entire tour group stares at me.

"Anyway," Toby continues, "we keep our water pretty calm, so the jellyfish here all have pretty short tendrils."

One woman murmurs to another, "I didn't know that," and I have to turn my face to hide my smile.

The final stragglers of the tour group come through, with Georgia bringing up the rear. She scans the room before her gaze finally catches on me, and she sidesteps the rest of the group while Toby continues to talk.

"There you are," she says under her breath. "I thought you might be visiting Jenny, but you weren't, so I had this extremely awkward encounter. She doesn't really talk, does she? I ended up literally backing out of the gift shop. Anyway, come on, we gotta go get ready. I'm gonna let you put makeup on me, I hope you're excited."

The blue light filters over us, making the room feel like a

dream. Georgia looks up at the jellyfish, translucent and slow-moving, placid in their heated water. For them, there are no seasons, no decisions, no passing of time. In here, everything is always the same. I feel an urge to rest my head against the glass and never move.

But Georgia's foot is tapping, one hand drumming a piano rhythm on her hip, the other fiddling with the end of her long, thick braid. Her eyes follow the jellyfish for a moment, her mouth opening slightly as if about to voice a thought, and then she looks down at me again.

"Caroline," she says, "come on, it's time to go. We have so much to do."

She stretches out her hand, callused and familiar. I take it and she pulls me up—leading me back into the world.

ACKNOWLEDGMENTS

Thank you to Annie Berger, Sarah Kasman, Cassie Gutman, and everyone else who touched this book at Sourcebooks Fire. I always assumed editing would be an anxious, scary process, and you proved me completely wrong. This book is so much better, and I am a better writer because of your work and your trust.

Thank you to Nell Pierce for your enthusiasm, kindness, and professionalism; for showing me a great bakery in New York; and, more than anything, for all the work you did to put this book into the world.

Thank you to Holly Hilliard, who had no reason to read this book and help me but did. I will always be grateful.

Thank you to two fantastic Durham coffee shops: Cocoa Cinnamon, where I started this book, and Bean Traders, where I finished the first draft. Thank you also to all the places in between where I worked on it: Hendersonville, Wilmington, Topsail Island, Holden Beach, and Raleigh, NC; Florence and Myrtle Beach, SC; Washington, DC; Boston, MA; St. Petersburg, FL; and probably many more places I've forgotten.

Thank you to my dog, Toast, for absolutely nothing. (Just kidding. You're perfect. Please don't eat this book.)

Thank you to everyone at Duke Young Writers' Camp from 2004 through 2008. When I think of being a teenager, I think of you, and I feel unspeakably lucky. Thank you especially to Barry Yeoman, the best teacher I've ever had, and Julia Howland-Myers, who held my hand when things got hard.

Thank you to Don, Janice, and Kym, for being the most supportive, loving second family I can imagine.

Thank you to Lucy, for twenty years of friendship.

Thank you to my Slack, my friends who are my family—Chloe, Nathan, Bethany, Melissa, and Sunny—for the love, humor, support, wit, questions, arguments, book recommendations, ham, pins, and pizza you bring to my life every day. You inspire me to be stronger and better in every way. You are more than I deserve.

Thank you to Mom, Dad, Allyn, and Scott, for so much. For raising me in a house full of books. For encouraging me in every creative pursuit I've ever tried, but especially writing. For a world-class education. For teaching me to be honest, direct, and hardworking. For cultivating a love of yearly traditions, live music, great ice cream, and stories. For always being weird, funny, and kind.

Thank you to Ben, my favorite person. Do you love me? I love you.

ABOUT THE AUTHOR

Sarah Van Name grew up in North Carolina and attended Duke University twice, once for a teenage creative writing camp and once as an undergraduate. She lives and works in Durham with her husband, Ben, and her dog, Toast.